The Heretofore Un-tolled History

of

THE INDEPENDENT REPUBLIC OF HARVEY MARKSON

The Inside Story
as told to
John D. Frankel

Order this book online at www.trafford.com
or email orders@trafford.com

Most Trafford titles are also available at major online book retailers.

Note for Librarians: A cataloguing record for this book is available from Library and Archives Canada at www.collectionscanada.ca/amicus/index-e.html

Printed in Victoria, BC, Canada.

ISBN: 978-1-4251-8870-2 (Soft)

We at Trafford believe that it is the responsibility of us all, as both individuals and corporations, to make choices that are environmentally and socially sound. You, in turn, are supporting this responsible conduct each time you purchase a Trafford book, or make use of our publishing services. To find out how you are helping, please visit www.trafford.com/responsiblepublishing.html

Our mission is to efficiently provide the world's finest, most comprehensive book publishing service, enabling every author to experience success. To find out how to publish your book, your way, and have it available worldwide, visit us online at www.trafford.com

Trafford rev: 8/7/2009

www.trafford.com

North America & international
toll-free: 1 888 232 4444 (USA & Canada)
phone: 250 383 6864 • fax: 812 355 4082
email: info@trafford.com

To my Bevy

TRUTH BE TOLD

Most storytellers lie. They twist things around in every direction. They exaggerate at every turn. The history of Harvey's Republic needs to be related in a straightforward manner and by someone who was there and knows what he's talking about, in contrast to, say, a financial journalist. Writers take liberties of all sorts. They pretend to know what's on this person's mind or that person's when, of course, they have no idea really. What they do is make it up or guess. It's astounding their pants don't catch on fire, frankly. Here, to have a reliable record—rather than a cheap piece of speculative mendacity—an unimpeachable source needed to be unearthed. Somebody who was on the scene, and on it 24/7.

No matter how calm our lives may seem from without, many a battle rages on inside. So it was with Harvey when events overtook him, as they do all of us from time to time. When it looks as if your world is headed for the abyss, do you not hear a voice, a very loud and very clear voice? Like some uninhibited know-it-all, does it not love to criticize every move you've ever made—or ever thought of making? Well, that's who narrates the events of Harvey's Republic, a space, as we say nowadays, where Harvey could be king—king of the castle. Even if he was short one castle.

I.

AN EXODUS OF ONE

Ahem. Anyway, to get started, Harvey was about to get out that night—and out for good. It was about nine in the evening, the Saturday before Easter. The limo driver on the way to the airport complained winter had overstayed its welcome. So had Harvey, perhaps. Wet snow had fallen earlier in the morning. But when the sun, in winter a nine-to-fiver at the best of times, quit for the day, darkness came on. A bitter cold set in and chased away every cloud, leaving the sky brimful of stars.

It was far from clear, however, exactly what Harvey thought he was about to get out of—or into. Make no mistake, Harvey's escape—or whatever you want to call it—bore world-shaking political consequences, at least for Harvey, though predictably, like Icarus's flight in Brueghel's masterpiece, his departure attracted the attention of nary a soul.

When that furtive, open-shirted, thick-necked, short-assed, drink-crazed, liar-womanizer, know-nothing journalist, the guy you'd see at all those corporate annual meetings downtown with his little spiral-bound notebook in hand and writer of the "Goings On" column for *The World of Finance* (paid circulation 289,000—including the free copies available at every car wash in the city), sat himself down on the other side of the airport bar, even he didn't offer the usual head nod or hand wave of recognition.

[To gossip on a gossiper, The Street has it that the journalist did not question—not for one single solitary second—the idea suggested by a floor trader in a bar just down the street from the stock exchange one night after work that as part of their strategic marketing plan, United Condoms (LAY: closing price: $28.75) intended to acquire National Caskets (END: closing price: $12:12) so they could get their customers both coming and going.]

No question this night signalled an important juncture in Harvey's life. On a slightly reduced scale, it bore all the ramifications of the French Revolution, the ouster of Marcos from the Philippines, the bankruptcy of the Soviet Union and the introduction to the financial world—Harvey's world—of negotiated brokerage commissions: brave but failed attempts at an entirely new kind of order.

But even people privileged to witness events of that magnitude report, time and time again, the need of the next day's newspaper to tell them what they saw. So insecure has the contemporary mind grown in its understanding of what goes on about it that it is unable—simply and completely unable—to grasp events that take place right before its very eyes and ears, especially events far from trivial.

Harvey, or anybody else for that matter, could get all worked up about a lavish cocktail party at Grace and Piggy Donnis's country place, with the whole world—*tout* Toronto—there, even though everyone knows in advance that oblivion awaits the passing of such a petty event every bit as much as it awaits the semi-colon. On the other hand, at some easily-identifiable, truly-significant turning point in someone's life, where a totally new arrangement with the universe has just been proclaimed—*Vive l'indépendance!*—it turns out that the poets have sadly misled us. No trumpets sound. No flags wave. No smoky smell wafts through the air as skyrockets woosh into the night and burst into blossoms of white, orange and blue followed by crackling of gunfire and claps of thunder. When somebody dies or marries, bells ring and ring and ring to let the world know something important has just taken place. But not this night. No bells rang out in jubilation. Not the clapper of even a small bell wavered, that you can be sure of. Harvey's departure went totally untolled.

Nature has laid out for our lives—if only to test our faith—the most magnificent array of prisons imaginable. The more publicized of these flaunt carefully masoned walls upon which drably dressed guards, a rifle slung over the shoulder, amble back and forth. Such institutions, I say, deserve their fame. They provide maximum security for us. And once inside, a person can lead a life free from the everyday harassment of the modern city.

Not for a single solitary moment do I claim you need to

experience The State's hospitality to recognize the total unreasonableness of the game we're in. We already know that most of the time that we do (that we put in) on this earth and most of things we do—"Look, I filled the hummingbird feeder!"—meet with utter and complete indifference. And by now we all know, and only too well, that neither high stone walls nor gap-toothed morons armed to their gingivitis-ridden gums, their fat fingers clutched to the canvas shoulder strap of a Kalashnikov, can restrain our comings and goings, our basic freedoms, one whit more than, say, hint of a severe financial reversal.

Or how about unabated lust? Whew! That can be worse than the lash. Add to the list ambitions, thwarted and unthwarted. Include timidity. The list of today's more popular penal institutions—usually one-man shows in which you get to play both warden and prisoner—runs on and on. At that, it probably would not identify (I couldn't figure it out myself) the one that had entertained Harvey the last few months so insistently.

Day in and day out, preachers and poets—those politicians of the spirit—try to convince us that we live in a benevolent universe, right? Get this: despite all Her well-documented dirty tricks—volcanoes, earthquakes, hurricanes, droughts, pestilence, economic forecasts and wrestling federations—we are supposed to believe that Nature is on our side. Really?

The preachers and poets on this planet want us to believe that despite the obvious ape-like crudeness of certain Homo Sapiens (for example, slick-tongued lawyers, slick-penned journalists and rubber-gloved periodontists), and despite the fact that the ideas of fairness and justice (vital to any kind of decent everyday existence) remain often no more than ideas, each, like a chrysalis, holding out great promise but at the same time raising grave doubts as to whether their cocooned beauty will ever, ever see the light of day—despite all that—they want us to believe that Nature's on our side? How in the world would we ever know that? How in the world would we ever know that She is glad to have mankind on board? Who but a nine-year-old computer hacker would believe in a user-friendly Universe? I mean, who's trying to kid who? Or whom?

On the other hand, we take it as no joke when things go right, right? Such as the day the price of the shares of Save Your Time Software Inc. ("Your Salvation in a Box"), which Harvey held in great number, surged six bucks. A little sign like that and it's as if Eternity has jumped into the palm of your hand. But here's a good question: How long do you get to stride triumphant upon the earth's surface? How long? Till the early edition of *The World of Finance* thuds against your front door the next morning. There, on the second to last page, a black-bordered paragraph titled "Oops" states in bold print that the previous day's closing price of The Save Your Thyme [*sic*] Hardware [*sic*] Limited was incorrectly stated. The correct closing price was $5.25, down a $1.25.

Incorrectly stated? The clappers in the bells of jubilation halt in mid-stroke—joyous interruptus—and life dissolves into a twenty-four hour infomercial for REALITY Inc. that asks where in hell you got the idea the world was meant to work in your favour. And while you sulk in front of the TV, some round-faced evangelist with a drawl, a squeaky nasal voice, a crop of imported hair and an oversized knot in his red tie points out that you are trying to celebrate the wrong life—wait for the next one. Good God! It makes you wonder how anyone without vestments or vested interests could possibly believe there's a deity in charge, or even on staff.

It's enough to destroy your faith.

No more rants, I promise. Forgive me.

Two double Manhattans on the rocks and then a third, an innocent attempt—what the hell!—to savour the sweetness of release had more than prepared our Harvey for this departure/escape. Without further thought, he put two twenty dollar bills on the bar. That meant an out-sized tip for the bartender, with whom, other than his drink orders, Harvey had exchanged not two words. Then leaving the bartender to munch peanuts with the mean-spirited journalist (forgive the redundancy), our Icarus picked up his notebook computer and sauntered out, his heels scuffing the terrazzo as he sauntered towards Gate 9D.

A tall, skinny man in a dark gray shirt and thin black tie, his arms held tightly to his chest, nodded his head in the direction of a pink plastic container on the counter. Harvey clunked in it all his loose change, along with a set of keys, a black pen and a gold lighter (a memento of the Saturday at the race track in the fall of '92 when Zygmunt—Zygmunt the Lucky—won five out of the last six races and eighteen thousand dollars). Then obediently Harvey slid the little pink container on to the whirring conveyor and marched straight through the green metal arch. Jesus! You would have thought the airport itself was about to take off. Buzzers screeched. Horns hooted. People came on the run from every direction. Harvey Markson had carried his goddamn laptop through the security arch.

At least as recorded in late-night movies, history has shown that security guards get duped far too often by friendly drunks. The security people must have taken Harvey's amiable demeanour as a cover-up. The skinny guard searched Harvey and all his belongings a half dozen times. He checked the initials on his handkerchief against those on his passport and against the signature on the $10,000 in Visa travelers' cheques. He examined the twenty £10 notes, the zinc throat lozenges, the Rolaids, and the two packages of Dunhill cigarettes. Three times at least, the fat guard, with the fancy gold epaulettes and gold on every other finger and in every other tooth, waved his magic detector around Harvey's body (twice very carelessly in the area of Harvey's crotch). Captain Vastly Overweight did everything except put the suspect himself on the conveyor belt and send him through the x-ray machine. Finally, finding not a thing to confirm their suspicions, Captain Vastly and his skinny sidekick relented.

And what do you think Harvey did? He thanked them. Harvey thanked them, for chrissake. How likely was that gesture to increase somebody's confidence in his ability to pull off this project? (Originally called Project Get-The-Hell-Out-Of-Here, later shortened to Project Vamoose and then, later still, as familiarity grew, extended to Project Vamooski, which rhymes with Rimouski)

At gate 9D, no other passengers remained to board. Yet no one chided Harvey for being late. That was nice. No one tried to hurry him along. His boarding pass was taken with a simple quick smile of gratitude. Harvey then walked down the long, enclosed passageway, a square tunnel with beige walls and green carpet, and stepped onto the plane. A flight attendant with very bright, electric bright, brown eyes and a Greek accent welcomed Passenger Markson aboard Olympia Airlines (flying from Toronto to London and then on to Athens). When Harvey asked her to verify what the travel agent told him, she confirmed that Olympia Airlines still permitted smoking at that point. Then she added, with a wave of her finger, "No smoking before the No Smoking sign was ecks-ting-wi-shed."

It was Easter time, to repeat, and everybody seemed to be fleeing the city. That's why the Greek airline's flight was the only one the travel agent could book with so little notice from Harvey. The only empty seats left in the brightly-lit first-class cabin were the two seats in the last row; the one next to the window was the one reserved for Harvey. No sooner had Harvey stored his computer in the overhead compartment, sat down and fastened his seat belt than the bearded purser arrived to welcome Passenger Markson with a stem glass of Pol Roger—fuel for an already well-lit fire. Then the flight attendant with the friendly smile came by and left next to the champagne glass on the fold-down table two small foil-wrapped Easter eggs. After what he'd been through the last months, Harvey had forgotten what a genial atmosphere felt like. You know what it felt like? Like someone had come along, pushed back some huge steel door—you could almost hear it clank open—and put an end once and for all to his captivity.

Not ten minutes later, as the plane climbed into the night sky, it began to lurch and shake and creak. The swarthy-skinned man across the aisle tilted his head toward his chest, his hands pressed together in front of his face. Harvey, for his part, reached up and turned on the overhead air vent full blast and let the cool air splash on his face. He loosened his tie, opened his collar and swallowed nervously. Once again questions arose about the merit of project Vamooski. Two minutes later the shaking subsided. Through a window across the aisle you could see the moon take back its rightful place in the middle of the sky. A gentle gong sounded. The overhead illuminated sign with the red "x" on top of a narrow white rectangle went dim. Immediately, Harvey took out the gold lighter from Zygmunt and lit the cigarette held ready for that moment. He drew in the smoke and, after a long pause, blew it back out and watched the smoke cloud disintegrate chaotically in the air stream from the overhead vent. Then once again, the plane began to lurch and shake. The captain's voice came over the speaker system; he nonchalantly introduced himself and announced the possibility of turbulence ahead.

Goddamn. Life seems such an up-and-down, on-again-off-again, in-and-out business. What accounts for the great marketing success today of astrologers, macroeconomists and so many of the other boondogglers is our unshakable desire to smooth out the cyclicality of life. One moment this, the next moment that, right up to the end, life bobs up and down—or as *The World of Finance* would put it, life soars and plummets, plummets and soars. What the hell kind of life is that?

Only with a disregard for the truth typical of *The World of Finance,* considered by some the Bible of financial markets, could one report that over the previous months Harvey's life had been bumping along. Thumping along, as in a migraine, would be more apt. Only a few days before Harvey flew out had the negotiations with Leon—Dr. Robert John Leon Kelpner, D.D.S., Dip. Perio.—finally come to a conclusion. Justice had not been served.

The negotiations ended not in the manner of an eye for an eye; they ended more like the experience of someone under Leon's dental care—a tooth for a wildly expensive dental implant. In these negotiations, even with his lawyer's meter ticking away, Leon, obsessively cost-conscious as he was, would recount irrelevant story after irrelevant story, each of which ended with a solo bray of laughter —his. To listen to Leon carry on, sitting at the highly polished oak boardroom table of Hammer, Drillon and Fisk, it would take a person no time to realize that neither love of money (the most logical guess), nor an inborn desire to alleviate suffering had attracted Leon to dentistry and then to periodontistry. The real motive must have been a deep-seated need to do stand-up comedy with a captive audience at his (latex-covered) fingertips.

Yet, in his roundabout way, it looked like Leon had sold his point of view to everybody. That included Robbie Elliott, Harvey's well-regarded but next-to-useless lawyer, who had never less than eighteen cases on the go at any one time. Leon (D.D.S., Dip. Perio.), the new major shareholder of the investment counselling firm of R. H. Winkes & Associates, claimed that, without the irreplaceable genius of Rupert Winkes in its service, due to an untimely death, the firm had little dollar value to anyone. How did he convince everyone? He wore their patience to the bone with utter nonsense and then quickly made a demand, which out of the sheer need for some silence was granted him. It was a typical legal process—a nightmare come to life.

After weeks and weeks of wrangling, Leon finally agreed to have the firm itself buy back with future profits Harvey's shares of R. H. Winkes & Associates in three equal tranches of $300,000. One up front, another in a year and a final payment two years hence.

For that, both Leon and the well-regarded Robbie Elliott, who was in East Timor at a law-and-order convention when the final agreement was reached, should have gone to jail, the one for theft and the other as an accessory to the crime. On a simple multiple of three times revenue, Harvey's five per cent ownership of R. H. Winkes & Associates, which managed $7.1 billion in pension fund assets as well as the portfolios of a few selected clients, such as that of Grace Donnis (but not, of course, that of her husband, Piggy, who headed a well-known brokerage firm) and several other of the city's outstanding citizens, was worth twice as much.

"Why would you say it's a good deal, Zyg?" Harvey asked, the phone coddled on his stomach, the television across the room rendered mute by remote control. "I was a full associate in the firm."

"You're kidding. You were one of the associates of Rupert Winkes & Associates? An associate? I always thought you were the ampersand," said Zyg. "Look, at least you get to pay off your bank loan. By the time Leon's through with Winkes the place won't be worth a goddamn nickel." That statement was quickly followed by a laugh one-half geniality, one-half arrogant certainty.

"You always have all the answers, don't you, Zyg?"

"Hey, why're you in such a flap?"

The phone calls, the waiting, the strategy meetings with the lawyers, Leon's total unreasonableness and his complete disregard for anything that resembled a relevant fact or truth all combined to wear down Harvey's tolerance. He had averaged less than four hours of solid sleep a night for the last three months. Usually he was up half the night, to pace up and down the long hall that connected the living room of his condo to the back bedroom. The fatigue and the uncertainty, the relentless goddamn uncertainty, ate away inside him like some flesh-devouring disease.

Zygmunt, the good friend, once he heard Leon had control of R. H. Winkes & Associates, had predicted to the letter—to the letter, mind you—the problems Leon would bring about. Zyg seemed more like a soothsayer who took delight in the deadly accuracy of his prophecies than a close and helpful friend. How nice it would have felt to have someone, or something, truly allied to Harvey's cause. Put another way, in the middle of those negotiations, had lightning struck Leon dead, it would have been a far more convincing argument for the existence of God than anything Aquinas or St. Anselm came up with.

Project Vamooski dictated that all the furniture bought just two years previously for his new condominium had to go. The whole lot, including the Louis Quatorze Bergere chairs, would return in the Prime Movers' moving van to where it had come from and in exactly the same excellent repair in which it had arrived. The only thing to get lost on the return trip back was Superior Interiors' exorbitant mark-up. Change, to make the point again, drives a very hard bargain.

To boot, Harvey had forgotten a few details vital to Project Vamooski, such as:

- Passport renewal
- Change of mailing address
- Cancel phone
- Ship books
- Get electricity meter read
- Buy £s
- Buy VISA travelers cheques

- Dry clean suits, ties
- Fix shift key on notebook
- Cancel cable TV
- Sell car
- $ for concierge
- Cancel magazines
- Airline reservations

The cancellation of magazine subscriptions, for example, is no easy task when these days the practice is to send you every other week from the day you subscribe a request to renew. One thing not needed was storage space. Not a trace of Harvey Markson's possessions was to be left behind. Each day the ever-present to-do list would grow longer. Most important of all, courtesy demanded his apartment had to be left spotless.

Thank God for Mrs. Avogadro. Even without a job description she accepted responsibilities for concerns far beyond soiled dishes, dirty laundry, un-vacuumed carpets and lingering dust. It was she, though not five feet high, nor a hundred pounds in weight, who lugged the suitcases up from the tenth floor storage room and got them packed and ready in time for the airport limousine.

To jump back a moment, about three years before, when Harvey was allowed to purchase shares and become a partner at R. H. Winkes & Associates, Harvey, tired of the never-ending sluggish stream of traffic from the house he rented in the north part of the city to his office downtown, bought a luxury condominium ("Central. Exquisite city view. 2 b/r, 2 ½ baths, f/p, vtb mortgage avail., asking $640,000"). The condo market had shown little signs of life after the collapse of 1989 and the $540,000 price, already reduced $120,000, dropped another $50,000 before Harvey signed the four-page Agreement to Purchase. The building that housed Harvey's apartment, the Tuscan Plaza, stood at the intersection of two of the city's main thoroughfares, Bloor Street and Avenue Road, almost.

Almost. Because the developers had to build the Tuscan Plaza around a small Anglican church that occupied the northeast corner of the intersection. No matter how hard the president of the development company, Integrity Development, of which Reuben Eldred "Piggy" Donnis owned 49.1 per cent, cajoled and pleaded, the parishioners of The Church of The Redeemer refused to sell. Even Piggy himself, outraged at this intransigence, got in on the negotiations, confident that he could, to use words said to be his, "blow them away." He pointed out to the church's finance committee the wonderful works the parish could perform with the proceeds from the sale. Besides financing a new building in the suburbs and the church's outreach program, they could go a long way, Piggy claimed, in the church's war on world poverty, a subject no one knew him to have paid much attention to before. But no matter how much influence he brought to bear on the local bishop and other church authorities, no matter how hard he huffed and he puffed, Piggy could not get the elders of the church to budge their House of God one single, solitary inch.

According to the account Harvey heard, in the end Piggy lost all patience and blurted out, "Why won't you move, man, for the love of God?"

To which the rector replied coolly, "Thank you, Mr. Donnis, I think you've finally begun to understand us."

Harvey's new home overlooked the little Church of The Redeemer from nineteen storeys above. It had a very clear view of the intersection, the museum across the street, the tall bank buildings that took up more than their fair share of skyline, and of the skinny, six-months-pregnant communications tower that on an overcast night would insert itself into the clouds.

You know what Harvey liked best about his new residence? Not the plushness. Not the affable doorman. Not the access to all the nearby stores—stores that stocked everything in the world that man had altered in some way and offered for sale—and restaurants just a step or two away. No, it was the freedom. The choices: He could drive to the office. Or walk. He could take the subway down. Or, if he was late and wanted to find out how to run the world, a five-dollar cab ride down would do the trick. This awareness of choice, where there had been none before, only hours of bumper-to-bumper combat, made him question for the first time, for the very first time, the hand-me-down values of the city. And in my opinion, this new awareness explains better than any psychiatric theory the etiology of Project Vamooski.

Grace Donnis got Zuzu Hornfeldt, busy as ZuZu was, to do the interior of Harvey's new home. Zuzu had done many of the city's most important homes, as well as decorating two foreign embassies and the lavish country house of Piggy Donnis (itself an embassy for Mammon). Zuzu was the president and chief executive officer of a three-employee organization she called Superior Interiors. And that's what her business stationery said, too. But everybody else in the city referred to it as "Inferiors" and had done so for so long the fun had gone out of it. Instead the name had become a shibboleth: if you didn't know what "Inferiors" was, you were from out of town.

At first it looked like Zuzu wouldn't be able to do Harvey's place she had so much work on her plate. She had taken the contract to decorate the rabbi's study, the library and the council room for the city's newest synagogue, Temple HaSneh, "The Burning Bush." Unfortunately, less than two weeks from completion of the structure, Temple HaSneh itself caught fire and burned to the ground. That left everything up in the air while the insurance companies argued over whether it was gross negligence on the part of the construction company or an act of God—again. Anyway, that freed up Zuzu to work the magic of her impeccable taste on Harvey's apartment.

Harvey had stressed the word *functional* to Zuzu. While that word is somewhat abstract, still, in all fairness, it does retain a rather particular meaning. Zuzu, however, chose to translate it into the French word *Louis* as in Louis Quatorze. The two wall tapestries, the purple-bordered white carpets and the white and gold armoire in the living room reflected, chez Harvey, the glory of the Sun King. That glory was also reflected in two horribly uncomfortable gray-green Bergere chairs and an ornate gold and black chesterfield with carved, scroll-like flourishes on its mahogany, paw-shaped feet. In the den/second bedroom, a French Provincial desk at a cost of eighteen thousand dollars qualified as the city's most expensive mini-storage space. It stored nothing other than, in one of its tiny drawers, a few unpaid bills that remained unpaid seldom more than a long weekend, even the gigantic ones in the beginning that came almost weekly from Zuzu (and later from the lawyers).

But it was Mrs. Avogadro—and not Zuzu Hornfeldt, who always claimed credit for it—who had introduced Harvey to Zygmunt. "You call Mr. Zygmunt. He nice man." At times Harvey disagreed with that judgment. At times he thought the only thing that Zygmunt and he had in common was Mrs. Avogadro, and the need for cleanliness and neatness in their living quarters.

If that woman could bring to the rest of the world the same of sense of sparkling order she brought to Harvey's apartment every Friday (though Harvey had to re-arrange the green Bergere chairs after every visit of hers), what a world we'd have—order everywhere. Mind you, she held very strong opinions, just as Zygmunt did, and she was nobody's fool. She told Harvey he was "crazy, much crazy" to abandon the city. She told him that not once, but every Friday from the time she first heard a hint of Project Vamooski, and she voiced her disapproval to his face, if he was there, or by phone to his office. One occasion she interrupted the Leon negotiations to tell Mr. Harvey to buy spray starch for his shirt collars, Lysol for the two and a half bathrooms and a can of Drano for his head.

When the time arrived for Harvey to say good-bye, Mrs. Avogadro kept her eyes averted. When he leaned down and hugged her—it was the first time he had ever embraced her—you could hear her take in a quick breath. When Harvey said he would write, she stroked her finger across her cheek just below the eye.

"No write, Mr. Harvey. You come back."

II.

EROS BOARDS

"Cup a tea for you, sir," said the purser in a deep, soothing voice.

Harvey pushed his tongue against the roof of his mouth to get a suggestion from his taste buds. "Little more champagne, please," said Harvey. As he spoke the plane shook again.

"Pardon, sir?"

Harvey raised his voice over the hum of the plane's engines. "More champagne would be nice. Thanks, no tea."

What would have really hit the spot at that point was a little feedback from the Universe. In those moments when nothing feels solid, when you feel the ground gone from under you, when everything feels up in the air, wouldn't you just love some sort of signal from Nature? She could say to you, perhaps in a deep, resonant, biblical voice like that of the purser's, "Hey, take it easy, you're on the right track. Everything's going to work out just fine. Not to worry." And then, in case you couldn't believe your ears, you get some sort of confirming visual sign; water would spout from a nearby rock, for example, to show that, yes, you were on the right track. Or the sea would part.

But no bells pealed out to indicate victory. No joyful trumpet blasts rushed in over the moan of the plane's engines to signal triumph to Harvey. When Harvey got up to stretch his legs a little later, no shrill whistles rang out, like those you hear when a political candidate approaches the convention's podium. No "oles" ricocheted through the pressurized cabin as they do through the plaza de toros when some poor dumbfounded, blood-spurting bull collapses to the ground.

Have you ever gone for a long time, for months, without a speck of good news? All you get is stressful bad news or no news which, of course, brings its own stress. Sometimes the stock market gets into a bad mood and each low point slides down lower than the one before, and there's no end. No matter how much you want some sign to tell you a reversal is at hand none comes, only a relentless slide that goes on and on until finally you feel disoriented. After all those months of delay, with Harvey now en route, wouldn't it be nice to know things were headed in the right direction? Was it really too much to ask for a little honest feedback, say, to have a cherub drop over for a short chat? At forty-two thousand feet above sea level, how long would it take for one to slide over from heaven?

We've stumbled upon a major problem here. You don't read much about this in your local newspapers. But we've got a little communications problem going for us here on earth.

God doesn't talk to us anymore. Someone pulled the plug on him. Maybe it was Eve. Or the serpent. Or, to argue, as Julian Jaynes did, that, at some stage in our evolution, a fluke change in human consciousness cut off the divine voices. Or, perhaps it was just a badly botched public relations scheme: "Eden Tiff Denied. Garden Talks To Resume Shortly."

"Some caviar or Gravalux?" asked the purser holding out a small silver tray of pinkish and black canapés spaced out on a white doily. Harvey shook his head.

Harvey by nature was a researcher. He trained himself to ask questions on top of questions about a company's future. On more than one occasion an exasperated chief financial officer half-drowned by questions about everything from balance sheet notations to employee turnover ratios had brought the meeting to a quick end or, in other cases, rudely hung up on him. But in this case, with his own future at stake, he hadn't bothered to pop a few questions to himself. Now that the project could not be turned off, some came to mind: How was he going to meet people in London? Where would he live? What would he do on weekends? A few loose ends like that and—wham!—in pops uncertainty. Put another way, as to the final success of Project Vamooski, at this point unquestionably well off the ground, and no one could deny that, the jury was still out. Nowadays juries take forever. It's a crime, really. We should sue Nature. The case is open and shut. But first you'd have to find a half-decent lawyer who'd return your phone calls. Talk about the impossible.

Zyg's offer to have Harvey stay home and head up the investment research department at Sheardon-Cassidy began to look attractive. What if, as pointed out to Harvey, the new job awaiting him in London turned out to be the same kind of nightmare R.H. Winkes & Associates had been these last few months? What if he never got to know anyone in London? It's one thing to visit London as a tourist and feast on its sites. It's another to live there from day to day like a native without the native's connections—and survive. Harvey needed a fully developed fallback plan. You'd do that in business, why wouldn't you do it in real life?

Harvey swallowed the last of the champagne, pushed the pull-down tray back up into place and slipped the glass into the seat pocket in front of him. As was his habit back in the condo at the Tuscan Plaza, he got up to walk about and think. It didn't look odd in any way. Passengers probably thought he was on the way to the lavatory, as the purser called it. Harvey strolled down to the cockpit door and then turned to walk back down the aisle towards the other end of the plane. To his left, in the third row, a woman seated on the aisle struck a match and lit her cigarette.

Not a dozen oil wells set afire by an Iraqi army in retreat, just the small flame of a match flared into existence. In that instant, all of Project Vamooski's history was rendered mere preamble, a simple going-through-the-motions, like the northern sun in winter.

Harvey cut short his stroll through the cabin and returned to his seat. What he had just seen was a regal-looking woman, thirty to thirty-five, in a well-tailored gray suit, brownish hair with a blonde streak about an inch and half wide leading back from the high forehead of a very handsome face. The overall impression was of a younger version of Grace Donnis. Or of the Duchess of Kent and the display of elegance the television cameras would catch each summer at Wimbledon when she presented the winners with their trophies.

Harvey leaned to his right out into the aisle to catch a second glimpse. All he could see, two rows down and on the other side, was her left arm, more particularly, a left forearm placed on an armrest like a sceptre of high office upon a plush velvet cushion.

Pale but not too pale, slim but not too slim, the forearm protruded from the frilled cuff of a white blouse, its outline expanding gently into a perfect fullness and then contracting. Light danced quietly upon the pale tanned surface that gave way now and again to a freckle. Its nakedness exuded warmth. No sudden rises or bulges of telltale effects of athletic activity carried to excess. The narrowest part of the forearm, a thin wrist encircled by a bracelet of twisted gold threads, continued on to a graceful hand with well-proportioned fingers curved inwards slightly, as if in a pose for Michelangelo, and which held the white cylinder of a cigarette just lit. Most wondrous of all, the third finger bore the jewel of jewels: no ring. Then, as if some concerned curator had come and put it safely away for the night, the forearm disappeared from view.

Two opposing desires clashed. On the one hand, lust—straightforward enough, surely. On the other, a deep-seated need to find out where things stood. Then out of nowhere came the idea that, if by chance Her Holiness should find her way to Harvey's bed it would signal—categorically, definitively, unquestionably—the success of Project Vamooski. It would signal to Harvey that he would get to live in a new world, no longer fettered by the constraints of his old world, no longer imprisoned in the small crevices between his fears, free at last to come and go as he bloody well wished, the end of life as a hobby.

In our hearts, we know the great poets lie to make a point. For the most part the world is changed not by great gestures but by the small unnoticed ones, a smile, for example, or a wink or, in this case, the wave of a forearm that launched Harvey as if upon some Holy Sacred Task.

And is it so farfetched, really, that Harvey in this high state of uncertainty would revert to such primitive means of resolution? In all fairness, when they don't know what the hell to do, don't people often fall back on some old piece of learned behaviour? One nice thing about this task-and-outcome ritual was that it required no special headdress, no rhythmic dance, no body paint, no sacred objects to shake in mid-air and no chants. Thank God for no chants; the other passengers would have thought Harvey had gone completely bonkers.

If not exactly Arthurian, still, The Task stood as a worthy challenge. How many times at Thrace's restaurant had Harvey seen Zyg, who hardly ever smoked, begin by leaning over to a woman at the next table to ask for a match and then end up with her back at his place later? The only time Harvey tried a trick like that was one night dining by himself at Thrace's; he leaned over to an unescorted woman at the next table, excused himself, and in the politest manner imaginable asked to borrow the small glass ashtray at her elbow. The women immediately called over the maitre d' and asked to be moved. Had Harvey not been well known to the restaurant, they would have thrown him out on the street. When he paid his bill and left shortly after, the pianist just back from her break played "Lover," barely able to keep a smirk off her face.

Get some total stranger to your bed, Harvey? Why not an

assault on the north face of Everest? Jesus-Jesus, where was your head when you thought that one up?

"We'll be serving shortly, sir," said the purser as he handed Harvey a large white napkin.

She had to be English. You could tell. She had just holidayed for two weeks with her married sister in Toronto. Now she was on her way back to her job as a medical researcher at the London School of Medicine. Probably nobility. Probably lived with her father in Kent, maybe in Tunbridge or Tunbridge Wells, and commuted to London by train. Her father, most likely, was a lawyer with a good sense of humour (we're dealing with fantasy here, don't forget) and sat in the House of Lords.

One thing had become obvious: the approach—the initial phase of The Holy Sacred Task—would require the utmost delicacy and diplomacy. The last thing Harvey wanted her to think was that this was an attempt to make an easy pickup. The trouble was a monstrous gulf—a monstrous carpeted gulf about two and half feet wide stretching two rows down—separated Harvey from this object of desire.

Nowadays monstrous gulfs exist everywhere. Things started to fall apart in the last century with a couple of world-class wars. People who used to steep themselves in the scriptures took up self-help books. Psychiatrists took over from shamans. Technology freed up Sundays for golf and sailing and coitus at the cottage. Governments took over tithing but upped the ante. Insurrectionists, terrorists and separatists sprung up out of nowhere. In previous times one prayed to be spared from trespasses (and plagues). Now people study martial arts. The sense of community has disappeared. Our confidence in The Good lies shattered. And we are left no choice but to rely on the ever-wavering self-confidence within. In North America today, most people believe there's only thing you can count on: You. In Europe it's the same. Separation has put us all in the same boat. The old sense of friendliness towards your neighbour you simply cannot count on these days, whether he or she be two or three houses down the street or two or three rows down the aisle of an airplane.

The clatter of trays and the crash of doors from the galley kitchen told Harvey that the pre-prepared "dining experiences" were about to be delivered to the passengers in first class. Harvey needed to act. He got up, stepped into the aisle, straightened his vest, much the way a matador about to enter the bullring nervously straightens his "suit of lights." And then he strode forward to confront the magnificent specimen of nature.

Toro, chi. Toro, chh-i, chh-i.

To succeed, he needed an approach bold, deft, graceful, intelligent, incisive and inventive.

"Excuse me. Sorry, sorry to bother you. Could I, ummm, trouble you, trouble you for a light? The purser's busy with dinner," said Harvey. As he released that last bit of fast-breaking news he tilted his head in the direction of the galley. "I mean, don't let me disturb you. I saw you were smoking. Just if you have a match, you know, handy."

Harvey stood erect, his shoulders straight, his hand rested, almost proudly, on the high back of the seat across the aisle from Her Holiness.

Ch-i, toro, ch-i.

She tilted her face towards Harvey. She looked up sympathetically. Then she paused, hunched her shoulders, and put forward her graceful hands, the palms upward.

"No paluki inglese," she said.

Ch-i, toro. Torito, ch-i, ch-i.

Harvey made a second pass. "Du feu, maybe? Avez-vous du feu? Haben Sie Feuer?"

Ole!

She stretched her hands wider apart and pushed her lower lip farther forward.

A third pass. Harvey pressed a thumb and forefinger of one hand together and stroked that configuration along the palm of his left hand. Then he brought the configuration slowly towards his lips to meet a V quickly formed by two fingers of the left hand.

Ole! Ole!

"No-no paluki inglese."

"Oui, je vois. Well, uh, thank you all the same. I'll get some from the purser. Dankeschön. Pardonnez. Excusa. Buenas noches."

Matador! Oy vay!

For God's sake, here's a communications problem to end all communications problems. You have Helen of Troy perched on your doorstep and all she speaks is ancient Sanskrit. "No paluki inglese. No paluki inglese," repeated matador Harvey to himself as he returned to his seat.

Before, with victory in sight, neither trumpets of celebration nor bells of jubilation sounded out. But now, not even the relentless moan of the plane's engines could drown out the catcalls or the shrill, derogatory whistles. If the seat cushions hadn't been fastened down, I swear they would have come flying into the ring.

Harvey rang for the purser and ordered not matches—nor a cape, nor a towel to wipe the gore from the vest of his *traje de luces*—only a simple blanket. Exactly the move suggested in the first place. And despite the purser's assurance of an exquisite (there's a word that's seen better times) gourmet meal, Harvey, the fight gone out of him, pushed his seat all the way back and fell asleep, swept into unconsciousness by alcohol, exhaustion and defeat—in the midst of the sky made to lie down in a green blanket courtesy of Olympia Airways.

Rule, Harvey. Harvey rules the waves.

Harvey never-never-never will be slaves.

So far the trip had been nothing to write home about. Not because it had been uneventful, far from that, but more because Harvey had no home to write to. Thinking back though, Harvey found it odd that Her Holiness had spoken to him in such a manner. The next morning, outside the Stansted Airport terminal, next to an impatient porter, with two huge suitcases, two small suitcases and a computer carry-on case perched on his cart, stood a very, very subdued Harvey, a blue Burberry coat hugged to his body. He was waiting for the Sheardon-Cassidy limousine that Zygmunt had arranged to drive him to his hotel in London. Periodic crackles of planes shot by overhead and drowned out the shriek of police whistles and the clatter of car horns.

"Excuse me, could you tell me, is this the spot to catch a taxicab for London?" a voice with a slight English accent asked from behind.

Harvey turned. The woman's eyes shot upwards.

"No paluki inglese," replied Harvey.

"It was self-defence. You were very drunk."

III.

VICTORY NIGHS

Even an incompetent exodontist could have extracted more from Ms. Paluki Inglese than Harvey on the way into London.

"Katherine."

"Katherine. What a nice name," said Harvey, Zyg's old line. "Katherine what, may I ask?"

"Well, at the moment I don't know really. It's a bit complicated."

She had a fairly full chest (quite astounding when you consider how close to it she played her cards). In profile, high cheeks rested on a softly curved jaw with a well-proportioned nose and flat temples that formed a backdrop for eyelids that struggled to stay open.

"Visiting friends here?"

"No, my aunt in London."

"For long?"

"She has a house in Mallorca, too. I'm taking her down there tomorrow."

"Where does she live in London?"

"Belgravia. Eaton Square." Katherine clasped her arms to her shoulders.

"Driver, could you turn the heat up a bit, please?" said Harvey who moved forward a little on the seat. "We'll go to Eaton Square first, driver. Then you can drop me off at the Dorchester." He turned back towards Katherine, "Where are you from?"

"I'm not sure. Nowhere at the moment." Her eyes closed.

"That must make your taxes reasonable," Harvey replied, but Katherine could not have heard a word.

The driver pulled the Bentley out on to the main highway towards London. And Harvey felt any chance of a relationship with Katherine whatever-the-hell-her-name-was was headed—to use an expression common in the investment world when the market drops—south.

Had a new Ice Age descended? What in hell was going on? A woman who doesn't care to give you her own goddamn name? A woman who displays all the enthusiasm for human existence of a security guard on night watch? Who falls asleep two seconds after the conversation begins? Fabulous forearms or not, lovely soft cheeks or not, enticing eyes or not, The Holy Sacred Task was off. If she needs help, she's got her aunt. The sooner Ms. Paluki Inglese was off the scene the better. The smart move—it was decided irrevocably—was to drop her off at her aunt's place and then deploy his newly acquired skill and vamoose. Vamoose to the hotel and into a nice warm shower before he froze to death. It was spring, but England can be cold no matter the time of year. Cold as hell.

Things were supposed to be different. Jesus, this was supposed to be a moment of rebirth, of exultation! Harvey had landed in England, for God's sake! Harvey was in England. England! Here was the old Harvey in his new world, seated in the lap of luxury in a chauffeur-driven Bentley with a woman as attractive—in a certain way—as any he'd met in his life. Here was Harvey en route to an elegant five-star hotel, gliding along the expressway through the lush countryside of England, but had anything about Harvey changed now that he'd left his old world behind? Had there been any hint of a regime change of some sort?

No, not really.

Just before reaching the outskirts of the city, the driver swerved the car into the outside lane to overtake a farmer's dawdling truck—lorry, in England—with a load of live chickens imprisoned in little metal cages. Their little red heads bobbed up and down. You would not need an actuary's help to calculate their life expectancy. They looked happy—the fate in store for them unanticipated. Maybe that's the trick. Maybe it's better to have no expectations. Expectations can be deadly. And none are more lethal than the ones we have for ourselves.

Then, after rounding a long curve, a policeman with white sleeves covering the arms of his uniform waved them back into the inside lane. The slowed traffic went past a brown van that had missed the turn and run straight into the trunk of a huge maple tree, the van's front end crumpled up like a page of yesterday's newspaper readied for the garbage. What expectations, do you suppose, the driver of the van started the day with? How many of us get up in the morning and say: "Well, I'll be losing an eye or an ear on the way to work today." (On the other hand, if a broker phones, it's not unreasonable to expect the loss of an arm and at least one other limb.) Nobody leaves after breakfast for work saying: "If I live, I'll be home for dinner, darling. We're expecting a dissident to set off a pipe bomb in the church basement this afternoon." We don't think that way. Yet a moment's thought would tell you we're all on the road to ill health. The rest is mere topography.

Under the gloomy sky, the English countryside had not looked that much different from the terrain, so familiar, around the Donnis's country place outside Toronto, except a little greener. The rolling fields looked the same, the trees—tall oaks and elms and maples—looked much the same, the placid Holstein and Hereford cows munching away in the fields looked the same. The one difference one might note was that the English bulls—no cultural slur intended—looked quite a bit more passive.

Harvey, already run down by preparation for his getaway, now added to that fatigue by contemplating the mile long to-do list that resided both in his own memory and in that of his notebook computer. He had to find a furnished apartment as soon as possible and stock it. He had a suitcase full of magazines and journals to read to get ready for his new job in London. And, as a favour to Zygmunt, who was coming over the following week to fire the current manager of Sheardon-Cassidy's London office, Harvey had agreed to interview the short-listed candidates. That's how Zygmunt justified the Sheardon-Cassidy limousine to ferry Harvey in from the airport to a suite at the Dorchester Hotel.

The limousine wound its way through abandoned streets in the heart of the city. A bowler-hatted man with an umbrella scurried carelessly in front of the limousine. The driver honked. Katherine opened her eyes and looked around, moving her head only slightly.

"There already?"

"Almost."

"Would you mind, Mr. Markson, letting me off down the street from my aunt's. She's elderly and wouldn't quite understand if a stranger in a big limousine dropped me off at the door."

As Katherine spoke, a small smile did slip on to her face. It was not a full smile by any means. Beauty makes us quick to forgive those who have trespassed against us.

"Why don't you get settled in at your aunt's. I'm at the Dorchester. I'll send the driver over later and we can have tea at the hotel. The Dorchester serves the best afternoon tea in London. And wonderful watercress sandwiches. And then we could," said Harvey, "catch a couple of art galleries. If you don't stay up the day you arrive, the jet lag gets worse."

"I can't run out on my aunt the minute I'm in the door."

"You're going to be with her two whole weeks."

"Eaton Square is the next street, sir," said the driver.

"Stop here, please, driver," Katherine commanded. She rested her hand on Harvey's arm. "I'd like to. I can't."

Chh-i, toro, chh-i.

Nothing to lose, all was lost. "Are you coming back to London?"

The driver had gotten out and stood there holding Katherine's suitcase. As she stepped out of the car she said, "Things are a little complicated for me right now, Mr. Markson." No smile. She took her suitcase from the driver and walked off down the street.

They might as well have brought the dray-horses into the bullring and dragged old Harvey out by his cloven feet.

Ciao, matador.

The limousine pulled away from the curb as if sliding into a funeral cortege. At any rate, The Holy Sacred Task, to get Katherine to his bed, was off, forgotten and buried. Celibacy seemed a far more sensible lifestyle.

About forty-five minutes later Harvey heard the phone ring as he got out of a warm shower. He took his time to answer, probably just the front desk about something.

"Harvey, it's Katherine. Katherine, you know, from the airport. My aunt had to leave for her house in Mallorca unexpectedly. She left a key round at a neighbour's but the neighbour's gone out. I waited. I'm so tired I can't walk."

"Take a cab over. I'll meet you in the lobby."

"You're very kind. I'm sorry to do this to you. I didn't sleep a wink on the plane. I've never felt so desperate in my life. I didn't even thank you for the lift in from the airport. I must look like a total ingrate."

Henceforth she was known as Katherine the Ingrate.

Harvey strode back to the bathroom, retracing the wet footmarks on the thick gray carpet, dragging his bath towel behind him not unlike somebody about to be awarded both ears—maybe even a little tail.

IV.

TO GO BACK

About a half a mile up the road from the harbour sits Toronto's financial district, which stole its name from the road—Bay Street. Just before you get to the old city hall, a lovingly ornamented brown, almost pink, stone building with copper roofs turned green by time and a clock tower that chimes every quarter hour just to remind you of life's ephemerality, five towering, brash oblong boxes-on-end, by the mid-1980s, had completed a highly successful takeover of the sky. Ever since (except around the height of day), the former lead tenant of the sky hardly ever showed its face and might as well have lived behind the moon.

The first box on the west side of Bay Street was gold. The next one, black. Then came the tallest one in white marble. On the other side, the east side, there were two: one silver box and the last, the fifth, whose architect thought the colour spectrum had more to offer, chose a facade of polished red granite. These boxes may have looked like the typical curtain-walled office buildings of concrete and steel covered over with glass and anodized aluminum or marble, the kind of building that nowadays dominates the skyline of the modern city. They were not.

These were the temples of the five largest money-changing institutions in the country, the five largest chartered banks that graciously lent their names to the boxes without demanding collateral of any kind. At ground floor level, four of the boxes flaunted *salons de banque* with ceilings lofty enough to impress the myriads of depositors and withdrawers who choose to come and go non-electronically. Above the banking halls (as in, over the store), dwelt the bankers themselves in spacious offices, accessible only to the few and only after attendants with amiable smiles buzzed open the glass entrance doors. Up there in the quiet, they were better able to figure out ways to raise their banking fees, as your bank statements invariably claim (as if these calculations were done without any thought to future bonuses or shareholder demands), "in order to serve you better."

These bank-boxes housed every manner of business and organization: law firms and accounting firms, corporate head offices and investment firms, a chaplaincy, immigration offices, companies that specialized in temporary office help, doctors' offices, The Toronto Stock Exchange (where the faithful learned never to doubt the centuries-old upward slope of stock markets) and almost all other forms of modern commerce except for heavy manufacturing, open-pit mines, timber cutting or any other enterprise that requires hard physical labour. To offset that deficiency, the inhabitant executives, professionals, salespeople, secretaries and computer analysts worked up a sweat in the district's fitness clubs. People plunked down plastic cards, green or gold, to jog on treadmills, ride bikes that stand still or chase a small black ball around a room—opportunities to exercise something other than their stock options.

Below ground level, beneath the salons de banque, a labyrinth of concourses and passageways connected the boxes together and offered every conceivable kind of store from fashion to photography. Close by, huge bustling food-eating areas called "Gourmet Centres" cooked up on a minute's notice cuisine specialties from every corner of the known world to be taken away in small, highly-lithographed cardboard boxes or consumed right on the spot amid the clatter, buzz and laughter of thronging crowds.

Far above those pockets of giddiness and impatience, on the fifty-first floor of one of the oblong boxes-on-end, the black one (the acid-rich city air vetoed Mies Van der Rohe's original design choice of a rich chestnut brown), resided the offices of R. H. Winkes & Associates Inc., Investment Counsellors.

Only in our bleakest moments—in a lurching plane or a lawyer's office—when Nature pulls another one of Her dirty tricks, do we regress to the belief that events are unconnected to any scheme, let alone to any Grand Schemer. Only on those days do our hearts protest against the shoddy, slipshod set-up of our world. And then our hearts, like some ill-tempered judges, silently scream out: Order! Order! We must have order!

To the average stockbroker, intent to gain his or her fair

share of daily bread or perhaps a bit more, and who has to gaze all day at numbers and symbols of one sort or another to tell him, or her, what has, or has not, taken place in the market, an order stands not as something to contemplate but as something to fill. When the price of last week's "investment idea" jumps up six points—soars, to use journalese—the broker never leans back in his or her stuffed leather chair, hands cupped behind the head, to stare at the ceiling and wonder whether there's a grand scheme afoot or a Grand Schemer at work. A broker knows without question that what was at play was his or her own foresight and keen intelligence.

As Jonathan Swift put it, "The power of fortune is confessed only by the miserable, for the happy impute all success to prudence or merit."

A plain, unembossed, black-on-white business card in one particular financial community, this one located in downtown Toronto, but it could be anywhere, announced an exception to that rule: Rupert Haldane Winkes, B.Eng., C.A., M.B.A., C.F.A. In the 1997 *World of Finance's* poll of Canadian pension and endowment fund trustees to determine the top investment counsellors, R. H. Winkes & Associates placed first in every single category save communications.

During the week, from seven in the morning until seven at night, at the earliest, but often until eight or ten—some said because of marriage held together more by loyalty than compatibility—you would find Rupert Haldane Winkes at his desk. With a sharpened pencil in his hand, his black, shelf-like eyebrows pointed down at a glossy annual report, which, as if a Talmudic scholar, he would always read from back to front. He began at the Notes to the Audited Statements and worked his way forward to the chief executive officer's message at the front, looking not necessarily so much for revelation as for deceit or concealment. How well had management walked that thin-thin line between the wrath of tax collectors and the demands of shareholders who might become disgruntled over the meagreness of earnings? How much credit did management take when earnings grew? How much blame when they shrunk? (Plummeted, in the words of *The World of Finance.*) Did the company attribute its fate to a rise in interest rates or to a slowdown in the economy or to the silly bastards in Ottawa, to borrow a commonly deployed Street expression?

Rupert would read with meticulous care, stopping every once in a while to tap some buttons of an antiquated gray Olivetti calculator and then to pull down its noisy crank. One of Rupert's arguments for keeping that mechanical relic was that it had no batteries to run down nor would it encounter any problems with changeover from 1999 to 2000. When he presented such arguments, a child-like grin would come on his face as if he had discovered humour for all of mankind.

Or you might catch Rupert with the phone nestled between his shoulder and the darkened skin of his neck rutted by time and the sun, with that black shelf of eyebrows pointed straight ahead toward one of the walls of books. As he listened intently, he would make brief notes on the yellow lined pad kept always at his right hand. He might for a second neaten the stack of colour-coded file folders on his desk. By Rupert's calculations, in a properly run business, you kept everything neat and in first class working order or paid a price. And you listened far more than you talked.

"Unn-hnn...Unn-hnnn...Unn-hnn...Thank you, we won't be interested. Unn-hnn...Unnnn....Unn-hnn... Thank you. Just not our kind of investment. Thank you," Rupert would say in his deep, stern, monotone voice that shared characteristics with a muted fog horn, and then lay the phone gently back in its cradle.

"Not our kind of investment" usually meant a lack of faith. "If management's not honest, you got to watch them twice over. How they run their business. And how they run their books. Each on its own's a full-time job. I don't have time to be a forensic accountant and an analyst."

High on the list of those Rupert found little time for were the cheaters, whose numbers never really added up. Nor the incompetents, who took full credit for the ups but, once earnings dropped, had a hundred reasons and excuses, all fully described in the "CEO's Comments" of the company's annual report. He claimed he never read a report that attributed the earnings shortfall to a lack of foresight or preparation. Not far behind on his list stood "lickspittles" (Where would he get an expression like that?) and those people Rupert referred to as the "merchants of mendacity" or "storytellers," people who made stories up about companies that bore little relation to the eventual results.

"What utter nonsense, Harvey, for God's sake!" Rupert might say after he finished reading the daily "Outlook" column of *The World of Finance* written by the Economics Editor, Lawrence Lipakowksi, B.A., M.A. (Econ.). "Lipakowski can't possibly know what's on Clinton's mind. Why do people bother with such junk? Beats me. It's nothing more than a gossip column on the future. Lipakowski can't write and he surely can't think. How does he get away with it? Look at this, Harvey, from last spring." Rupert plucked out from a lower drawer of his desk a file labelled "market predictions," and from it took a newspaper clipping, the date carefully written on the upper right-hand corner. "Last spring he said rates would go up. They went down. Then in the summer he said the market would continue to rise and it dropped eight per cent in the next three weeks. Then he tells his readers to get into gold. What does he know about gold? Next time he calls looking for a quote from me, I'm going to tell him: You ought to include an offer of free towels with your columns, 'cause one thing's for sure, Larry, anybody who listens to your predictions will end up taking a bath." All this delivered with a face as straight as that of Moses coming down from the Mount. Then he continued. "What utter nonsense. I'll tell you one thing: not in his lifetime will anybody accuse Larry Lipakowski of having to fend off omniscience."

Rupert said he read Lipakowksi's columns because he considered a Lipakowski "buy" recommendation an unusually reliable signal to sell. "If it weren't for the distortions those journalists bring to the market," he said on more than one instance, "we'd have to work twice as hard. There'd be no one to spread the pessimism or the euphoria," Rupert would reach for his pipe and put it in his mouth for a moment and then return it to the unsoiled ash tray. Never once did tobacco find its way into the pipe.

"Harvey, see? The last thing we need around this place is an economist. They're only good for using up newsprint. And for window dressing." That child-like smile returned to his face accompanied by a little laugh, "Larry Lipakowski's very own window dressing made from pure sour grapes." He sucked on the pipe again. "I'll tell you, if he could sell cars or computers anywhere near as well as he merchandises his mendacity, the man would be in the Forbes Four Hundred Richest."

Larry Lipakowski trying to fend off omniscience. What a scene that would make. Larry of all people. Jesus, if Rupert only knew, if he only knew what happened to his beloved Winkes & Associates he'd resurrect himself tomorrow.

"Wrong-heads like Garzarelli, Granville, Russsell, or Lipakowski think they can predict the market. They can't. At this point in time, nobody can. Maybe the computer guys will come up with something someday. Chaos theory or maybe some genius mathematician will, we'll see. At least we know we're not smart enough to do it. That's where our edge comes from—from being stupid. Although I say one thing: whenever the brokers start hiring people left and right, you know the market's about to take a good tumble."

His sermon ended, Rupert took out a large red handkerchief, the kind farmers wear around the neck, and blew his nose. That nose took a sharp drop halfway down and which, along with his large black, moist, all-seeing eyes, provided reason enough for his fellow Street inhabitants, especially Zygmunt who had a label for everybody, to call him The Hawk or The Owl. But nobody did. Nobody referred to Rupert as anything other than Rupert. Even the parking lot attendant and the barber used the name Rupert, although usually preceded by "mister." Only on the rarest of occasions, in the five years Harvey worked with Rupert, did he hear Rupert have to use his last name, let alone spell "Winkes," even with people never seen nor met. On The Street all rights to the name Rupert belonged to one person and one person alone—Rupert Haldane Winkes—in the same way that there is name reserved for G-d and nobody else.

When not at his desk in his corner office, Rupert liked to sit over in the outsized red leather chair that could accommodate comfortably his six-foot-four body. That was Rupert's throne. Nobody else ever sat in it. It formed an arrangement with two smaller chairs and a long couch, all in red leather, which stood as a foursome around a black marble coffee table, an arrangement placed far enough in front of the book shelves to allow a person to pass behind it on the one badly worn part of the maroon rug. Thirteen years before, as a temporary measure for the overflow of books, Rupert, indifferent to the loss of prestige, got special permission from the landlord and had freestanding book shelves installed along the glass wall that faced the gold tower across the street. That turned his corner office into a cave, a place of refuge for the intellect.

The huge white *Webster's Complete Dictionary* and the *Manfrost World Encyclopedia,* both of which spent most of their time on the coffee table open to one reference or another, plus a few other compendia as well, were perhaps the only books in Rupert's library that had not been read at least once by him from cover to cover. Books not read in their entirety simply did not qualify for shelf space.

The section for business books included all of Peter Drucker's publications, several books on strategy, such as Kenichi Ohmae's *The Strategist* and Peter Senge's *Fifth Discipline,* at least a dozen books on marketing, including Porter's *Marketing Mystique,* and a whole shelf on organizational strategy. Dozens of other books had offered themselves for these walls through junk mail circulars, all of which Rupert perused quickly in the day's mail file; but seldom did the candidates nominated by glossy brochures make it to those walls that Rupert referred to as his "knowledge warehouse." The section on investments held only a well-thumbed and well-marked-up copy of Graham and Dodd's work on investment analysis. Most of the other published material on this subject including past copies of the *Financial Analysts Journal* were kept in the company's main library, three doors down the hall. Among his many accounting books, Rupert did make room for R.Y. Maningo's *Reality and Generally Accepted Accounting Principles,* according to Rupert, unequalled for flawed logic.

On the high shelf in the farthest corner sat the works of Malthus, Ricardo and Adam Smith, but nothing about economics, micro or macro, from Keynes on. Another section held dictionaries and *Fowler's Modern English Usage.* And a real Bible. When the Bible came up in conversation with some broker, to introduce a little surprise, Rupert would pull it down from the shelf. Most of colleagues on the Street would have expected *The World of Finance.* The only book in stock under the category of "Religion" in the bookstore on the concourse level of the black bank tower was Arthur Cranston-Naismith's *Comfort in the House of the Lord,* a smallish book that dealt with the profitability of converting unfrequented city churches into condominiums.

Rupert always referred to one part of his bookshelves as his rainy day section. You would find there, with the exception of Schliermacher and Schopenhauer whom he detested, writings of many of the great thinkers: Plato and Aristotle, Plotinus, Maimonides, St. Thomas, St. Anselm, Descartes, Locke, Spinoza, Hume, Hegel, Kierkegaard, Nietzsche, Bradley, Josiah Royce, William James, Buber, Russell, Bergson, Teilhard de Chardin and many of Heidegger's works including *Sein und Zeit* and several commentaries on it as well as his *Introduction to Metaphysics,* a half dozen contemporary works such as those of John Rawls and Julian Jaynes, four of the latest books on Chaos Theory and a complete set of Copplestone's *History of Philosophy* in rather old, mottled brown paperbacks. Three bin-like sections contained the contemporary reports on the state of the world from six daily and three weekly newspapers and the latest editions of some thirty monthly magazines (not bad for a man who held no love for journalism). It often seemed as though he could retain the thoughts behind every word he read for months and months if not forever. Some people thought he knew everything.

While many people on The Street had some difficulty understanding the word integrity and some when they had occasion to write it used only "i's," such was not the case with Rupert. If its press releases suggested for one second misrepresentation of facts or conflict of interests, Rupert would not spend a second on the company's annual report. "Where there's no integrity, you get only short-term thinking. That's okay in some businesses. Maybe if you're selling beer. But not if you want to stay in business for any length of time. Cheating is a surefire formula for bankruptcy." He scribbled those last words down on his yellow pad as a reminder to add them to his notebooks.

He missed out on many flash-in-the-pan opportunities. He didn't buy a single share of Air Ungava because the president sold one of its planes from inventory to raise cash and then persuaded his accountants to allow the profit to be counted as ordinary profit, though it was in the notes. "Airlines aren't in the used plane business, now are they?" Rupert said and shook his head back and forth as he did whenever he found some company cooking their financial statements. At the first sign of inclement financial weather for airlines, Air Ungava filed for creditor protection.

Another hot stock that he claimed he got a dozen phone calls about was Mirth Financial Services, a chain of financial planning boutiques that delivered fantastic profit margins selling mutual funds. He remembered a story, and even dug it out from an old copy of *The World of Finance,* how the president had charged double commission when investing the insurance settlement of a woman rendered paraplegic by a car accident. Never invested a nickel there. And he wouldn't put a nickel in any company associated in any manner with Piggy Donnis. Put another way, whenever the Donnis group of companies tried to sell a new or secondary issue of shares to raise capital, not one share found its way into the portfolios managed by R.H. Winkes & Associates. Put yet another way, whenever Piggy went to market, Rupert stayed home. And although Rupert admired Donnis's wife Grace (who didn't?), he would not have accepted her as a client except for Harvey's long-standing friendship with her and her niece.

No one on the Street would be surprised to find a whole shelf of books dedicated to environmental concerns. Letters to the editor from Rupert often appeared in the morning paper all making the same simple point: it was bad corporate management to ignore the environment. And for the last three years, having previously served on many, the only charity he worked on was the Nassagaweya Conservation Association, a charity set up by him to protect wildlife in the township where his farm was.

And there was the famous shelf with a dozen and half notebooks labelled "Insights" in which he had recorded, in pencil, thoughts—his, but mostly those of others—that seemed to sum things up. One entry of his read: *The Street is nothing more than a feast of hope. When the market charges ahead, everybody hopes to make a killing. When it starts to tumble, they pray to God not to get killed.*

His office was an island. No, it was a lonely beach on which one individual calmly put forth an ocean of effort trying to figure out what in hell was about to roll in next. Around the office, seemingly immune to Nature's whims, Rupert, the captain, walked the maroon decks of R. H. Winkes & Associates offices with absolute confidence and seeming omniscience. Away from his ship, however, with only a few exceptions, he acted the duck out of water.

After a sentence or two of small talk, Rupert would direct the conversation to topics like some shortcomings of Modern Portfolio Theory, Chomsky's comments on the undemocratic mindset of the media or, if you preferred, Heidegger's failure to produce, as promised in *Sein und Zeit*, an analysis of Time. Either that or the conversation collided with embarrassing silences while Rupert twisted his body back and forth, his hands in his back pockets like a farmer in overalls. On the other hand, if he got to a third sentence as he did at the annual meeting of Cryogenics Diversified in April of '94, he cut to ribbons the proposal of Neville Kent, Cyrogenics' chairman, to assign special voting rights to the A shares, held mostly by the Chairman and his supporters.

Would such a change of character make Rupert that much different from anybody else? Aren't we all environmental chameleons? Bold here, meek there. Grandiloquent, conquering heroes in our studies and warm showers, yet, outside, confronted by some fat-fingered traffic cop, more often than not, we become self-defeating stammerers. It was only on those odd occasions that Rupert seemed human. The rest of the time he seemed like some indestructible god.

Most days as the venue for lunch, Rupert would select his sturdy, well-shined, mahogany desk. From the black tower's penthouse restaurant, three floors above the Winkes' offices, the busboy with his timid smile would bring down "the usual": simple consommé soup and a sliced chicken sandwich on rye toast, no butter, and definitely no "marge." Not an extra gram of fat resided in or around Rupert's tall body. Fastidiously, he stood guard against the entry of even one unnecessary molecule of cholesterol into his cardio-vascular system. Working around his farm as hard as he did on weekends and holidays kept him twice as fit as Harvey who, twenty-five years younger, played squash or tennis, jogged or worked out a couple of times a week. It was of course not a matter of vanity with Rupert but judgment. Certainly his sombre neckties, not quite snug to the collar, gave no indication of a man concerned with appearances.

"As far as I can tell, of all the things I've invested in, good health's given me the best return by a mile," Rupert would say in defence of his eating habits. Although Rupert received enough lunch invitations to last through this life and the next two, usually from brokerage salesmen assigned to the Winkes & Associates account or from a colleague who wanted him to sit on some industry committee or from people who just wanted to pick his brain, seldom did he go. He treated time with reverence and rationed every second of it for good use. On the rare occasion when he did go out to lunch he would never let anybody else pay for his. That was an oddity in a community of people who pursued, with the all determination of Arthurian knights, the holy grail of a free lunch, preferably a risk-free, free lunch (such as a "best efforts" arrangement when underwriting a new share issue for some company).

By the end of the five years the two men worked together, at least two dozen of the books on the shelves of the TV room in Harvey's apartment bore the same titles as those found in the non-business section of Rupert's office. At a strategy lunch with Rupert the specialty was never the soup du jour, nor the plat du jour, but the intellectual catch of the day.

"What are we, Harvey?"

"Investment counsellors," answered Harvey uncomfortably, as if part of a Socratic dialogue.

"No, we're vultures." Typical Rupert. "We prey on other people's ignorance." Rupert would start off slowly, scanning the menu as he talked, his head down, his voice in a matter-of-fact monotone. "We're scavengers. We look for situations people have given up for dead. If we thought the other investors knew what they were doing, we wouldn't touch the bloody stock. Why do we stay away from gold? Because we're ignoramuses about gold. We'd get eaten alive. But take that idea you brought in last week, Lehigh Robotics, why are we looking at it? Because we figure, at this point in time, we can understand that company better than any other investor around. By the time you're through, if we decide to invest our time—and it will take plenty—we'll know the company inside and out, almost better than management itself. You know, Harvey, what I think we are? Slow-buck artists." Rupert laughed. "Yup, we're probably the only slow-buck artists on The Street."

Rupert made one feel like he was a pipeline to the truth. He might say something like "the trouble with organized religion is that they promise you an 800 number to God and instead give you a 900 number." Or, "religions are fine right up to the point they get organized." Or, in mid-conversation, he might throw in a La Rochefoucauld-like aphorism: "Of all the tools at our disposal—the hammer, the saw, the knife, the wheel, the computer—the one the most under-designed for the job it's to do, is the mind." If he did not a hold a broker in high regard, Rupert would never call the man stupid or dishonest. He once said of Ferdinand Swasont that "the notion of honesty was simply not a candidate for Ferdy's consciousness."

Not a candidate for consciousness? That was vintage Rupert. At times, Harvey felt that Rupert could have written the Ten Commandments.

Those who knew Rupert, or of him, fell into two camps: In one, stood the admirers of the power of his exceptional mind that held fear for no one. In the other, those who took it as self-evident that the higher powers on The Street ruled not out of privilege but by divine right saw him as an arrogant and stubborn troublemaker—an outright heretic, always questioning the system.

Even some of the followers of the latter camp re-arranged their Saturday golf games and drove the thirty-five miles along Highway 401 west to Campbellville for the brief memorial service. No casket, no hymns, only a few brief words from a neighbour, whose voice cracked whenever he used the word integrity. The service was short. None of the attendees was invited to gather back after at Rupert's farmhouse up the road.

As far as the police could determine, two nights before, driving north at the speed limit along the Side Road Number Sixteen on his way to the monthly meeting of the

Nassagaweya Conservation Association, of which he was founder and chairman, Rupert had swerved to avoid a white-tailed deer. The car hit the deer, then slid off the rain-covered pavement and tumbled eighteen feet down a steep embankment landing upside down on a huge boulder which crushed the car's roof into the floor boards. As if his old Volvo was some kind of fast-acting crucifix, in one swift, ill-designed moment the omniscient, omnipotent Rupert Haldane Winkes was slipped into non-existence. A kind of *deus ex machina* in reverse had been introduced, and rather than resolving things, it complicated them.

An announcement with a black border around it—the border twice the thickness a newspaper uses when admitting mistakes—appeared in *The World of Finance* and two other newspapers. It stated that, out of respect to the loss of their leader and friend, R. H. Winkes & Associates would remain closed that Friday and the following Monday.

One change changed everything. Everything became new. Everything old looked new and unfamiliar—a sort of orderly chaos.

Harvey went into the office on the Monday to write a letter of condolence to Rupert's wife. After eight revisions on his word processor, he wrote it out in longhand and sent it off. (He never received an acknowledgment.) Before starting work on his to-do list, he walked down the empty hallway, the phones silent as if in mourning, and into Rupert's corner office. He sat down on the red leather couch in the corner, not in Rupert's desk chair, left neatly as always square to the desk. That would have seemed sacrilegious.

The big leather chair, the throne, the seat of power, sat in its stillness like a museum piece speaking only of the past, not, as before, about the shape of the future. The mahogany desk, the birth site of dozens and dozens of insights and solid, studied opinions could never regain its prestige. Death had aged the old black Olivetti calculator and transformed it from a lively curiosity to an antiquated oddity. Before the death, each book sat neatly in its place on the dark-stained shelves, sat there not as paper and glue and printer's ink, but as Rupert's allies that could be called upon at any moment for support. That alliance between Rupert and his room, which now smelled like the stale air of a church basement, had fallen apart and revealed its symbiotic weakness. The book spines of simple black, dark blue or washed-out brown, their gold or silver titles almost worn off, stood now as mere decoration, as so much wall covering to be bought or sold by the foot through "Inferiors" or one of its suppliers.

No book had gained acceptance to those shelves unless cherished. Any book that Rupert read or perused and could not find a use for was driven, twice a year in his eight-year-old Volvo station wagon along with the other unsuccessful candidates, to the Campbellville Public Library.

One book, Heidegger's *Being and Time*, sat on the coffee table. Harvey thumbed through it and found annotations on almost every other page: sometimes nothing more than a "!" or a "??" or a "wow!!!" Sometimes a scrawled "word play." Rupert lived in his books. But without Rupert to wield them, the books and the papers and magazines were lifeless crossbows, catapults, lances, spears—outmoded weapons—their efficacy stolen from them by change. And Rupert was no longer there to say whether the change was for the better. Or for the worse.

V.

REVELATIONS

"Hi, Harvey. Leon Kelpner, Roberta Winkes' brother," the man by the window said as he looked up from reading *Being and Time* and crossed the room, his hand held out. It was Tuesday morning about nine thirty. A breakfast meeting of the trustees of the Museum's endowment fund had gone on longer than scheduled and kept Harvey late.

"Harvey Markson."

"Did Rupert really understand any of this bunk?" said Leon laughing, as he tossed the book down on the coffee table and seated himself in Rupert's armchair over by the bookshelves. "My sister told me you and Rupert talked a lot about abstract things. She also told me Rupert claimed he couldn't run this place without you."

"How is your sister doing?"

"She's still in shock really. Rupert was in such good health she had never given a thought to his not being around to look after her."

No doubt serving the same function as labels mothers sew on their children's clothes for camp, the right cuff of his pink shirt proclaimed the owner to be RJLK and it half concealed a white handkerchief that peeked out from under.

"We worked well together," said Harvey. "Rupert was exceptional. Nobody on The Street understood the numbers—or The Street—better than Rupert."

"Look, I have to be back at my office. I've got patients coming in at eleven. So I don't have much time this morning. I wanted to bring you up to date. Have you got a minute?"

"Sure, of course. Let me tell them at reception." Harvey picked up the phone, tapped the zero key and then said softly, "Hold calls, please."

"My sister doesn't know the first thing about this business or, for that matter, any other business. At this stage in her life it's a little late to learn, wouldn't you say? She'll probably move to Florida or maybe Nassau. She always hated the winters here, even more so since she broke her hip last year. I don't blame her. Just to talk of winter gives me the shivers."

Leon pulled out the handkerchief out from under his shirt sleeve, dabbed both sides of his nose, then stuffed it back under. An inch or so of it still showed.

"My sister agreed to sell me Rupert's shares. I've always been intrigued by this business. Managing other people's money is the business to be in today. Everybody's getting older. They have to save for retirement. The market is huge. And, you know, I always felt Rupert didn't promote this company nearly well enough. Whoever heard of him outside of Bay Street?" Leon leaned closer. "But I don't want to be involved in the day-to-day stuff. I'm a periodontist. I know gums. But I've got a ton of connections. I'm a director at the Academy of Periodontology. I know a ton of journalists. And I've got some ideas that'll make both of us a lot money." Leon brushed back into place the gray and black cowlick that had fallen over his forehead. "I want you to run the company. When things settle down a bit we'll talk salary and share options and all that stuff. For now let's just see what we can get going. I always think it's better to go steady before you get married, don't you?"

Then Leon laughed. It was a loud, pneumatic laugh, the sound of a jackhammer biting into concrete or of an oversized outboard motor starting up on a still lake at dawn.

"I don't know what to say about the guy. In some ways he seems okay. But, God, he keeps a handkerchief tucked in his sleeve. What the hell is that all about? Then again, the guy grew up in Montreal, what can you expect? It's all show business with those guys," Harvey said. "Old Rupert never talked about his wife let alone his brother-in-law. Rupert was such a, you know, private person. Always referred to her as Mrs. Winkes. I didn't even know her name was Roberta. Somehow I suspected she had a drinking problem. Never knew a brother Leon existed. I don't know what to think. Seems more like a car salesman than a dentist."

"I'll tell you what to think," said Zygmunt his words broken by the intake of large gulps of air as he placed his squash racquet beside the couch he was on. "Think about getting the hell out of there. A.S.A.P. Can you seriously imagine any man saying 'lets go steady before we get married' for chrissake? I don't know if there'll be any marriage, but I do know one thing. Somebody's going to get screwed." A few more gulps of air. "Before that somebody is Harvey Markson, sell him your Winkes shares, get your dough, pay off the bank and get the hell out of there. I don't care what you do. Come and work for us. Go back to managing bond portfolios at some insurance company. Blow town. Go and live in Tokyo. Istanbul. Nairobi, if you like. London. Paris. Rome. Find yourself a nice woman. Not that there's anything wrong with Sara, except she's fallen in love with her career." Zygmunt leaned forward not unlike Leon did. "You know, Harvey, today, with your talent, your experience, the fact that you worked with Rupert for five years, goddamn Rupert H. Winkes, I mean, you could work anywhere in the goddamn world you wanted to. All's I'm saying is your first move is to get the hell out of Winkes & Associates."

Contrast Zygmunt's approach with that of Rupert's. If you had a problem or a proposal or an idea of some sort, Rupert would sip his tisane tea and listen to you quietly, always with concentrated eyes and an intensity that made you feel nothing else in this world mattered to him. At the end of each point or sub-point the person speaking made, Rupert, in his deep voice and slow manner, would ask a brief question or utter a "u-hnnn" of suspended judgment until a line of action of some sort, interim or final, was reached. And those solutions always sounded simple and completely devoid of uncertainty.

"Get the hell out? Sure. Why not? What do I care about our clients? What do I care about the staff? What do I care about making a living?"

"Steward," Zygmunt said in a raised voice to the white-coated man a few feet away behind the bar, "two club sandwiches and two sodas with bitters. A squirt of lime juice in mine. Two cubes of ice. Lime not lemon. Right, steward?" In a whisper, out of earshot, Zygmunt added between gasps for breath, "He'll get it wrong. Ten bucks?"

In long, slow strokes Zygmunt ran a towel, first down the back of his neck and then around his face, each corpuscle brilliant red from overwork. "Admit it, Harvey, that last shot was a mis-hit. A definite mis-hit. You meant to take the ball down the wall. That's the third goddamn week in a row you beat me. You know, Harvey, I'm getting Susan to do your horoscope. I'm not playing you again while your luck's running this hot."

"Who's Susan?"

"Don't remember the last name? It's Italian. Susan Arrivederci or something. I met her last night at Thrace's, at the bar. She loves astrology. Women that believe in that psychic junk are always, always the easiest to bed. It's a sure sign. That or an ankle bracelet."

"I thought you were going to the opening of *Ragtime* with the woman from Winnipeg you met on the plane."

"The Pig and his goddamn management meetings they go on and on. I had to cancel and send her to the show with her roommate. The goddamn thing started at three and didn't end until after nine." Zygmunt blotted his face with the towel. "Can't get over it. What a total jerk The Pig can be. Good thing he owns most of the joint. Sometimes I think I'd be better off as his goddamn secretary. I want you to do this, Zyg. Do that, Zyg."

"You were at Thrace's?"

"Just for a nightcap. On the way home. This Susan woman I met and her friend came back to the apartment and did my horoscope. We got pretty drunk. No beddy-byes with the friend there, of course. Next time for sure. Only problem is I can't remember what the hell I did with her phone number."

"What's The Pig on about now?"

"Things haven't looked this good for Sheardon-Cassidy in five years. We're going to make a ton of dough this year, I know."

It was shortly after twelve-thirty noon on a Tuesday. Every Tuesday, if they were both in town, Harvey and Zyg would meet at The Bay Street Squash + Fitness Club, three floors below street level in the white bank tower in which Sheardon-Cassidy International Limited (known to The Street as "Sheer Mendacity"), Bay Street's largest independent investment dealer, had its good offices and that of its new, youngest president ever, Zygmunt Adams.

Zygmunt referred to this weekly meeting at the club as a "contest of mind and body." It began always with a game of squash as the "body" part of the contest, after which, puffing and groaning, the two mean would flop themselves, exhausted, on the chrome and green leather loveseats on either side of a low, bleached-oak table with a built-in backgammon board. As the "mind" part of the contest, they would play backgammon. That turned out to be either a game of unusual mental adroitness or of sheer luck, depending on whether Zygmunt won or lost. Simple rules: the loser of the squash game paid for the drinks, loser at backgammon paid for the sandwiches. After, they would shower and head back to their respective offices, usually no later than two o'clock.

In squash, as in many racquet sports, C is the grade

awarded a player of mediocre ability. The club pro had assigned Harvey a C. Zygmunt called himself a "high C." On talent alone he deserved an X or a Y. For his Nietzschean will to win, however, he'd get an "A++." No matter how far behind in the score, Zygmunt would charge around the court with all the elegance of three-legged rhinoceros, yet out to win every point, never letting up for a second. Harvey usually won the squash games, though not without a struggle. Zygmunt with his love of risk usually won the backgammon.

As he rattled the dice, Zygmunt acknowledged with a nod two men lunching on the other side of the lounge area, a mandatory gesture of recognition to fend off accusations of arrogance. Then as he contemplated the lay of the backgammon board, Zygmunt said, "Watch this—double sixes." The dice crackled across the board and settled. "Goddamn, another three."

A loud, sharp thwack came as a racquet smacked against Court Six's glass back wall to the side of the backgammon table. The muffled thud of a body against that wall followed by the usual sounds that punctuated lunch in the Bay Squash + Fitness Club player's lounge and often accompanied by groans of dismay—"Dear God!"—the cries of men abandoned in their moments of need.

The steward brought over a tray with two tall glasses on it.

"Which is mine?"

"That would be the one nearest you, Mr. Adams."

"Good-good," said Zygmunt as he scribbled a large Z on the orange chit. The diamond on his small finger flickered in the light that spilled through the glass back wall.

"Mr. Oink smells something's not quite kosher. Sweet Jesus.

We're starting to make dough everywhere but Europe. You think I'm a bad loser, you should see him. He can't stand to lose a single goddamn nickel. Of course, the Swasonts agree with him all the way. Ever since Donnis brought those two goofballs on the board, there's absolutely no reasoning with him. Anyway, I gotta shake things up in the London office for sure, probably Paris, too. When I handled the territory my best account over there was a guy named Gottfried de Holger. Ever heard of him?" As usual, Zygmunt didn't wait for an answer. "Every financial guy in Europe would give his oldest son to do business with de Holger. And looks like Jean-Claude, my guy, can't even get the door open. I mean I'm not saying The Pig doesn't have a point. It's just the way he goes about it."

Zyg took a sip of his drink and spat it back into the glass. "Ee-yihh! You owe me ten bucks, Markson. This is lemon. Taste it, for chrissake. Ten bucks. Cash. I don't take plastic. You can pay me in the locker room." Zygmunt took a second sip to confirm. "Steward." The people at the tables nearby turned around. "Steward, we agreed on lime, didn't we, steward? You promised. Steward. You, the one person in the world I thought I could trust."

Zygmunt grabbed the leather dice cup. He shook it and created clucking sound.

"On top of that, The Pig wants to take a software company public. It's a Blester deal. 'Member the guy I met at the racetrack? You know the guy that'd started up his own software company. He had this program called Save Your Time. Remember? I used to call it The Saviour? I thought it was going to make me a packet of dough just when I needed it."

"I thought that deal died a quiet death months ago."

"They finally got a marketing guy who knows what the hell he's doing. We got some venture capital for him, a couple of million. He needs a little more. The stock'll quadruple in the next year. Best software program I've ever seen. Absolutely fabulous. It'll save companies a ton of dough. It's a kind of project management tool that gets everybody in a company working on the right priority. Get rid of all that bureaucratic crap. Just think of what that would do for productivity. And you know what their slogan is? *Give yourself the time of your life.* Brilliant. Gotta be a winner. Gotta be."

Zygmunt shook the dice cup again and then tipped it to let the dice scramble across the board. The near one showed two dots, the far one only one." He took a sip of the drink the steward handed him. "Now you got it right, steward. I always said what a wonderful man you were, steward."

"How's the program work?" asked Harvey.

"It makes you figure out your priorities. Then it teaches you to break down the parts and go after them in the right order. It'll be the hottest piece of enterprise software on the market. Once they get some volume, the margins are absolutely stunning. Once the program's written, you just have marketing costs and it's just a matter of how many sales you can make. Then all the upgrades you can sell after that are practically pure gravy. Best part, it's going to change our lives."

"Yours maybe."

"Yours too. You'll invest."

"Not in some start-up with no earnings."

"This time you will. I'm putting more dough in it. If you had a nice little nest egg in the bank, you could tell Leon what the hell he could do with his Winkes & Associates," said Zygmunt turning his gaze down to the backgammon board.

"Hey, are you going to roll those damn dice or nurse them back to health, I have to get back to the office this year, you know. You don't have to rush. You're leaving anyway."

"Leaving what?"

"Winkes."

"Oh good, I thought you meant you wanted me to take my squash game on the pro circuit."

"Jesus, Harvey, how someone as naive as you survives down here baffles me. You needed Rupert and me both looking out for you. And now Rupert's buggered off and I have to do it all myself. I don't know if I'll have time for Sheardon-Cassidy."

"Zyg, look, I appreciate your concern. I do. Really. But I am perfectly capable of figuring this whole thing out for myself. I just need to get the lay of the land first."

"Give Kelpner two months and you'll be the lay of the land. He'll screw you blind. But you won't listen. You're so goddamn independent. You hate it when someone tells you what's good for you. You know, Harvey, not everything can be analyzed. Sometimes people just know. They just know. I haven't scratched my way up from nowhere to president and not learned a goddamn thing along the way."

"It's disgraceful the university hasn't offered you the Chair of Philosophy."

"I think they're waiting for me to graduate high school first. Watch this—double fives." The dice clinked and scurried across the table. "Son of a bitch!" Zyg moved one disc five spaces. "You may not know much about squash or backgammon, but you're as good an analyst as there is on The Street." The last words said slowly for emphasis. "But a library is not the only place in this world that has answers." Zygmunt started to wave a forefinger at Harvey. "Kelpner's a hustler.

Simple as that. I know hustlers. He'll screw you somehow... sometime. If not today, tomorrow. If not tomorrow, guess when? Next month. And if not next month, next year."

"How the hell do you know, Zygmunt? How can you be so sure? You're just guessing. You don't know the guy from Adam."

"There's where you're wrong, Harvey. I know all about Adams. That's my last name, you know." His late start on English showed up again. "Leon's a fox in sheep's clothing."

"You've never even met the guy."

"Don't need to," said Zygmunt as he rolled the dice and moved one of his disks. The steward placed the sandwiches down on the table. Steward, didn't your mother tell you limes are green and lemons are yellow."

"Zyg!"

"Your luck will turn, Mr. Adams," said the white-coated man in a strong Lancashire accent, not taking the situation seriously. "The drinks and sandwiches for your account this week again, sir?"

"The match is far from over. Far." Zyg took a bite of his sandwich. After replacing the ashtray, the steward moved away. "That business you told me about with the handkerchief tucked up his sleeve. Who does he think he is, Merlin the Magician? Jees-us. Who's he trying to kid? He's short. Full of energy. Exactly like me. I wouldn't trust the guy if he was the minister of the local church."

Zygmunt was often a little slow to reveal the supporting material for his judgments. "I thought I had Kelpner right on from what you told me on the phone. Just to be sure, I checked with our guys in Montreal. Seems..." Once again a racket smashed against the glass wall. Zygmunt raised his voice. "Seems Leon had a dental practice in perio... perio... gum specialist. Made a good living at it. Wouldn't match what you'd make on the squash circuit, mind you. He worked himself in as one of the directors of the Quebec Society of Dentists or whatever. One of his patients got him into real estate. Then the two of them put together a condo project in Ottawa which they flogged as tax shelters, mostly to Kelpner's dentist buddies in Montreal who couldn't wait to get their dough out of Quebec."

"What's wrong with that? You guys sell tax shelters."

"Yah, but we always overprice within reason. What I'm telling you is that every last one of those little Montreal dental lambs got flossed. The condos were way, way overpriced. Leon's partner made a nice little chunk of dough out of it. The architects and the developers did very nicely, thank you. And friend Leon? Well he made a packet, too. His colleagues didn't fare quite as well, unfortunately. That was back in '89. Some of them, they tell me, are still paying the bank off. Then for some reason it struck your esteemed associate, Dr. Kelpner, it might be a good idea to move his practice. Like here. The referrals had dried up."

"That's wild. You believe all that? You've told me yourself the minute a doctor loses a nickel he yells Cheater! Cheater!" Harvey finished his soda and bitters. "Look, Leon may be a promoter, but he doesn't need to cheat. He's got a profession."

Zygmunt didn't say a word. He shook his head back and forth two or three times. He blinked twice—slow blinks. Then he stared straight ahead, as if wondering whether his friend Harvey had spent the last ten years on The Street or in some adult daycare centre.

VI.

A NICE FRESH START

Is it the fascination of a new job that makes things in the early going work so well? Is it because a fresh start carries no backload of past sins? Is it because it's a sort of renaissance?

Whatever the reason, the new arrangement at H. R. Winkes & Associates seemed, in the beginning, to fare well. With all of Rupert's responsibilities added to his own, Harvey's day began in the office at seven—shades of Rupert—and ended in exactly the same place twelve or fourteen hours later. There were dozens of client calls that had to be taken or made. On top of that, research reports prepared by the firm's junior analysts and which were carried back and forth in the brown leather attaché case (a birthday gift his friend

Sara bought at the MOMA museum in New York), made up his bedtime reading. In the early days of the Rupert-less regime, Harvey needed all his energy to keep his to-dos at all manageable.

The disciplined investment approach, the almost maniacal attention to detail, everything checked and double checked, and the track record which put R. H. Winkes & Associates in the top decile of "Penfacts Survey of Investment Managers" five years straight, had won enough respect for the firm that clients appeared in no hurry to leave. But the money sharks smelled blood. Even in the random gathering outside the Campbellville Community Centre, before the memorial service for Rupert and after, people were making themselves known to other people. Vice-presidents from the Max Blugen Group, from PMS Inc., from Hargrove-Canning and the president of Latham, Sommers and Wilding all must have managed to get a word in with the many chief financial officers and dozen or so chief executive officers who had come that day to pay their last respects to their wise and trusted counsellor.

When it comes to the question of money—given its history, reputation and influence—we know loyalty has a half-life of about 3.5 nanoseconds. Six weeks later, even though Leon almost developed severe palsy over the salary involved, Harvey hired Richard Leiryter (pronounced lee-riter), who gave up his own consulting business to come and run the "bond side" for Winkes and take on some of Harvey's research work. Harvey's coup—ten or twelve firms including Sheardon-Cassidy would have hired Leiryter in a second to look after their fixed income portfolios—impressed even Zygmunt and, for a while, reduced to a trickle his predictions that if something drastic wasn't done the future path of R.H Winkes & Associates lead "south, very south."

Richard moved into the spare office, Harvey kept his old one and Leon took over Rupert's and made a few changes to it. The big mahogany desk now faced the wall. The small refrigerator in the lower corner of one of the bookshelves and which had never held anything other than fruit juices and mineral water, now contained bottles of Chablis and Meursault, not of recent vintage, and a tall bottle of Noilly Pratt Vermouth that had to be tilted to fit in. The bottom left-hand drawer of the desk where Rupert kept the Winkes monthly financials close to hand gave way to bottles of Chivas Regal and Seagram's Golden Gin. The cost of these new acquisitions got charged to a newly created expense category called "promotion."

As if legalized theft, nothing seem to give Leon more delight than a tax write-off. The "promotions" account grew quickly in size. Hundreds and then thousands of dollars for meals and drinks at Leon's golf club, bills from The Port Credit Golf and Sailing Club, began to show up every month. And as the golf season wound down, the names of journalists, public relations practitioners and the occasional marketing consultant or "guru" (Leon used the terms interchangeably) appeared on the American Express slips for Harvey's approval.

"Leverage, Harvey. We gotta leverage this high-priced talent we got around this joint."

For all the joy those write-offs gave Leon, they produced only one small new piece of business: a deferred profit-sharing of a James K. Butler Ltd., a clothing manufacturer run by an old friend of Leon's and which had a patchy profit history.

Wednesdays at eleven, Leon would leave what he called

"my cash flow machine" referring, of course, to the three oral hygienists in his employ, in order to come downtown to the Winkes offices for the weekly executive meeting in the company's cramped boardroom, which doubled as a reference library. The meetings were scheduled to start at noon. Sometimes they did, sometimes they didn't. It all depended on whether or not the Unbelievable Discount Mart on the concourse level, next to the parking garage elevator, had sidetracked Leon. Once, a saving of almost a dollar on each of four packages of Gillette Mach III razor blades delayed the meeting thirty-five minutes. Another time, a delay of twenty minutes resulted from the unusual opportunity to save twenty-three cents on a bottle of Grecian Formula hair treatment. During the golf season, no meeting went beyond two o'clock; Leon had a regular game that teed off at two forty-five.

In the executive meetings with Harvey and Joanne Patton-Userkawicz (pronounced "pat-on user-kawicz"), the senior secretary and office manager, Leon seldom hesitated to compliment Harvey's accomplishments—"Terrific stuff!" "Brilliant!" "Nicely done!" "Pure genius!" "Right on!" "Way to go, hero!"—as long as the commended feats required no additional outlay of money. Leon was never able to find time to read Harvey's memos or the minutes from the meetings or the notes from Harvey's meetings with Richard Leiryter. Once in a while Leon did delve into the reasons behind the purchase or sale of a stock like Cryogenics Diversified or Commonwealth National. An "Oh, I see" punctuated every thirty seconds of explanation. Often Leon would pull his handkerchief-from-the-sleeve trick and blow his nose. In fact, the main function of the meetings became the education of Dr. Leon Kelpner. D.D.S., Dip. Perio. on how to invest professionally. Had his patients any idea how slow he was to grasp even the simplest investment concepts (earnings multiples, discounted cash flow, book value) they would not have been caught dead in his motorized dental chair. And, as Harvey found out later, they would have had to search the city high and low to find a periodontist with higher fees.

Under Rupert, the board of directors of Winkes, composed of Rupert as chairman, Harvey as a second director, and Ms. Joanne Patton-Userkawicz as secretary-treasurer, met once a year to go through the annual ritual required by corporate law to accept the minutes of the previous year's annual meeting, the year's financial statements and to re-appoint the auditors. Within six minutes, there being no further business, the meeting was adjourned. Rupert and Harvey would sign the minutes that Joanne had typed up ahead of time. (She was quick, meticulous and loyal. The only objection Rupert ever raised was that after her marriage, the former Ms. Patton had to spend half the day on the phone spelling her name. Zygmunt claimed she had the best legs on Bay Street and in the days when she was just Ms. Patton, it was with a sense of respect and constraint seldom displayed by Zyg, that, on his visits to the Winkes office, he had not approached Joanne on matters totally unrelated to business.) Like so many boards, the board of directors of H. R. Winkes, de facto, directed nothing.

When Leon made himself chairman, president and chief executive officer, he installed as part-time treasurer an accountant he knew from the golf club with an eleven handicap. Harvey insisted there be no reduction to Joanne's salary. As a trade-off, Leon convinced Harvey to accept a small interim salary increase of $25,000 until they got a "better handle on how profitable this little joint's going to be, it's kind of a start-up at this point." When Harvey's business cards should have read Executive Vice President instead of just Vice President, "Use your old ones," said Leon. "Titles don't matter around here."

Except for expenses incurred, Leon never questioned anything Harvey did nor even glanced at any of the office correspondence. What a far cry from Rupert. Rupert had to know every detail. Not a cheque, not a purchase order, not a letter, not a report went out of Winkes without a neat RHW scribbled on the file copy.

"You think he didn't want you to get new cards to save money, Harvey?" Zygmunt's Lightning moved smoothly out of the Ontario Place marina one warm Thursday evening in July shortly after six o'clock. "What kind of raise did he give you for all your new responsibilities?" asked Zyg as he headed the boat out into the lake.

"Small. We have to see how things go first," said Harvey sloughing it off.

"Same old crap. Try now, pay later. That's Leon. He reminds me of a business broker from Vancouver I once got to know too well. If by dinner time, the guy hadn't cheated somebody out of something, he felt he hadn't done an honest day's work."

"I ever speak of Rupert's friend from London? Norman James?" asked Harvey, to change the subject. "Very British. Very much the gentlemen. He wrote me the nicest letter. Almost outright worship of Rupert. The postscript said if ever I got fed up here he'd have a job for me in London anytime."

"Take it."

"Things don't look so bad right now, Zyg. And we've got such a great staff. Leiryter may be young, but he's really, really bright."

"Can't be that good, you haven't been at Thrace's for a month. When was the last time you left your office at a decent hour?" Harvey took the tiller while Zygmunt turned off the motor and pulled down on a halyard, hand over hand, to raise the mainsail.

"Without Rupert of course it's a lot tougher. Sometimes I walk down the hall to get his opinion before I remember he's not around. For that moment the world doesn't make much sense. But I've got so much to do I just don't have time to think about that sort of stuff."

"Harv, what I'm going to do with you?" said Zyg as he retook command. "Coming about!" The boom and sail swung gently to the other side of the boat, making a thump at the end of its short journey. Harvey and Zygmunt moved to the windward side.

"Remember how Rupert told you that honesty was not a candidate for Ferdy's consciousness? Well, try and get this into your head." Zygmunt paused. "Fairness never was, never is and never will be a candidate the consciousness of Dr. Leon Kelpner. Can you not see that? Do you need an auditor's report, for chrissake, before you believe anything?"

The only sound to follow was the lap of waves against the hull. The fresh breeze that had carried them so promisingly out beyond the harbour, like an unhappy employee, had quit on the spot. The two men sat becalmed, the canvas sail above them flapping indifferently.

Zygmunt ignored the luffing sail and talked on "D'you see The Saviour closed today at three fifty. Good volume, too. We're going to be rich. Nice and bloody rich."

"But I don't know how I let you talk me into betting on something as wild as that. Do those guys really know what they're doing?"

"That Saviour's going to make us a pot full, Harvey, trust me." The two men sat motionless in the total calm. "I've always wanted to just take off. Sail to Africa or around South America or some place. You know what? When our ship comes in I'm gonna get rid of this tub."

On a Friday morning late that September, a sunless dawn disclosed a city drenched from rain. The streetlights had just gone out as Harvey's taxi drew up in the middle of a puddle beside the red bank tower. The ill-humoured taxi driver, an expert in international trade agreements ("Why should we ship all our jobs to Mexico?"), had forgotten to convey his thanks for Harvey's overly generous tip. Harvey had come down to the office to clear up a few things off his desk before the two-hour seminar he was about to present to the Financial Analysts Society of Toronto. The lights in the office were already on. Harvey walked down the corridor past the open door of Rupert's old office.

"Hi, Butch. Come on in a minute."

Leon didn't cross the room in his usual way with his hand outstretched. Instead, he remained by the window, the city behind him forming a sullen backdrop. Like some minister in contemplation of passage from the bible, Leon held Rupert's copy of Heidegger's *Being and Time* as if with a second try he might make some sense of it.

That same tableau, detail for detail, with that same mock-earnest grin, with that same lock of hair arranged to hang down over his forehead as it probably had back in high school days forty years before, a small rose in the coat lapel, the handkerchief peek-a-booing from under the shirt cuff, and, no doubt the same *Being and Time* of Rupert's, appeared in a photograph on the inside cover of a flimsy, black and orange promotional brochure entitled "H. R. Winkes & Associates: The Professionals." Inserted into that title by way of a carat were the hand-written words "World's Oldest" on the copy Zygmunt sent "fresh off the press" to Harvey eight months later.

"Anybody understand this gobbledygook? Probably the guy that wrote it didn't even." Leon yanked the cord on his pneumatic laughter.

"Rupert seemed to," said Harvey.

" 'So it is fitting,' " read Leon in a slightly pitched voice, 'that we should raise anew the question of the meaning of Being. But are we nowadays even perplexed at our inability to understand the expression "Being"?' " Then Leon added, "You bet we are." And he laughed again.

Harvey didn't.

"If Rupert was so goddamn smart, why would he waste time on utter crap like that?"

Leon pushed the book back in its slot on the shelf and then, with his hand, motioned towards the couch. "This'll have to be quick, Butch. I gotta catch a plane for Chicago. I'm in charge of hospitality suite at the AAP conference."

"AAP?"

"Fair enough. The American Academy of Periodontology. What's with those guys, I don't know. Every year I have to run the hospitality suite as if I'm the only guy in the whole shooting match that can fix gums and make people feel good."

"Sorry, Leon, I'm a little rushed. I'm giving a seminar on performance measurement in a half an hour," Harvey inserted.

"Sometime you'll have to explain all that to me," said Leon. "I bought us each a coffee. I wasn't sure if you wanted one."

"No, no thanks. I'll be drinking it all morning at the seminar."

Leon sat down in Rupert's old armchair. He took a sip from the paper cup, the back of one hand acting as a safety net against spillage. He put the cup back down on the coffee table and pulled out his handkerchief from under the shirt cuff and dabbed his mouth. Harvey seated on the other side of the coffee table in the middle of the red leather couch thoughtlessly spread out his arms across the back as if readying himself to be mounted on a crucifix.

"I've got some fabulous news, Butch, absolutely fabulous. I wanted to make sure you didn't get wind of it from somewhere else." Leon gave a little double cough. "When we lost the Municipal Workers' pension account last month, I began to think, hell, Harvey's no salesman. He may be our genius portfolio manager. But a salesman? Uh-uh. He shouldn't be out knocking on doors. That's silly. Complete waste of his talent."

"The Municipal Workers made the decision months ago. They told Rupert they wanted to take their portfolio in-house. That happens all the time. That's part of this business. Pension funds grow."

Leon got up from his chair walked over to the window and then back. "Fair enough," said Leon, "but how we gonna replace that business. You got a big account you can land us tomorrow?"

"I'm working on one."

"Who?"

"The Ontario Librarians' Association."

"Jesus, my cousin's a librarian. They're worse than lawyers. It takes them six generations to make up their minds." Leon came over and took another drink of coffee then returned to the window. "Look, plain and simple, you don't have the time to sell. I don't have time to either. I could, you know. I put myself through dentistry selling time-sharing packages. No, we need help. We need somebody who knows the right people, somebody who can open doors and tell our story. H.R. Winkes & Associates has one helluva nice track record. We have a great, great story to tell."

"That's not H.R. Winkes' track record. It's Rupert's. It's too early to go out for new business from people who don't know us. For the next while we need to concentrate on just holding on to the business we have. You were at the funeral. All kinds of people will be trying to take it away from us. We need time"

"How much?"

"A year. Maybe two."

"I understand your line of reasoning completely. But the only line I'm really interested in is the one at the bottom of our profit and loss statement. Two years is out of the question. Six months is out of the question. I've got a fortune tied up in this company."

"We have to confirm the track record. Nobody new will come with us before that. That's the way it works. It took even Rupert—and he was the best in the business—almost a decade before the big players began to believe in him. It just simply doesn't happen overnight."

"No," said Leon. He got up out of the chair. "Rupert didn't take the track record to the grave with him. The track record belongs to Winkes. Same system. Same discipline. Same approach. Rupert explained all that stuff to me one night. I fell asleep halfway through, mind you, but I got the idea. You buy good companies in businesses you understand. At a good price, of course. Doesn't matter whether Rupert does it or you do it or the man in the moon does it."

"That may be. But, unfortunately, Leon, that's not the way pension fund trustees think." Harvey's words became firmer.

"Bull crap. We gotta start to toot our own horn—today. Now. Before someone else like the Municipal Workers jumps ship." Leon moved away from the window. "This little company's a gem, you know that? I've looked at tons of companies to buy. This is a gem. Unlimited potential. But Rupert was too low-key. So goddamn low-key that ten blocks from here nobody knows we exist. We gotta make noise." Leon sat down again and leaned back. Without looking up he said, "D'you know Lawrence Lipakowski? You know, the guy that writes all that economics stuff in *The World of Finance?*"

"Larry? Of course."

"Well, yesterday he agreed to come with us. He's the kind of guy who can put Winkes on the map. He knows everybody. Everybody. He knows every bank president on a first name basis." Leon paused. "This's going to make you a very wealthy young man. Very wealthy. I wanted you to hear the good news. That's why I came down here. Just imagine, Harv. With Larry on board we'll..."

On board? Molten blood surged down Harvey's arms, his stomach seemed to drop away like the bow of a ship lurching through heavy seas.

Negative news. A private Hiroshima. Another senseless Nagasaki, as senseless as the first one. An invisible Chernobyl.

The phone call, back in grade seven, to say that the wheel of a ski tow had severed the right arm of his best friend.

The day after Harvey's fourteenth birthday, his father's announcement in a lowered voice that he was moving out of the house permanently.

Back in university days, when Harvey learned first-hand that two large hazel-green eyes could take control of one's will—"Love, first learned in a lady's eyes"—and then the owner of those hazel-green eyes, on the third date, could tell him not to waste his time. "Men," she said, "did not and would never really interest her." God took leave that day.

The senseless, numbing death of Rupert.

His unrelenting absence.

No! No-o-o-o-o-o!

Shards of absurdity that pierce the heart and scar the spirit. Noiseless, world-splintering explosions.

From *The New York Times*:

> A speeding object from outer space that struck the earth 65 million years ago in a cataclysm that may have wiped out the dinosaur...produced what was

> perhaps the largest explosion to rock the planet since life began. The energy released by its impact is now estimated to be equal to the detonation of up to 300 million hydrogen bombs, each about 70 times more powerful than the atomic bomb that destroyed Hiroshima.

From a well-diversified portfolio of disasters, Nature can choose at anytime to smite our very best plans (and us, too). Are we not bloody fortunate when things do come together in our favour, even if it's only for a moment or two, now and again, every once in a while?

Of course, the fact is that at the moment things are not coming together for us at all these days. The tired, worn-out nation-state has been replaced by the person-state (except for soccer and the Olympics). Normally now, each of us moves about as an independently owned-and-operated political entity. Each of us finds himself, or herself, alone, in combat with a Universe unreasonably frugal with contentment and comfort. City-states offer no better alternative. They have turned into nothing more than four-lane battlefields for battles fought in low gear with our fellow man.

"Sorry, Zyg, traffic was godawful," said Harvey as he took off his coat and handed it to a young blonde woman in a light blue uniform with white lapels.

"Never mind, it's only the third inning," said Zygmunt as turned to the blonde hostess who tended bar in the Sheardon-Cassidy box that evening and said to her, "I'd like you to meet the person who was my best friend until you came along..."

"Marianne," said the hostess and held out her hand to shake Harvey's.

"Marion, I'd like you..."

"Marianne!"

"That's right. I'd like you to meet Harvey, my former best friend. Sadly, he doesn't care enough to phone me and tell me what the hell's going on in his life. He won't take the time to tell me, his best friend, that his company has just hired one of the great, great talents of modern finance. That, I have to hear that from our traders."

The men sat down each in a large Chinese-red chair, the kind of chair you'd normally find in a living room. This living room, however, had only three walls. Beyond the missing wall, at the far end of the room, as if from some cave, an expanse of green was interrupted only by large orangey-brown squares. Spotted here and there were men, most of them dressed in gray, though one was in white and three wore black jackets.

"Leon only told me early this morning. Out of the blue. I had an all-day seminar."

"Larry La Lip? Where the hell was Leon's head when he thought that one up? You'd think at this point in his life Leon would want to make a career change out of being a complete idiot."

"Leon thinks Larry will bring in a ton of business."

"What'd you tell him?"

"I told him it would have been nice if we'd talked it over first."

"Good-good."

"I said Larry may be a widely-read journalist and a trained economist, but Rupert did not have a great deal of respect for Larry's understanding of investments."

A boisterous cheer like some Greek chorus drowned out Zyg's reply.

The Sheardon-Cassidy box—twelve seats for viewing the field, a seating area with four large armchairs and a bar with three stools—overlooked the diamond from an ideal location halfway between home plate and first base. A fact, which at that point in time, made little difference to Harvey and Zygmunt. They paid no attention to the game.

"And?" said Zygmunt loudly, as if he was saying it for the third or fourth time.

"Leon said, 'Well, that may be very significant if Rupert were here. But he's not. So his opinion doesn't matter much.' And then he went on and said something like: 'Look, my bright young friend, you have a major, major contribution to make to this organization, we need you here.' Then he began to wave his finger at me. Then he went on and on about how the number of shares he owned said that he controlled the joint and he would decide what's best for best for the company. And then, 'If I have time discuss them with you, fine. If I don't, that's fine too. We can't afford the luxury of all-day workshops for decisions.' His voice became louder at the end. Then he backed off a little and said, 'Let's talk about it when I get back from Chicago, Butch.' And then he gave me a wink. One of those winks, you know, the kind you give somebody as if you're good buddies."

The crowd moaned.

"Where's that leave you?"

"I don't know. I really don't know. I can't just quit. How about the other people there? How about Joanne? And Richard? I just hired the guy. And the clients, what would they do? And where would I go? Every cent I've got is tied up in Winkes or in that stupid software company you got me into. And I owe the bank a ton for my Winkes shares. And, maybe I'm wrong. Maybe Larry might work out all right. You have to admit he's got terrific connections. He knows everybody. He could sell sand in the desert, just like you. As long as he doesn't start messing around with the portfolios, it could work. Who knows? But sometimes I think, I think, oh god, poor Rupert would die."

"He already did. That's the problem."

Harvey stroked the side of his head and ran a hand down the back of his neck. "Maybe one of the insurance companies will buy Leon out. They were always after Rupert to sell."

"Leon'd never sell. He's in love with the power. It's a big step up from writing prescriptions for dental floss. I saw him at lunch the other day. The way he had those waiters hopping you'd think he was Mr. Oink himself. Only brute force'll get him out of Winkes. Brute force, the Securities Commission or bankruptcy."

"Norman James, that friend of Rupert's from London, called today to ask if I knew anybody on Salomon's foreign exchange desk in New York. He repeated what he said in his letter. If I ever want a job, there's one waiting in London."

"I know you're going to say no, but why not try this on? Come on over and run my research department. That assembly of know-nothings on the nineteenth floor spews out nothing but absolute crap. Totally pathetic. The industry ratings for research departments came out yesterday. Our guys finished nowhere. You don't have to give me an answer right now, just give it some thought. You owe me that. Don't forget, I got you in here tonight for free."

"Zyg, I'd have to be completely out of my mind to work for you."

"Try to do a guy a favour and what do you get? Insults. Just think about it for a day or two, okay Harvey?"

As Zygmunt got up to go to the bar for another scotch the crowd's roar grew to frenzy. "Sara coming with you to The Pig's tomorrow night?"

"If she's back from New York in time. I'd like to skip it, but I told Grace I'd be there. Sure don't feel like talking to the Swasonts and everybody about how things are doing at Winkes."

"When I was with that woman I met at Thrace's last week I should've invited her. She studies astrology. You'd like her. She's read everything anybody ever printed on the subject. The only problem is I still can't remember her goddamn name to look up the phone number. I went through my Palm Pilot three times. Couldn't find it anywhere. Might have to bring Marion."

"Marianne."

"I'd better get her phone number just in case."

Harvey hardly heard the crowd's burst of glee. Nor did he take much notice of the two men down on the field in white uniforms jogging about. Explosions crackled through the night air, lit up by bursts of white, red and blue. Then a lazy cloud drifted into the sky as if everything had gone up in smoke.

VII.

BON CHANCE

The township of King lies twenty miles north of Toronto. Real estate ads for properties in that region always refer to the terrain as "rolling." Unlike the advertisement that led Harvey to his Tuscan Plaza condominium (written with the usual hyperbole—"outstanding craftsmanship"—a claim brought into contention by the original buyers and their lawsuit for $2.25 million over a couple of minor points, such as the second-rate detail work in all the kitchens and a plumbing system that leaked on every floor but one, a total misrepresentation by the builder, Integrity Developments, a company, you might remember, 49.1% owned by Reuben Eldred Donnis personally), "rolling" does, in fact, accurately describe the countryside of King Township. Tree-covered hilltops gracefully give way to low-lying fields in which groups of indolent, tail-swishing cattle, mostly Holstein, some poled Herefords and, occasionally, Charolais stand around still ponds. Ontario Provincial Highway Number 400 and its eight lanes of high-speed impatience—cars, trucks and flashing ambulances, hurrying to and from more northerly parts of the province—splits this undulating oasis of King Township into a less desirable eastern part and the more desirable western one.

If you've come up from the city, you turn off Highway 400, then go west a mile and a half along a paved, slender road, the King Sideroad, and then turn north again up the 7th Concession Road. Not forty feet after you turn, the macadam surface gives way to dirt, which is most likely to remain dirt, as long as Reuben Eldred Donnis puts his weight behind the local residents' association, which fights every attempt by the Township's works department to upgrade the road network of western half of King Township. Donnis, with first-hand knowledge of how developers can destroy the tranquility of a district, dug his hooves in at every mention of improving any road in his proximity.

At the next east-west sideroad, the standard mile and a quarter north of the King Sideroad, a freshly-painted, white, three-rail fence greets you on the left and for the next half mile accompanies you down into a treed valley and then meanders off over the next hill. (In contrast to the injured feelings that resulted whenever Donnis cut a deal in the city, on his country estate not one single fence stood in need of mending.) You then come to a short patch of well-tended lawn alongside the road with three mail boxes spaced about fifty yards apart, all painted in chocolate brown with white letters. The first one announces: "J. Duggan, Farm Manager." The second "A. Miscotti, Head Trainer," and finally with no proclaimed status, "Bon Chance," probably the sole recognition by Ruben Eldred Donnis, that something other than his own wit might have accounted for his out-sized fortune.

A few feet past the Bon Chance mailbox, Harvey turned in. He drove along the freshly paved driveway (evidence that Donnis bore no objection against asphalt itself), past a yellow field shorn of its hay, another with tall corn stalks, past an enclosure where, as the car approached, an aristocratic mare pranced away, her blonde mane spread out, toying with the breeze, then past a field of gray-white, unperturbed Charolais, some standing, some lying down, through a woods of birch and sugar maples, a few of their leaves already yellow and red, and over a small idle stream in which a pair of ducks with luminescent green heads and invisible means of locomotion floated up and down in search of a late afternoon snack. Then the woods opened onto a large span of immaculately groomed lawn. Harvey's car bobbed over a speed bump and then wound its way up a curved road, which reversed itself near the top and then—suddenly—presented the main house, which, with the help of long terraced gardens on either side, took up the better part of the horizon.

The house, bedded into a hilly perch, loomed over the fields in front of it as imposingly as a castle. The limestone of its gray walls came from the same quarry used for the town jail. So did that of the stone chimney, as well constructed as the rest of the house, if not better. On top of the chimney, the black silhouette of a cock stood upon arrows pointed in the four different directions each with a letter attached—N, E, S and an O—Eldred's little joke, brought back on one of his trips to France. Beneath the gray, slate-tiled roof, copper eaves, green with time, flowed into downspouts that dropped down past white-framed leaded windows guarded by large black shutters. A portico half concealed the front door of this magnificent chateau-house—an attempt, quite in the spirit of a French king, to show the world a thing or two about designed elegance.

A young blonde-haired girl in jeans and a white shirt far too large for her, with one of those friendly smiles common to country dwellers but seldom seen in modern cities, greeted Harvey with a wave and directed him towards the house rather than the field down to the right, which held four or five rows of cars. Harvey followed the driveway around, past Zygmunt's red Porsche parked sideways against the eight-door garage as was the large-model Mercedes of Roi Swasont. (As the story goes Swasont's birth certificate shows his name clearly as Roy St. John Swasont, but in his brief and unsuccessful fling as an actor, he changed the spelling to Roi. Only Zygmunt, with his European upbringing, and slight tendency to mock, gave it the French pronunciation close to "rw – ah.") The two men did share one thing in common: neither would allow another human to drive his car, let alone a makeshift valet service.

Harvey brought his unwashed blue Buick Regal to a stop under the portico. Instantly the car door was swung open by the farm manager's son, who Harvey knew from a night spent calving the previous year. The two chatted a moment. Harvey looked around, then took a deep breath of the grass-scented air, unexpectedly warm for that late in September, and walked to the front door as his car was driven off. A small brass plate hung on the doorknocker instructed guests to walk right in.

His late arrival meant that the brass-banistered stairway

that swept in full majesty up to the second floor was the only greeter in the entrance hall. He walked on through the arched oak doorway towards the buzz and cackle that formed the background for piano sounds of Jack Black, who always played for the Donnis parties, and the familiar admixed smell of cigarette smoke and alcohol.

Brass medallions, which in former days decorated the harnesses of carriage horses, hung along the long dark wooden beams that traversed the room below the pitched ceiling. Above the buzzing and cackling carpet of humanity could be seen the tops of large seascapes and landscapes and winterscapes at far end of the room. At this end, more sparsely populated at that moment, hung abstract paintings, most of them done by two well-known Canadian artists. Here and there hung muted Aubusson tapestries Grace Donnis had brought back from Europe. A Henry Moore maquette rested in a lighted recess of an oak-paneled wall. A small Renoir hung on the south wall as if its sole purpose was to match the blue of the Persian carpets.

A young man in a white pleated shirt, winged collar and red bow tie approached Harvey with a tray of champagne flutes, some pinkish others golden. Behind the waiter, a maid in a black dress and frilly white apron held a silver tray of chopped egg whites and yolks, finely cut up onion, a huge mound of black caviar granules surrounded by small squares of bread.

Such, the late September afternoon, was what Zygmunt referred to as "The Sty."

After so many visits, Harvey had come to feel quite at home with the honed-smooth luxury proffered by "Bon Chance." Here, at one reception or another, Harvey had met: Edward

Heath, former President Gerald Ford, the Archbishop of Canterbury, Prince Andrew, any number of lords and ladies, the Marquis de Beauveau and the Marquise (Grace's cousin) over from France to look at some show horses entered in the Royal Winter Fair. And Harvey had met ambassadors, consuls, cabinet ministers, members of parliament, film stars, actors, directors, good authors, bad authors, CEOs and CFOs by the dozen, almost any type of person that had had his or her hands on the wheels of power. You needed only a limited amount of exposure to the polish and charm of such people to learn how to conduct yourself in such social situations.

But whatever Harvey had learned from those experiences he had forgotten this night. Earlier in the day a barbarian economist had invaded his world. Harvey had nothing more to offer the other guests than a handshake and a quiet "hi."

The fondness Eldred's wife Grace held for her niece, Sara, seemed to transfer over to Harvey. Grace became not only a friend but a client when her father died and left her the proceeds the sale of the family home and a life insurance policy he paid into for almost forty years. The big financial trick for Harvey was to dissuade Grace from taking the year's profits and more for her "special causes": women who were victims of any kind—addiction, abuse or simply abandonment. That meant semi-annual lunches of reciprocal mentorship at which confessions and admonitions traveled in both directions, signs of a deep friendship. Had not time, with its typical indifference, put twenty years between their birthdates some other sort of relationship might have developed.

That attraction might explain Harvey's instant entrancement by Katherine the Ingrate, some months later on the getaway plane to London. There was a definite resemblance between Katherine and Grace. Well-kempt hair. That high-shouldered, regal bearing. The alert eyes. The patrician forehead slightly flattened at the sides. The same soft and unhurried movements. While Katherine seemed to have no need to watch her diet, Grace certainly did. Grace's passion for good food seemed the only aspect of her being not entirely within her self-control. A glass of wine in her husband's hand might not last sixty seconds; in hers it could easily last the whole evening. "I always like to remain mistress of myself," she would say in her soft, smooth voice. In contrast to Katherine, however, Grace had quick and ready smile for all except "miscreants" and that smile could put anyone at ease from her gardener to a member of the royal family and back down again to the stable hands who mucked out the stalls, and down further to economists and financial journalists.

Harvey had come this evening solely because he told Grace he would. Eldred's power and influence when combined with Grace's taste and spiritedness meant that an invitation to "Bon Chance" for any "function"—a party, dinner, gala, barbeque, fundraiser—was seldom refused. Grace seemed to find inactivity unbearable. So that if she was not promoting a social evening of some type—a table at the Latin Ball, a group for opening night at The Royal Winter Fair, The African Medical Relief Gala or The Junior Committee's Annual Costume Ball at The Art Gallery, bidders for The Children's Aid Society Silent Auction, ticket sales for The Ontario Cancer Society's Night of Fashion or the Anglican Church's chilli-cooking contest, or had no dinner party of some kind to go to—Grace did not stand still. She'd start a party herself.

"Harvey. Nice to see you," said of one of the guests.

"Hi, Harvey, Grace's been looking for you," said another.

"Hi, Harvey. Weren't you supposed to come in for a checkup last week?"

"I thought Sara was coming with you?" stated an older woman wearing ruby earrings and a very large matching ruby brooch.

"Couldn't make it back from New York in time," Harvey answered holding his glass above his shoulders to slip by.

"Harvey, don't forget our squash game Thursday."

Harvey thought he replied to those voices, but had no idea whether he had in fact spoken the words out loud, whispered them—or just thought them. He was searching out Grace.

Though Bon Chance had at its disposal eighteen hundred acres of the earth's surface, the guests had crammed themselves together in two large living rooms, not more than several hundred square feet.

"...those idiots in Ottawa..."

"...Elsie got her hearing back. And know the best part? She was in England and the government health program paid the whole shot. It didn't cost her a dime. Not. A. Dime."

"On the eighteenth I needed a birdie to whip this guy, so I said to my wife, Maureen, hand me..."

Familiar topics: health, the incompetence of government, newly discovered bargains and the favourite of all topics—the recent history of the self—the truth, you can be sure, adulterated no more than necessary to make something completely trivial seem important.

Harvey had no small talk in him.

Grace, on the far side of the huge living room, acknowledged Harvey's presence instantly with a smile and moved towards him. Ferdy Swasont (Roi's brother), joined her on her way over to comment on a new Bokhara rug in the library. The only rug on Harvey's mind was the one Leon had pulled out from under him the day before. And the only consolation was the thought how Leon would have given his eye-teeth—as well as those of many of his patients—to be hobnobbing at Bon Chance.

Had some embalmer come along and drained all the energy out of Harvey? His shoulders felt heavy and tight, his voice as if unable to project sound. The Monday before, he'd assured Grace he'd be at Bon Chance. Somehow he didn't feel very present.

When Ruben Eldred Donnis flunked out of Upper Canada College, a school attended by the sons of the more affluent and those that aspired to be such, where else would he have gone but down to The Street. He started as a "chalk boy" scratching the latest stock prices all day long on the huge blackboard of Frank Undershot Limited. Donnis's father had stumbled upon a small fortune shortly after the Second World War when the city sprawled out to meet his hundred-acre pig farm. Old Mr. Donnis sold it for a huge sum and retired. When young Reuben Eldred Donnis discovered how much more than his father the developers made out of his father's land, Donnis, at that point in his early twenties, took whatever money he could raise and bought a small "strip plaza" developer called Integrity Development Ltd. He liked the name. The company grew in the boom years of the sixties. It established his name in real estate and eventually as well on The Street, when he took his company public in 1969, pocketing millions for himself.

The Street People never reached unanimity on the origin

of Eldred's nickname. One school of thought said it derived from his father's occupation of pig farmer. A second school supported— enthusiastically, too—the notion that it came from Eldred's porcine-shaped ears, pointed at the top as they were, and turned slightly forward, plus the fact that he often pawed at his nose with his stubby fists. The old guard, those who knew him from high school days as Ruben, swore the nickname originated from Donnis's incessant talk of wanting to pork this or that particular student from the nearby sister learning institution. No one nominated avarice. Anyway, The Street People don't care much about the etymology of a name, where it came from is not nearly as important as where it can get you.

Would it not be safe, then, to conclude that when the Bishop of Abitibi who, some thirty years before, joined in holy wedlock "Pig" Donnis and the lovely Grace Susan Constance Barrett he had no difficulty whatsoever retaining his belief in the mystery of union?

"Harvey. I was beginning to worry," said Grace as she approached, her cheek angled for a greeting kiss, her pearls swaying on a simple black embroidered silk blouse. "I always admired you for your punctuality. Now I'll just have to find some other admirable quality. If there is one, that is," she chided, her finger waved in mock anger.

"Had a meeting with the lawyer at three. But he didn't get back from lunch until four. I'm sorry." (How often we suffer shame and embarrassment for actions of those under oath to help us.)

"If things aren't going so well without Rupert, it might be

a good thing later to talk to Eldred for a minute," Grace said quietly, moving a little closer to Harvey and looking across the room rather than at him as she spoke. One small comment about a lawyer and she knew something was up.

With his wife and over-flowing supper plate in hand, the president of one of the major banks began taxiing towards Grace from the other side of the room.

"Spend a little time with Aunt Viv, please Harvey," Grace whispered quickly. "You know how she loves you. I want to make sure she has a good time. I'll call you next week. You and I haven't talked since Eldred and I got back from the Bahamas. We should. I need to do a little capital un-preservation. Call me. And get yourself something to eat before it's all gone."

In a month, neither a battalion of troops fresh from battle nor a half dozen football teams could have consumed the food Grace had laid out for her guests that evening. Candelabras and large bouquets of purple rhododendrons and white lilies formed a row down the middle of the end-to-end oak refectory tables which, along with a few dozen oak chairs, Grace had "stolen" at an estate sale in Surrey, England, said to have belonged at one time to John Paul Getty. In the blink of an eyelash, she could put forth abundance.

"Cold dinner down this side, hot down the other," announced out one of the waitresses.

The near side began with six different salads—crab, Caesar, pasta, artichoke and tomato, avocado and eggplant, and spinach. Next on silver platters came sliced turkey, cold roast beef fading from pink to dark gray, lobsters sliced in half, salmon filets, olive foccacia and three other kinds of bread. On the other side, the same salads and four large silver chafing dishes, and the accompanying oily smell of burning Sterno, filled with broccoli, eggplant (Eldred's favourite vegetable), sautéed potatoes, frenched green beans with almonds, and the choice of lamb, pheasant or trout, to be accompanied by mint sauce, hollandaise, béarnaise, apple jelly, chutney, horseradish and several other condiments and sauces.

We all have areas of frugality. True, Eldred had more than most. Any frequent guest to Bon Chance would know that the contents of the decanters on the sideboard would, in Ferdy's words, disappoint. Eldred's taste ran more to single malt scotches. A more notorious area of frugality for him was in the area of charity. Many a fundraiser found Eldred's cheque, if it ever did arrive as promised, a greater a disappointment than any decanted wine. Acts of generosity, beyond lavish parties, which seemed only to give him an excuse to drink, came from Grace's resources.

Plates on their laps, wineglasses nearby on a table or on the floor, people in circles of five or six scattered themselves throughout the mansion, some in the dining wing, some in the second living room, some in the first living room, and there they chattered on about their worlds. The bank president, loud as ever, spoke about the government's latest attempt to separate him from $1.38 for the half dozen slices of smoked salmon he had at lunch that day by means of a "hideous" new tax.

In this sea of plenty, only places to sit fell into short supply.

On the very top of the stairway that wound its way up to the second floor, having climbed as high as he could, perhaps a social habit, like some king overseeing his vassals, sat Roi Swasont. His business card, which he handed out generously, stated that he was chairman and CEO of Swasont and Partners, a family-owned brokerage house that employed nine people including a part-time receptionist. Beside him sat another CEO, Zuzu Hornfeldt, in muted colors of beige and taupe, the restless proprietress of "Inferiors."

"This is such fun? I don't want it to end," said Zuzu. "Why don't we get a gang together later and go back to Thrace's for a nightcap?"

Two steps lower on the stairway stretched a woman in fingernails—very long, very red fingernails. Her dress was equally red. A thick pink stripe outlined her mouth. Very little of her ample chest was concealed. She had long legs and wore heels long enough to hold down railway track. It was Marianne, the hostess from the Sheardon-Cassidy box the night before. Below her, leaning against the wall in a semi-crouch, sat the president of Sheardon-Cassidy, Mr. Zygmunt Adams himself.

The lowest member of the party sat with legs crossed was Roi's brother and business partner, Ferdinand Daniel Swasont, to most just "Ferdy." He was quite able to balance a dinner plate on his knee and at the same time transport a glass of red wine to its destination, the middle of his flushed, road-mapped face. As a result of a couple of great deals that fell completely apart in Ferdy's hand, to Zygmunt he was "Senor Fkup." To add a dash of gossip, rumour had it that Ferdy had sought the assistance of a sex therapist.

When Harvey first came upon that summit gathering, the members were all smiles for the roving photographer who squatted lower down the stairway. With a burst of light, he captured for history that tableau of power and suspected impotence.

Zuzu blew Harvey a kiss as he took up a dining position just below Ferdy, who winked. Roi was too engrossed with Marianne's red fingernails to say anything.

With a smirk of accomplishment, Zyg simply pointed to Marianne and swung back into his conversation with Ferdy.

Nobody thinks they can identify that all too common species of man—homo incompetens—more quickly than The Street People. "...If only those silly bastards in Ottawa had their heads screwed on," said Ferdy continuing to talk. A large piece of lettuce fell from his fork as he waved it to emphasize his point. "Why would anybody invest in this country, when all we've got here is sheer...what's the word I want? You know. Not monarchy..."

"Anarchy?" Zyg offered.

"Exactly," said Ferdy. "Sheer an-archy."

Roi and Ferdy behaved as if wealth had nestled into the Swasont family generations before—always nattily dressed, always members of the most important clubs, the Cherry Beach Golf and Yacht, the Provincial Club, The Indoor Racquets, and always on the committees of the big charities (for business reasons). They owned big homes in the more expensive parts of the city—Roi's was up on the Post Road and Ferdy's in Forest Hill. Yet both had been seen on more than one occasion driving their Jaguars up and down the city's streets looking for an unexpired parking meter.

In fact, wealth had spent no more than a half a generation among the Swasonts. Fortune had not shone upon the two until the late nineteen eighties when a mine called Pas d'Or, 300 kilometres northwest of Kirkland Lake, Ontario, a stock that they had promoted vigorously, produced, to the surprise of everyone, including the Swasonts, core assays of between .2.89 and 7.38 grams of gold per tonne of ore. And things started to look up for the Swasonts. And the more things looked up for them, as the social axiom goes, the more they looked down on others.

Red Marianne formed the swingman between Roi's monologue and the little chat group of Zygmunt and Ferdy. In earlier times to increase his cash flow, Ferdy had modeled for a series of ads for men's overcoats. He had developed a very distinguished look about him, especially when his temples began to gray. But his blue eyes moved lazily, without spark or sparkle. While big brother Roi never smiled, Ferdy did hardly anything else, but you never knew for what reason. Like his brother, since the gold strike anyway, he had his hair trimmed and his nails done at least once a week at Antonio and Baliegas' salon ("Tony and Baloney's"). And like his brother, he bought all his clothes at Jimsmith's where the green and white "Jimsmith Ultima" stitched-in label accounted for a large part of their price.

Roi had a triangular face, next to no hair on top, a thin moustache and small, unfriendly eyes. In a business meeting if you asked him a question, he would stoke the back of his head, just below the remaining ribbon of hair, with a freshly-sharpened pencil like some befuddled grocery store clerk. Then from his mouth would rush spurts of air that sounded like one of those old steam engines revving up for some great journey across the land. But the facileness of his answers told you the train never got far from the station.

One night at the Royal Ontario Museum ball, quite by chance, as the story goes, Roi was standing next to the bar carrying on his usual conversation about the "crazy bastards in Ottawa" when the chief financial officer of Antler Creek

Explorations came up to get a drink at the same time as the president of Mincorp Mining. Roi introduced the two men to each other. Out of that innocent act, came a handsome fee, mostly in escrowed shares, for the subsequent acquisition of a majority interest in the Pas d'Or mine. When the assays came in, the stock, trading over the counter at the time, went from thirteen cents to eleven dollars. That was in '89. The real gold, however, came because it established Roi as an expert dealmaker. At least a dozen and a half similar financings followed. Those deals only enhanced the reputation of the chairman, CEO and president of Swasont and Partners, though judging from the turnover in personnel neither Roi nor Ferdy found time to hone their leadership skills. Didn't matter. The Street only judges managerial talent on the basis of cash flow.

"Ferdy, listen for once," Zygmunt demanded. "This goddamn software program organizes everything but your sex life. The next version will probably do that, too."

"I like my sex life the way it is," said Ferdy and straightened his tie.

"Well, a stud like you, Ferdy, wouldn't need the upgrade." Zygmunt held a straight face. "But do you know how much of the workday a manager should spend organizing himself? Twen-tee per cent. Read the business school stuff. Twent-tee per cent. Nobody does that, of course. So they waste time on all the wrong things. Save Your Time cuts your organizing time to five per cent. Fi-ve per cent. You don't go to your office any more and feel overwhelmed. I call it The Saviour. It gives you a whole new outlook on life. A whole new way of life. Don't you see? People will line up at the doors."

While Zygmunt took a gulp of wine he held up a finger

to keep Ferdy silent. "God, can you imagine if all that effort that goes on in those giant banks was channelled in the right direction? Can you imagine what would happen when this stuff gets all those crazy bastards in Ottawa your brother talks about organized? Jesus. This stuff's gonna change the world, I'm telling you. One little blurb in Computer Universe and requests came in for beta sites from all over—Japan, Denmark and Tasmania. One little goddamn blurb..."

Harvey constituted a third group. A silent one.

"Productivity tools are the new gold, Ferdy. They're the new Pas d'Or's. What the hell could be more valuable than a software program that can organize your life? You can make those little disks for a dollar and sell them for a hundred or a thousand. Just like those glass makers in Venice took plain sand and made it into pieces of art."

"When I walk into a computer store I see millions of software programs on the shelves. It's worse than a giant book store. If your program really was any good, how would anybody ever know? You'd have to spend millions on advertising," Ferdy retorted.

"You're right, Ferdy, but think of it this way. The Saviour does one thing different. They figure it can save any executive, any manager, an hour a day. One...hour...a...day. That's like going on Standard Time every day without switching your clock back."

"I just got burned on some high-tech crap. Maybe we could talk in a couple of weeks when I get back from Vancouver."

"This software...is...a...money...making machine. It manufactures time. Time is gold, Ferdy. And nobody knows better than you what a little gold can do for you."

"Put something in the mail and I'll take a look at it."

"The pro formas look sweet, Ferdy. Really sweet. You've never seen anything like them. We're only looking for ten million. I'm in. Eldred's thinking of taking a big chunk."

"Okay, courier it over tomorrow first thing?"

"Even good old Harvey who only bets on sure things is in, aren't you, Harvey?"

Nietzsche erred. All is taste and tasting, he wrote. Maybe that was so in his time. In ours, all is sales and selling.

When Harvey came in, Aunt Viv was sitting by herself in the library on one of the flowered loveseats next to the fireplace. One of the help had just thrown a birch log on the fire and then taken away her dinner plate. The log smouldered for a moment and then flared as the bark caught fire. Harvey sat down in the loveseat facing her. A maid brought by a silver tray with coffee in gold rimmed white cups. Aunt Viv poured in a splash of cream in one of the cups and took it off the tray, her hand quivering a little as she did.

"Coffee, Mr. Markson," asked the maid.

"Thanks, Lydia. Just black."

Aunt Viv waited a long moment until the maid left the room.

"Harvey, I've never seen you looking so tired."

"A little burnt out, Viv. Lots of changes. Without Rupert, I'm a little snowed under."

"A shame we lost him. What a brilliant, brilliant man he must have been. Absolutely brilliant. He didn't care that much for Eldred, though, did he?" Aunt Viv gave a short laugh. "I shouldn't be so hard on my nephew, I know." Her eyes scanned Harvey's face. "You need to get away. Why don't you take my condo in West Palm for a couple of weeks? Whenever you want. With this stupid hip of mine, I'll never get down there this year."

They talked for a while, but when the maid came by a second time Aunt Viv asked to have her car "brought round." Refusing Harvey's help in favour of a thin black cane, she raised her small body from the loveseat and began to limp out of the room. "Hate driving in the dark, but I guess I'll have to," she said and took Harvey's arm. "I'll never find Grace. Call her in the morning. Thought I heard Eldred's voice in the hall. I'll say goodnight to him at least."

She walked out to the door of the library. Out in the hall Donnis, his back to Aunt Viv, was talking to the bartender.

"Never. Never, goddamn it, does my bar run out of Glenfiddich," said Donnis in a very loud voice. "I have carloads of the crap in my cellar. I mean, is it really too much to ask you people to use your head? Too much to expect one of you to come and get me to fetch up a bottle or two? If that's too much trouble for you, you just let me know..."

Aunt Viv turned in the opposite direction, toward the front door. "I'll phone tomorrow," she said and continued her small-stepped shuffle. "My coat's in the front hall. My seniority around here means I don't have to take it upstairs. I'd never get through that crowd on the stairway, anyway."

The stairway crowd of the Swasonts, Zyg et al chattered away. Harvey looked up at them as he helped Aunt Viv on with her coat and then walked her out to the waiting car. They pressed cheeks. "Don't be crazy, call me about the condo, Harvey. I'm serious." Aunt Viv shoved the cane in the back seat, got in the car and drove off, negotiating the driveway so carefully you would think she had never driven it before.

Harvey did not go back inside. Instead he walked up the stone steps beside the house, across the red-tiled terrace and onto the lawn that sprawled its way from the back of the mansion down to the lake. From under black coolie-hat reflectors mounted on poles, yellow light spilled out onto the lawn and into the neatly edged flowerbeds. The summer chairs and tables had been put away for the winter. A half dozen leafless maples, their trunks illuminated, had to serve as reminders of the times spent in their shade drinking Bloody Marys and Piña Coladas and Kir Royales. But the frogs were still around and, at that point, in the midst of their nightly concert. They filled the warmish air with loud deep gulps while the contrapuntal sounds must have been coming from grasshoppers and cicadas.

Harvey stepped out onto the wooden dock, which sank down with a wooosh sound. He walked past the bathers' bench (really a pew that Grace had bought some years before when a small church over on the next concession was decommissioned) and over to the edge of the dock. A prowling fish poked its nose through the water's surface and set off a series of ever-enlarging concentric circles picked up by the light of the dock's lantern. Not ten seconds later a black bug with long legs and large flimsy wings crash-landed on the lake—like Icarus—not an inch or more from where the fish had surfaced. Timing is everything.

On the far side of the lake, a few hundred yards away, one of Bon Chance's gentle rolling hills hid in the darkness, a couple of clouds loitering above it reflected the lights of the city thirty miles away. Against that backdrop Harvey could just make out the silhouettes of the herd of Charolais on top of the hill, another one of Bon Chance's "diversions." In fact,

Reuben Eldred Donnis had assembled for himself on this property every conceivable diversion that might bring him a moment's contentment—a lake large enough to water ski on, a covered swimming pool, a polo pitch, an indoor riding ring, stables for fifty horses, tennis courts, a nine-hole golf course, and, in the basement of the main house, a movie theatre and a billiard room. Why, then, did The Pig have to flee the place every night on the diaphanous wings of Glenfiddich Single Malt Scotch?

Harvey lit up a cigarette. He took four or five steps across the dock to the pew-bench and laid down on it, on his side, his arm acting as strut for his head. But he could not see the tranquil beauty about him. Instead Leon's press release kept racing through his thoughts. "H.R. Winkes & Associates is proud to announce..."

From the pew, he stared out at the lonely valley. He stared out across the still water. And at the pasture which in daylight was so green.

At least The Pig had his staff to comfort him.

VIII.

AN ALTERNATIVE LIFESTYLE

Two or three times a week, in the good weather, a hunched-over man in black and red sneakers—one black, one red—would approach the corner of King and Bay, the tools of his trade in hand. When he got to King Street and to the proper place on the sidewalk terrace in front of the fifty-seven-storey silver bank tower, to the very foot of Canadian financial power, he would open the camp stool he carried and sit down.

Another piece of his equipment, a blue baseball cap, the white front panel so soiled that the emblem stitched on looked more like a back hoe than a bird, he would remove from his head and place upside down on the terrazzo pavement. Then, around from his back and on to his knee he would swing a guitar, its black veneer scarred by wide yellow scratches. He'd look around for a moment and then begin to slide one hand back and forth along the fret board. The other hand pumped up and down across the sound hole, all in the hope that a tiny fraction of The Street's cash flow that day would find its way into the hat and from there into his pocket and from there into...

These were not bad times for The Street. Stock prices had risen almost steadily since their sudden collapse in 1987. Dividend yields were low by historical standards, but most of the market strategists still saw, as they always do, room for the market to move upwards ("Lots and lots of upside." L. Lipakowski, *The World of Finance,* September 26, 1998). A herd of the smaller investors had jumped, not sauntered, back into the market full force. The balance sheets of banks and brokers looked strong again. Business was good.

In the Sheardon-Cassidy's monthly newsletter, chairman Donnis used the cliché about how "the company's most important assets took the elevator down each night." (What was less clear, however, was how crazy chairman Donnis was about those who had not increased his net worth that quarter, taking the elevator back up the next day.) And while the executives of companies like Sheardon-Cassidy practiced Street Utilitarianism—the greatest happiness of the greatest shareholders—some of wealth must have trickled down into the hands of the most important assets as well. Yet, that particular night, so desperate were the important assets to scamper home, they could not find the time or spare change to express their gratitude for the good fortune that had befallen them the previous eleven years.

For Segovia it was hard times as usual. And ask any musician about the wear and tear, performance after performance, has on an instrument. So it was with Segovia's. But when a guitar string broke, strangely enough he experienced no drop in gross revenue. So with all the shrewdness of a chief financial officer, he must have decided to reduce his overhead. When a string broke, he didn't bother to replace it. Simple as that. Finally, on close inspection, there was not one string left on his guitar. Not one.

Good times or bad, one thing about Zyg, in a hurry or not, at least whenever Harvey was around, he'd throw five or ten dollars into the inverted baseball cap on the sidewalk. He claimed his early days in Canada washing dishes in the racetrack cafeteria taught him the importance of luck. "Goddamn it, Segovia, you gotta get strings and change your luck," he'd say.

Each time, Segovia would nod in agreement and then reply, "Gad love you, lad." But he always seemed to find other ways to deploy his capital.

All the same, every so often, probably from habit, Segovia'd bring the guitar up to his cocked ear to check for discordance. And every few minutes, he'd stop, swing the guitar around on to his back again, rub and wiggle his fingers, and stroke the gray stubble that surrounded a gap-toothed mouth not covered by any corporate dental plan. Like a true performer, he would smooth down on his bald head the dozen or so long strands of gray hair. Before concluding the intermission, he would remove from the baseball cap all signs of pettiness. He left only the large coins to demonstrate his talent had not gone unrecognized. Other people on The Street do the same. That was no different than the stockbroker who leaves his BMW, or a securities lawyer his Jaguar, parked in the driveway rather than hidden away in the garage. Could the real difference between the street people and The Street People be only a matter of capitalization?

Of course, nobody showed much interest in Segovia's history. One broker-type, not so young either, hypothesized while walking along just in front of Harvey one day, that Segovia had been a bank manager who cared about customers. Certainly nobody knew why Nature had smitten the man so. Could it really be that even before birth, old Segovia was set up for a life of poverty? His small, pale, vacuous eyes, only half-focused on the world, told you that he had accepted that fate, that he had accepted a life completely devoid of dignity, that he accepted a life that made his standard of living totally dependent on the generosity of The Street. Sweet Jesus!

At least from an anthropologist's point of view, there can be no great a difference in the size of Segovia's brain and that of some bank president on the fortieth floor of one of the towers. But bank presidents get to spend their days arranging golf games in Florida at Loxahatchee or tennis in the Bahamas at Lyford Cay or duck shoots at a private marsh not an hour's drive from downtown. Was it just a fluke of Nature—say, a slight shortage of neurotransmitters, a few drug-damaged neurons or synapses, some malformed gene, a blow to the head, or some other crushing event—that kept old Segovia from being up there in a security-protected, oak-paneled executive suite, up there away from the acrid smell of frying meat and spent diesel fuel, up there where the only honking he'd ever hear would be when a fellow gun club member called in on his cell phone from a duck blind?

Nevertheless—get this—Segovia always wore a smile. Always. Heaven alone would know the worry that went on behind that smile, worry about where his next meal would come from or if it would arrive at all, about whether that night he'd have over his head a roof or a train trestle, about whether his peers might beat him up and steal his coins to buy from Pride of the Peninsula Wineries (Symbol: PP. Share price 31/12/98: $32.40) a bottle of the cheapest wine available. (The Swasonts, even though they'd wait for the freezing of hell before they drank the stuff, claimed they made enough on "Peepee" to pay for vacations to all the great vineyards of Australia, California and France.) Perhaps in his own meek way Segovia believed some day he'd inherit the earth. In the meantime, he strummed away stringlessly. And you could tell from his pursed lips that, for a value-added throw-in, he liked to hum. (If he could haw, too, any number of legal firms in the area would have had a permanent spot for him.)

Nor would a regular observer of The Street scene find Segovia's behaviour exceptional. On many a sunny day The Queen of Sweden with her thrice-dyed yellow hair, in baggy blue sweat pants and a yellow and blue T-shirt emblazoned with a silver-foil emblem of Helsinki or Stockholm, might render The Street a visit. She would shout Scandinavian slogans of protest, expletives and curses, directed against god knows who or what. Her utterings lost nothing in translation. No one around could translate them. And no one quite knew if she was simply venting her anger or running for office. The passing pedestrians and foot couriers paid almost no notice and seemed to take it all in stride.

Anyone who worked in the bank towers in those days would be familiar with Whistler's Brother, a man whose distinguished dress suggested he had known significant power at one time or other. He would show up on The Street every year in early spring, in an impeccably tailored gray suit and an immaculate gray fedora with a small red and green feather in the hatband. He would stand in one of the street-level alcoves of the red bank's stone facade and, with an arm raised in a fascist-like salute, direct loud, shrill whistles, alternated randomly with low-pitched sounds from a mouth kazoo, at the white bank tower across the street. Street speculation had it that this mating call was directed not so much at the white bank itself as at one of its loans officers. Many years before, the story went, the loans officer had put to voice his own kind of un-mating call on the telephone late one Friday afternoon to alter a financial "friendship" of two decades by calling in Whistler's Brother's loan and forcing him into bankruptcy. Who could or would blame Whistler's Brother for dropping by now and again to say, in his own special way, hello?

It was late on the Friday afternoon, the day after the Donnis's party. Leon was out of town that day at another convention, so there had been no discussion with him about the press release announcing Lipakowski's appointment as president of R. H. Winkes & Associates. Harvey was leaving his office just before six to meet Zygmunt for drinks and dinner uptown at Thrace's. As he approached the intersection at King and Bay, Harvey spotted the Swasonts, Roi and Ferdy, diagonally across. At that moment he had no more desire to talk to them than he had had the night before. So he waited for another turn of the traffic lights.

On a third corner of the intersection the encamped Maestro Segovia was busy accompanying The Street's nightly horn concerto, the "Abandonment Concerto," a strident composition put together by mobile anarchists whose cars, on all four sides of the intersection of King and Bay, stood absolutely motionless as usual.

The few shafts of light that made it past the tall bank boxes onto the sidewalks elongated the shadows of the fast-paced walkers hurrying to catch their commuter trains. The air was cool. And the mood was surly. The market, no matter what measure you chose, except for the precious metals index, had dropped for three days in a row. It was that hour when The Street People abandon The Street, not one at time, as in the manner that Segovia's guitar strings had most likely snapped apart, but all at once, like a torrent from a burst dam. People—those most important assets—streamed hurriedly down the sidewalks of Bay Street in parallel rivulets to catch their trains. Between those fast-flowing sidewalks, the main traffic artery, coagulated with an excess of iron, moved not at all. The frowns on the faces of trotting walkers revealed intense displeasure, even though their co-workers and the local merchants had spent much of that day instructing them to have a nice weekend.

In the distance, an ambulance broke into a high-pitched squeal. Finally, every last one of the assembled vehicles chimed in and began to honk as if this hastily composed cacophony would somehow, with the same luck as at Jericho, overcome the attendant problem. Regardless of what op-ed journalists and other commentators on morality say, neither theft, nor murder, nor coveting a neighbour's wife, nor fiddled financial reports—in other words, nothing—provokes the same outrage and protest as does stagnated traffic. Impatience holds the modern city hostage.

To digress for a moment: on another afternoon, earlier that summer, on their way to tour one of the plants of Canadian Carbonated Beverages (Symbol: CAN. Share price 31/12/98: $12.40), an investment candidate for several pension fund portfolios managed by Winkes & Associates, Rupert and Harvey left the office shortly before five and drove right square into the teeth of the Bay Street rush hour. At the first intersection, King Street and Bay, rather than follow the car in front through the orange traffic light, as—in all fairness—was customary practice in the region, Rupert drew his car to a complete stop. The car behind began to honk. Clearly, his fellow traveler had taken Rupert for a complete imbecile (which implied, technically, an instant reduction in IQ of at least eighty points). Looking in the rearview mirror, Harvey could see an arm shoot out the passenger's window of the car behind. The middle finger of the hand was held vertical, the other fingers clenched to the palm. Then the hand pumped up and down three times through a short arc of about forty-five degrees. Unbeknownst to Rupert—the omniscient Rupert—in plain daylight, for all The Street to see, someone had just thrown him the proctologist's salute.

What genius man has in his hands! In one simple gesture he can signal instantly to the world—to the universe at large even—his profound dissatisfaction with the circumstances he confronts. With one simple gesture he can signal his rejection of that which his soul finds totally and profoundly unacceptable. How wonderful! At the same time, as part of this digression, is it not a question worth asking, why we don't have a signal of some sort, say, placing the back of your hand to your forehead and waving your fingers, to convey a message such as: "I was dead wrong. You have every reason to be upset. No question. How stupid of me, really. I don't blame you in the least. I was totally in the wrong. Please accept my sincerest apologies for any inconvenience my actions caused you. I sincerely hope that nothing I did will spoil one second of the time that remains before the sun sets. In other words, for whatever remains of it, I beg of you, have a nice day."

To return to Harvey standing on the corner: In the midst of the late afternoon traffic jam, Roi, with his slight limp, the result of an old injury he claimed came from football, though others said from a ping-pong accident in his basement, brother Ferdy Fkup at his side as always, sneered at a driver who had bellied the nose of his Jag into the intersection. Roi, no doubt, was on his way home to wash up and change for some black-tie event like the Royal Winter Fair, or for another elegant dinner party like the one the night before at The Pig's Sty. On the other hand (and on the other corner), Segovia would probably skip the wash up that night, as he probably did most nights. If his luck was in, he might go on from his place of toil straight to the prayer-for-fare hostel and there he'd be force-fed cold slop and warmed-over words by zealots plying the core competency of all religions—making the unacceptable acceptable.

Even in bad times, Roi Swasont would take home four or five hundred thousand dollars a year, one way or another. In good times, when the markets were running strong, he'd take home five times that, maybe more. Well, not necessarily home, mind you, more likely to a tax haven in the

Cayman Islands or in, as he referred to them, the Turkeys and Cacaos. But forget about the offshore bank account and the bank cards. Roi St. John Swasont would carry more cash in his wallet, would have more cash on hand that is, than the whole Segovian Enterprise would touch in a year, maybe two years—though it would take a skilled economist indeed to determine who contributed less to the country's Gross National Product.

Seeing the affluence of Roi oozing from the maroon silk handkerchief in the breast pocket of a sand-coloured alpaca overcoat, Segovia, inspired like some mutt-dog happy to see its owner, like a stock broker uncovering a hot prospect, began to strum away with all his heart. His hand moved confidently up and down across the narrow part of the guitar box. Above the noise of the intersecting rivers of iron, above the foul, piquant odour of freshly-spent diesel oil from the plodding buses, rose, that evening, the plaintive cries of Segovia's soundless composition.

What happened next embarrassed even the brazen sun, which went into hiding behind the black bank tower. As he walked by Segovia, Roi turned his head toward the stalled traffic. Roi turned not only blind eye but a deaf ear as well. Roi, Roi-Boy, Roi St. John Swasont pretended not to hear Segovia's plaintive notes. But, of course, there was nothing to hear. Nothing.

For Harvey, that was the end of The Street.

He crossed the intersection, threw a twenty in Segovia's cap and, almost in the same motion, signalled a taxi over to the curb.

"Lord t'undering Jesus," said Segovia, "you're a kind man, b'y."

"Be faster to walk, buddy," said the cabbie, the drivers behind blasting their horns and more than likely blaspheming, too.

"No hurry," replied Harvey and got in.

"Harvey, Harvey, where is your faith?" asked Zygmunt, his arms spread wide. Then he slurped a watery oyster into his mouth. "You see the Bloomberg today? Some software mail-order house in Ohio ordered fifty thousand copies of The Saviour. Fifty thousand. That's enough to keep the company on its feet for six months, probably more. Why aren't you eating your oysters?"

"Just want to slow down a minute. Everybody's seems in such a bloody hurry."

"Even that nerd-jerk, what's his name? You know the guy who writes that computer column for *The World*, even he thinks we're on to something," Zygmunt said as he squeezed lemon juice on to a second oyster. "You know what they're doing for the upgrade? A built-in mentor. And decision-making theory. Sometimes the thing will tell you that you need more information. Or it might make you list your options. Or it might just tell you: cool it. You don't think that'll sell? Microsoft's already sniffing around. Even The Pig liked it. You should have seen old Monsieur Cochon grunt when he saw the numbers the Save Your Time guys came up with." Zygmunt leaned back against the banquette and took a sip of wine. A knowing smirk perched on his face. "Stock's up to ninety cents. Year, year and a half, it'll be twenty bucks. Minimum."

"You think so?"

"The Saviour, for chrissake, is going to save our bacon. Maybe even save The Pig's. One thing for sure, it will get that goddamn creep from the tax department off my back. He was after me again today. I just sent them another ten thousand last month."

"Every time you fall in love with a stock you figure it'll make you a fortune."

"I'm not like you. I don't want to be some sort of financial guru or a rocket scientist. Or a quantum mechanic. I just want to be good and rich. Forget the good. How do you think Jimmy got this place started? From dough I could lend him 'cause a stock of mine took off."

Zyg had gotten to know Jimmy Thrace at the race track. Jimmy, christened Dimitri Popadopolous Thrasymachus according to his passport, in 1984 began a new life in a new homeland with a new name, as a dishwasher at the New Woodbine racetrack. Three and a half years later, Jimmy had worked himself up to head waiter at The Orchid, a restaurant very popular at one time. The owner, fatigued from two decades of days that started at 9 a.m. and ended seventeen hours later decided to sell to Jimmy. Zygmunt had just made a small killing on Pre-Cambrian Gas and Oil (Symbol: PCGO. Price 12/31/98: $48.50) and lent Jimmy enough for the down payment and helped him get a bank loan for the rest. Jimmy changed a few things about the place: he put in new soft brown carpet, painted the walls a soft beige and the trim an off-white, bought new chocolate brown coats with black lapels for the waiters, added a doorman, hired a big-name chef, added a few Greek seafood specialties, particularly "Thracian Shrimps" (about which the "Inns and Outs of Dining" column of "Life in the Big City" section of *The World of Finance* commented: "Five stars for the Thracian Shrimps. Try 'fore you die."). Along with the new specialties, Jimmy introduced five-star prices. Within a month, no matter who you were, you couldn't get a reservation unless you phoned a week in advance. An exception, of course, was Zygmunt who was also the only person allowed to run a tab, which always got paid off, though not always promptly.

"Where in hell's the salt? Ten guys come by with pepper grinders, but no one ever thinks someone might like some salt. Remind me to tell Jimmy." Harvey took the salt shaker from behind the small vase of yellow freesia and handed it to Zyg.

"Wait 'til you see Monday's paper. He made Lipakowski president—president and chief investment officer. All Leon told me was that Larry was coming with us."

"Jesus, I told you. I told you. But I'm not gloating. The best orthopod in this city couldn't find an honest bone in your friend Leon's body. And Larry? Just like Leon, Larry's walked over more people than the Flying Walendas. Why would he make an exception in your case?" Zygmunt shook the salt shaker. Nothing came out. "Hey, what kind of contraption is this?"

"You got it upside down," said Harvey. "It's not Leon. It's not Larry and his phony English accent he picked up in the year he spent at the London School of Economics. I ever tell you he told me he was the father of that new pricing model your options guys use?"

"If he was the father, it must have been by artificial insemination. He wasn't even around when our guys put that one together."

"Let me tell you what happened on my way here. You

won't believe it. I was outside my building at King and Bay. Who do I see coming along the other side of the street? Your pals Roi and Ferdy. And you know what? They walked right by Segovia as if he didn't exist."

"You are on to something, Mr. Markson." With his forefinger held over his thumb Zygmunt drew a line in the air. "Roi Swasont Withholds Charity. That's hot news. Where's my cell phone. I got to call city desk at *The World* right now and tell them." He took another sip of wine. "I told you a hundred times: Roi's so tight he has take valium for his fist muscles."

"Will you just listen one second, chrissake? There's Segovia pretending to play his guitar. And then there's Roi pretending not to hear. That strike you a little odd?"

"What would you expect?"

"You don't find that very strange? Here's some poor guy strumming away on a guitar with no sound and here's another guy walking along as if he's deaf. You think that's normal."

"Who cares?"

"Then I looked around the street and everybody—everybody—was pretending. Like walk-ons from a movie set. Everything slowed up like a dream. I couldn't even hear the traffic. When I looked up at the bank towers, I found them faking it too. It all happened in probably a split second."

"Hold on. Hold on. We're not talking about orgasms. How the hell does a building fake it?"

"They start to look like giant cut-outs. You know, like that odd feeling you get driving into a strange city, all the shops and stores along the way look like stage sets, facades with nothing behind them. I felt like a tourist in a city I'd never seen before. The streets, the stores, the buildings, the signs—the things I see every day—looked completely unfamiliar. I felt like a tourist. A goddamn tourist and I lived here almost all my life."

"Harv, I heard about a really good shrink in our building. All this Leon stuff has buggered your mind."

"Can't you be serious?"

"Look, just hang in 'til The Saviour gets on track. Then cash in and go live someplace more to your liking. You could go and live in Disneyland or with Santa at the North Pole. You know, someplace where there are no Rois. No Ferdy Fkups. No Leons."

"All I'm telling you is the city's changed. No, that's not it. It's too much the same." Harvey's raised his voice. "All I know is I want the hell out."

"God, those oysters were good," Zygmunt said running his tongue along his upper lip. "What have you got against the city all of sudden?" The waiter refilled the crystal wine goblets. Zygmunt took a sip. "Nectar, Arthur," he said. "Pure nectar."

"We blow fifty bucks on a bottle of this stuff. Fif-tee bucks," said Harvey as he fondled that napkin around the bottle. "With fifty bucks in his pocket Segov wouldn't know the difference between here and heaven."

"I knew something special was up but, frankly, I had no idea this was a get-together to revive the communist movement," Zygmunt argued with a straight face. "Look, we deserve privilege. We work bloody hard. And how many years have you spent as the financial guy on the Hospital Board? Why do I do all that crap for the United Way? Here's an idea. Why don't I get Jimmy's brother over there to phone a leper colony and book us in for a couple of years? We need more misery in our lives. That's our problem. We need more misery and perhaps some poverty. You'd love poverty, Harv." Zygmunt took a big swallow of wine. "You know what your problem is Harvey? You have to analyze every goddamn thing. Nothing can be what it is. Everything has to be broken up until little pieces so's your brain can examine it like some high-powered microscope."

"Just tell me one thing. Why are you and I here sucking down Belons, drinking Meursault and then there's Segovia down eating god-knows-what at the Brothers of Man Hostel? Who the hell's in on the decision-making process for all that?"

"I heard they want to change the name to the Brothers and Sisters of Men and Women Hostel."

A slender, attractive dark-haired, dark-skinned woman, with whom Zygmunt had had a short affair a couple of years before, sat down at the piano bar and adjusted the microphone up towards her lips. In a rhythmic, throaty, mellow voice she said over the sound system, "Good evening, Mr. Markson. How very nice to see you here again at Thrace's." Then she played a few notes of "Hello Dolly." "And a good evening to you, Mr. Adams," she said with a nod, and then followed with the first bars of "Colonel Bogey's March."

The waiter brought the entrees, slightly pinkish rack of lamb. Zygmunt didn't wait for the ratatouille or petites pommes. He carved off a chunk of lamb and stuffed it in his mouth. Then the empty wine glasses were taken away and replaced with fresh ones. A bottle of Margaux was shown to Zygmunt, who nodded his approval, and upon taking a taste, signalled his final approval with a forefinger pinched to his thumb, the other fingers raised.

While the glasses were filled, Zygmunt said nothing.

Then he asked, his mouth half full, his knife pointed towards Harvey, "What's up with Sara? If you aren't nice to her niece, The Amazer will take a sharp stick to your heart. I'd rather have The Pig after me."

"Sara's in the middle of an affair with art galleries. She decided she wants to be a curator. She's taking every curatorial course she can. And with my workload at Winkes these days, we talk, sure, but hardly see each other. You know why she wasn't at Bon Chance last night? She's in New York again. Know why? She's checking out another course she wants to take there next year. Sara doesn't do things in half measure. But you're right, that wouldn't stop Grace from trying to kill me."

"No, The Amazer wouldn't do that, she likes you too much. The one to look out for is Mrs. Avogadro. She's going to poison your food one day when she's over cleaning your joint. She thinks you should marry Sara."

"That's another thing I can't stand about this town. Everybody wants to run your life. Mrs. Avogadro's a wonderful woman, but she doesn't know Sara from Adam or Eve, for chrissake."

"Of course, she does. Sara used to sneak over to your place for a nap between classes on Fridays. They'd have afternoon tea together. Oh, Jesus, I almost forgot, Mrs. A. called me today. She left you a voice mail at your office, but just in case, she told me she needs spray starch and Clorox."

"I got her message. That woman should give seminars on communication techniques."

"Mrs. A. says you'll never find a better woman than Sara. But..."

"But what?"

"She can't figure out why Sara would want to marry a dipstick like you." Zygmunt laughed.

"Mrs. A. called me a dipstick?

"Yes, she did."

"Jesus, has her English improved."

Twenty minutes later, Zygmunt fished a toothpick from his pocket and with his hand barely covering his mouth took two or three furtive swipes at his teeth. Then he finished off the wine that was left in his glass. Once he caught the waiter's eye, he held up the empty glass and pointed to it.

"No more for me. I'm going to make it an early night," said Harvey.

"It's ten after nine. What the hell's the matter with you, you sick?" Zygmunt shook his head and then turned his head towards the waiter. "Okay, Arthur, just bring me a Remy in my coffee. And don't chintz."

The pianist sang: "Right in the middle of my dai-ly strife, Somebody real walked into my l-i-i-fe. Somebody real. Somebody real..."

The maitre d', known simply as "Jimmy's brother" because nobody could pronounce his first name, seated two women at the table next to Zyg and Harvey's. Harvey took no notice.

"I'm gone. I'm not playing third stooge to Larry and Leon. And once you've worked with Rupert where else in this town is there to go?"

"You'll be lucky to get a nickel from Leon for your Winkes shares. Wait 'til The Saviour comes through and then you'd have the dough to start up your own shop. You'd have no trouble getting clients."

"You know what I think? Everybody in this goddamn town wants to tell you what to do so you can be just like them. You know what I think? I think in this goddamn town the individual is an endangered species."

"You know what I think? I think Jimmy's brother just hit the jackpot for us. Don't look, but you should see the two he's put at the next table. This is our night Harvey," Zygmunt said and pumped his right fist back and forth in jerky jabs like hockey players do when they've just put the puck in the net.

"Not tonight, Zyg. I'm sort of out of it."

A few moments later, Zygmunt took a small cigar from his inside suit coat pocket and leaned towards the two women at the next table. He spoke with a French accent, obviously phony. "I am not able to catch za waiter's eye. Pardonnez, you have some, some feu. Some fire?"

The woman along the banquette from Zygmunt laughed at this obviously phony accent, reached into her purse and brought out silver lighter, which she flicked into flame.

Zygmunt paused. "Ça ne vous dérange pas? Z'you don't mind?"

"No, I adore the smell of cigars," said the woman as she fingered her simple gold necklace.

"You are ve-rey kind. Mille mercis." Zygmunt settled back in his seat, a grin of accomplishment covered his face.

"Leon has no choice. He has to buy my shares. It's in the agreement I had with Rupert. The company has to buy my shares over time."

"He won't pay up."

"There's a formula on earnings."

"By the time Leon's through there won't be any earnings. That's what I'm trying to tell you."

"For God's sake, Zygmunt, let up, will you? Do you have to have all the answers?" Harvey shook his head. "Did you graduate from the London School of Economics with Larry or something?"

"Look, Harv, listen to me. I'm just trying to help. There aren't many people I give a good goddamn about on Bay Street, okay? All's I'm saying you can't count on Leon for anything. The Saviour is a much better bet, believe me."

"I'm not counting on Leon for a goddamn thing other than what he owes me. I've made up my mind. I am gone. I want the hell out. I want out of this city. This place has turned into a jail. I'm gone. It's not *if*—it's when."

"You're just in a mood. Where the hell would you go?"

"A couple of the guys at Nomura Securities told me they could put me in touch with the right people in Tokyo."

"Just because you've got shares of Sony and Matsushita in your portfolios doesn't mean you could survive in Japan. Jesus Christ, you don't even speak the language."

"I'd take a crash courses. I've always been fascinated by Japan."

"Not even you, Harvey, could learn Japanese overnight. On second thought, maybe you're right," said Zygmunt. "You could live there and put down new roots. Buy a couple of rice paddies, open a sushi bar. Or why don't you go to Australia and live upside down for a while and see how you like it."

"That's how stupid I am. I never thought about doing anything except working with Rupert and living here."

"I gotta get over to London soon and get rid of my manager there. Sir Curly Tail is less than thrilled with our European operations, let me tell you. If you won't run our research department, why don't you take over our London office? At least you wouldn't have to learn Japanese. You'd like the English. They use many, many of the same words and expressions we do every day. You could take a crash course in learning to speaking English-English. Probably take half the time of Japanese."

"A city brimful with LSE graduates and Englishmen that talk like Larry? Not bloody likely."

Zygmunt casually shielded his mouth as if he was going to bring out a toothpick again. He spoke slowly, his eyes straight ahead. "They're both winners, Harv. They must be models or something. Jesus! I'll bet they're from Calgary. Too friendly to be from around here. With women from Calgary, I never miss. They've all got over-developed libidos."

"Zyg, mind if I wander on? I'll catch the tab next time."

New political arrangements seldom begin with shouting in the streets and the sound of gunshots. More often they begin with a quiet refusal. Or a metaphysical spasm. More often, they begin quietly, very quietly, out of a sudden awareness that something is wrong, unacceptably wrong and that some new arrangement is sorely needed. But new political arrangements demand a mountain of faith because usually at one point or another everything ends up upside down, like living in Australia. Regime change is notoriously difficult when "the ousted" and the one doing the ousting are the same person.

IX.

VICTORY NIGHS AGAIN

Katherine the Ingrate, exhausted, had in fact come to Harvey's queen-size bed at the Dorchester Hotel. You'll remember The Holy Sacred Task Harvey had assigned himself on the plane: to get Katherine to his bed. Success was to be taken as a sign that his project—this escape from the old order—was, indeed, on the right track. So with The Task accomplished, by hook or by crook, could we not then say: Yahoo! Phase I of Project Vamooski (rhymes with Rimouski) had been successfully launched?

Pas exactement.

True, Katherine was in Harvey's bed at the Dorchester. Demonstrably, verifiably, empirically so. No judge, no jury, no prosecuting attorney could possibly disagree with that fact. No matter your definition of the word *true,* no matter the context or use, "Harvey had gotten Katherine to his bed" was in fact a true statement. If you understood English, what you would expect to find on hearing that group of words uttered together was exactly what you would in fact find: Katherine in Harvey's bed.

So far so good.

By design, Project Vamooski was not for the timid. It was a high-risk venture, a shot at rebirth, at renewal, at resurrection of the Marksonian spirit. Surely, Harvey had not traveled all that way across thousands of miles of ocean to live with his old contemplative habits of hesitancy and delay. Had he not come, this Easter weekend, to this new world to change those sorts of things forever? To live. To reach that mystical state of existence we call being alive. To arise in a new life, free, unfettered by the old walls of fear and conformity. The new Harvey was to ascend again, like in the old days with Winkes & Associates, to the captaincy of the ship—his ship, his own ship. *Maître chez lui.*

Rule, Harvey. Harvey rules the waves.

Harvey never-never...

Hold on! Hold on! Whoa!

A synechdochal—forgive the word—error has arisen. Not unlike those strange pronouncements in Greek or Shakespearean tragedy, a part has become confused for the whole. "Harvey's bed" meant more, one hell of a lot more than "Harvey's bed." In truth, we have this wondrous, incontrovertible fact—Katherine *était au lit d'*Harvey—and yet we know in our hearts the real task at hand had yet to be carried out—consummated, if you like. So, in truth, the jury on the Project Vamooski case was, in fact, still out. Only some half-sane litigator would argue The Sacred Task had been completed.

Harvey had gone down to meet Katherine at the front door of the hotel, a rivulet of leftover shower water running down the right side of his face.

"You're very kind. I'm sorry to do this to you. I've never felt so desperate in my life. I only have a few pounds with me. No credit cards. I never imagined my aunt wouldn't be here when I arrived. I phoned Mallorca. No answer. I don't know a soul in London. Not a soul. I didn't know what to do. Still don't. I'm freezing to death. I'm absolutely dead tired. And I'm not even sure I can walk another step."

With one hand Harvey picked up the black suitcase of Katherine's and with the other clasped her left (magnificent) forearm and led her towards the elevator. The grin on the face of the elevator operator seemed gratuitous. Once in the suite, Harvey guided Katherine to the bedroom and handed her his blue silk dressing gown that he had left draped over the bed when he changed to go down to the lobby. He left the bedroom. A few minutes later—three maybe four—he knocked softly on the door before opening it. Katherine lay asleep in the bed—Harvey's bed. From the bottom drawer of the bureau he took out a green woollen blanket and threw it over her.

Harvey closed the door scribbled a note on a piece of buff-coloured hotel stationery.

> K.
> Back shortly.
> H.

Remaining true to his theory to stay awake the first day rather than catch a nap, Harvey slipped out of the suite for a late morning stroll.

What would happen when she woke up? What would she do? Rush off to the airport? Ask for a loan so she could get a room of her own? Get in contact with her Aunt in Mallorca and somehow get a hold of the key to her aunt's house? Ah, but what if she stayed? Then one of them could sleep on the couch and one in the bed. Or both in the bed. Or both on the couch. The possibilities seemed endless.

Why bat your head against a brick wall? (Project Vamooski, remember, was created to destroy walls.) No, Harvey dreamed up a strategy, elegant for its simplicity: he would bide his time.

It was Easter Sunday around eleven o'clock. The sun had risen well above the rooftops. The city had begun to warm up. London, perhaps tired from six preceding days of havoc, seemed relaxed, at home with itself. Almost no horn honking. Instead, plaintive church bells, from this direction and that, called the faithful and the faithless to come in their new hats and bonnets to church and contemplate the possibility of resurrection.

The trees in Hyde Park had uncoiled their spring leaves and with the sun's help displayed all shades and hues of green and yellow. An old, gnarled oak stood guard at the entrance gate to the huge park across from the hotel. The gigantic lawns beyond lolled contentedly. Here and there small groups of people, families mostly, sat on blankets, wicker hampers beside them. Three young boys in short pants laughed and hooted and taunted each other as they skidded a Frisbee back and forth through the air. At the intersection with another path, two elderly couples, the women in church-going hats of dark blue straw, passed in front of Harvey. It was an idyllic picture. Everyone seemed in his or her proper place—or on the way there.

Harvey was about to give in to fatigue and head back to the hotel to sleep for a while.

"How can you sleep?" a voice shouted at him. "Zimbabweans cannot. How can you rest? Zimbabweans dare not. While you doze off, our Mister Mugabe, our Mister Robert Mugabe, continues to oppress, to torture and to bring death and despair to his fellow Zimbabweans. Harare has given birth to a tyrant of exceptional cruelness. Given birth not to a saviour of the people as promised. No, to a ruthless tyrant. The nightmare began a decade and a half ago and has never ceased to be anything other than a nightmare. Wake up, you and you and you," the man said as he pointed his finger at Harvey and at two of the others that had gathered. "Wake up. Wake up you people, for God's sake. For God's sake."

The voice of the black man who stood on a blue plastic box grew more and more shrill. He shouted over the heads of the half dozen people that formed a loose semi-circle around him. "We must stop Mister Mugabe. He leaves us no choice. We must fight him. Fight with everything we have..."

At the Speaker's Corner section of Hyde Park people had gathered in several pockets—little hurricanes in reverse—each with a calm periphery but a maelstrom in the eye. Harvey walked to the edge of another group gathered about a tall, bald-headed man with a long gray beard who stood on a wooden crate. The man held his arms above his head in a V and shouted, "Labour has let us down. I say that, but let me tell you that no one supported the Labour Movement more than my family. My mother devoted her whole life to Labour. But my mother made one mistake. One very big mistake. One very big mistake."

"Should'n slept with your father, mate," a heckler inserted.

Further along the asphalt path, pigeons strutted back and forth, pecking at strewn crumbs. Beside a fence stood a pasty-faced, short man, hair down to his stooped shoulders, wearing worn brown sandals with ankle-length black socks and who looked completely intimidated by the world, even by the strutting pigeons. Then he got up on his pulpit-crate and began to shout.

"Fornicators! Fornicators! All you fornicators, let me ask you this: have your forgotten?" A swoosh of people as if addressed by surname rushed over.

"Have you been too busy lately fornicating your bloody ears off," shouted the speaker. He looked directly at Harvey (how unfair—the thought is not the deed, god knows). "Have you been too busy, my friends, to remember," the man's voice dropped to a whisper, his lisp became more pronounced, "what this day, my friends, is about? Too busy?" He began again to shout. "Today is about...sin. Sin! And sin, my friends, is nothing more than...a surrender of faith."

A blond, very overweight female accomplice took her place next to the speaker and held up several thin booklets with washed-out blue covers. She pointed to the title "Faith is the only Freedom" just above a large 2 preceded by the £ sign.

"Faith set me free," the man on the box said still shouting. "It will free you too. Without faith, you, my little fornicating friends, you are eternal prisoners." He looked straight at Harvey.

"You know what really gets you down? You know the real

killer in my opinion? Cancer? No. Heart attacks? No. Traffic accidents? No, my friends. Uncertainty. Ruthless, relentless, unceasing uncertainty is today's mass murderer! Medical science has never taken the time to figure out the wear and tear uncertainty inflicts upon on the human heart. We are drowning in doubt these days. The more answers we come upon the more questions we come up with. The old truths from the old sacred writings no longer seem to work. And you know what? Nature rejoices in our befuddlement, it's obvious. She just loves to shove all that uncertainty down our very throats. And then," the speaker dropped his voice, "then every once in a while, you are given a dollop of hope. But what is hope but junk food for the spirit. Can you feast on hope? Can you eat hope for breakfast. Or luncheon? Or supper? Who can live on hope?"

The unjustly accused, jet-lagged fornicator, Harvey, was willing to give it a try.

With a cat-burglar's cautiousness, Harvey stole back into his own suite. Then, and with a similar degree of stealth, he edged open the door to the bedroom, unsure that, while he was out for a Sunday morning stroll filled with accusations of sin (no wonder people stay in bed), the woman of his hopes and sinful dreams had not herself stolen away.

But, no, she had not. Katherine lay fast asleep. So Harvey released the knob slowly so that the door lock's tongue slid silently back into place. Only the screeching wheels of what sounded like a housemaid's trolley out in the hall interrupted the silence. Harvey switched on the television in the corner of the living room, the sound muffled. On his way past the marble coffee table, he picked up the information-laden note left for Katherine which time had rendered, as it does with so much of what is written, obsolete. He rolled it into a ball threw it, first try, into the wastebasket by the desk. Then he lay down on the couch.

The situation reminded him of the old days back not so long ago back (a week?) lying around his condo in his old world waiting for Leon and the lawyers to come up with an offer for his Winkes shares. Here though the couch was more a loveseat. Harvey had to coil his knees up under his chin. And instead of soft blanket crocheted for him by Aunt Viv, he had to use a Burberry coat not up to the job of covering at the same time both his shoulders and stocking feet. On the television, Chelsea United was about to play a European Cup match against a German team in Dusseldorf. As the players lined up at centre field for the opening ceremony, some Chelsea United fan with a trumpet played a few bars from the anthem of The Republic of Harvey Markson—*Rule, Harvey. Harvey rules the waves*—only half heard by The Republic's President, who was in the act of surrendering to the prince of sleep.

What awoke him a few hours later was Katherine on the phone in the next room. Hurriedly he threw his pants back on, just before Katherine, fully dressed again, opened the door in that stealth-like manner the suite had become accustomed to.

"Sleep okay?" asked Harvey.

"I always sleep wonderfully well in stolen beds."

"Reach your aunt?"

"Yes, her friend is out of trouble according to the doctors in Palma. I'll fly down in the morning on the 8:30 flight we were supposed to go on."

"She gave me the number and address of her char out in

Hammersmith who has a key, but there's no answer. It's the right number. I checked it with information."

"I'll get you a room."

"It was all very last minute. No credit cards. I have a bank card, but at the moment there's not a great deal in there."

"Don't worry."

"That wouldn't be right."

"Send me a cheque sometime."

"The char, she'll be home sooner or later."

"You're welcome to stay here. We seem quite capable of working out the sleeping arrangements. I've grown to like the couch," said Harvey as he plumped up one of its cushions. "What are you going to do? Go out to the airport and sit around all night."

Once they had your name at the Golden Guinea, where the Dorchester concierge had made reservations for Harvey et al, they knew how to use it.

"Good evening, Mr. Markson." Then a discreet bow in the direction of Katherine. "Would Mr. Markson like...? What does Mr. Markson think madam would prefer...?"

"This isn't a restaurant, it's a men's club." said Katherine. "Why do they ask you what I want? Do they think I don't have a mind?"

The walls in maroon brocade, the trim around the doors and windows frames painted a glossy black, the banquettes covered in a dark red flock, and the maitre d' and waiters in white tie created a fitting background for Katherine's aloofness. She ordered a vermouth, specifically Noilly Pratt, and soda, lots of soda, in a tall glass, which she emphasized by holding one graceful hand above the other graceful hand, her forearms undulating gently, gracefully, magnificently.

Not until the waiter brought the drinks and Harvey had taken a couple of sips of his Manhattan did he feel somewhat at ease in the presence of the great Katherine.

"What I meant in the limousine this morning by 'a bit complicated' was I've just broken up with my husband. At least, I think have. I hope I have. My aunt's a specialist in these matters. She's been through three husbands. When I phoned last Monday to tell her, she insisted I come over for Easter. She bought the plane ticket. She thought I should rest up before I took the world on again, as she put it, 'single-mindedly.' "

"Will you get a job?"

"Oh, yes, of course."

"How long has it been?"

"Since I worked? Five years, perhaps six." She spoke with that slight English accent of hers, her voiced sporadically altered by huskiness. Some of the blue of her eyes overflowed on to her cheeks. Her upper lip was narrow and tense with determination, a small flaw easily overcome by the elegant straight lines of her nose.

"What does your husband do? Or did he do? Mind my asking?"

"Full-time? He thinks he's the Holy Trinity. On the side, he's a neurosurgeon. Lord and Master of the Toronto General Neurological Unit. The Generalissimo of The General, I used to call him."

"Where's all that leave you?"

"A woman."

"For a living, I mean."

"He didn't want me to work. He liked me home. To serve

and obey." The ice cubes crashed against the side of Katherine's glass. "The only problem was he was a closet tyrant. His real first name was Tyrone but I used to call him Dr. Tyrant. He didn't care for that. And then there was this peculiar preference of mine. I like to come and go as I wish—within reason, of course. He was even less fond of that than being called Dr. Tyrant. I don't know what it is about me but I can't stand being ordered around. I abhor oppression of any kind. Especially when the one oppressed is me. I just abhor it."

Sound familiar? Have we not heard the same kind of talk somewhere before? Say, at Thrace's back in Toronto in a conversation between a certain gentleman and Zyg Adams, a few months earlier? Was it not the motive, the very motive that led to the founding of The Republic? Nothing, absolutely nothing, promotes the prospect of union so much as a common cause.

Harvey began to see Katherine the Ingrate in quite a different light. Rays of blue, pink, yellow and pure white danced off her face.

"He was just so wound up in his work there was no room for anything or anybody else. It was equally my fault, of course. I should have fought back a lot sooner. I don't want a cent from him. I gave him all his credit cards back. That was stupid. No one would issue me one in my own name without a credit history. I might accept a ride in from the airport, even the use of a stranger's bed," another smile accompanied Katherine's words, "but I do have pride."

"Pride's a notoriously poor provider, I'm told."

"I have a Ph.D.," Katherine said, her back straightening.

"That's not necessarily the path to wealth either. In what?" asked Harvey.

"Economics."

What? Economics! Was God about to take all the first-born sons again? Everywhere you looked, economists. First Larry and now Katherine. Everybody lauds the plagues sent to persuade the Pharaoh of Egypt. But does anyone ever stop to think of the poor Egyptian farmer who woke up happy one morning, opened the front door of his small hut only to see an endless buzzing, green-black carpet in his fields? Do you think he said to his wife, "Darling, this is truly wonderful, now the Pharaoh will have to let the Israelites go."?

"And what will economics degree do for you?" Harvey's voice quieter.

"I'm hoping, quite frankly, it will improve the money supply. My money supply."

"How?"

"With a job somewhere?"

"Where is somewhere?"

"Don't know. Maybe here. My aunt arranged an interview with some insurance people in The City when we're back from Mallorca. Maybe in Toronto."

By the time dinner and a bottle of Gevrey-Chambertin 1993 had been consumed, Harvey's enthusiasm was back full force. Katherine would wave those stunning forearms of hers to emphasize a point, wave them gently, softly, as if conducting a quiet religious ceremony—undulatingly, softly undulating.

Katherine slept in Harvey's bed that night. Harvey did not. He slept on the couch again. Had he been able to get his hand on some powdered rhinoceros horn, it might have turned out differently. But at the end of day that Easter Sunday, she played the fatigue card once again and refused the offer of a nightcap in the suite.

Goddamn! Beauty is supposed to bring warmth and light to the world. Beauty is supposed to be the tipoff that something greater than what meets the eye is at play. If you listen to the mongers of religion trying to increase their market share, beauty is supposed to signal that beneath the chaos of everyday life, beneath the frenzied confusion of everyday urban life, some sort of order exists.

The idea of a liaison of any sort with Katherine could only have been conceived by a mind numbed by alcohol and drunk with newfound freedom. What's more, the thought that such a liaison was to be an omen of any kind reeked of desperation. One of those ideas which, upon reflection, makes you ask yourself, where in hell did I get that idea from?

The next morning when Harvey put her in a cab for the airport, she looked as unhappy as she did when they drove into London. It seemed the only thing that would make her feel on top of the world would be a successful expedition to the North Pole.

The Holy Sacred Task was stricken from his list of to-dos.

X.

INTO THIN AIR

What has not been explained yet is that this elegant suite at the Dorchester, which cost £490 a night, and which Katherine had taken so for granted, was being paid for by Sheardon-Cassidy. The hotel was Zygmunt's favourite in London, and he stayed there on every visit except in 1990 when it was under renovation. Zygmunt had insisted that Harvey stay there in return for doing some advance interviews with the candidates for a new managing director of Sheardon-Cassidy's London office.

Zygmunt was about to shake up the company's European operations. His partners at Sheardon-Cassidy, of which there were thirty-seven including the largest shareholder who was also the Chairman and Chief Executive Officer Eldred "Piggy" Donnis (Sir Oink, as Zygmunt sometimes referred to him), were very unhappy about the money the London and Paris offices had lost the previous three months. While brokerage houses like to advise clients that the best chance for gain comes from thinking long term, for their own account the same advisors show a marked preference for the short term. The Street hates to tie up its own capital; that can be risky. And, in the words yelled out by Chairmen Eldred, "We don't buy risk, for God's sake, that's what we sell!"

With the introduction of the new Euro currency, the European operations were beginning to look risky. Even though the European office had been a profit-earning part of the company over the last twenty years, according to Zygmunt, the partners wanted to know why they should hold on to an operation that lost money three months in a row.

In the financial world, now is everything. Yesterday has a half-life of about twelve hours.

Zygmunt had established most of Sheardon-Cassidy's important current European clientele himself in an earlier era as the executive vice-president of sales. Later, as president, he had beefed up the London and Paris offices. That had paid off handsomely the first two years, but it had not done so of late. His partners, especially the ones whose opinions he tended to ignore, blamed the losses on Zygmunt's rashness though, oddly, they had never given him the least credit in the profitable days (the joy of leadership). The Pig and the other partners wanted something done—now. Right now. Right goddamn now. Period. End of discussion. Period. Now. Period. Period. Not tomorrow.

To mollify them, Zygmunt, was going to London and

Europe as Monsieur Robespierre of the Committee of Public Safety to make a few heads roll. To hear him tell it, he was coming over to have a little tête à tête with the manager of the London office, which would turn out to be a tête à sans tête. Nor was it unlikely at some point that the head of the Paris office, who of late had found more time for horses in the Bois de Boulogne and women in the *boîtes de nuit* than for clients, might also find his head under the knife. At least that's what the rowdy, unruly peasants who called themselves Zyg's partners, screamed for. Evidently, even the head bond trader demanded an end to the inequity of having money he made for the company lost through the indolent hands of the European operations.

A recruitment firm had lined up a list of six candidates—Zygmunt insisted on six, no mistakes this time—for director of the London office. But when Zygmunt realized he wouldn't have time to interview them all, he wanted Harvey to narrow the list from six down to two or three. Zygmunt was to interview the final candidates, make the final selection and negotiate the employment contract. For Harvey's participation, Sheardon-Cassidy would pay for his suite at the Dorchester no less, since the interviews could not take place at the lavish London office before the decapitation of the current managing director, they had to be conducted, nevertheless, in an appropriately lavish-appearing setting.

That Monday, after breakfast, Harvey phoned Norman James's secretary at Ponton Greenwell Utterbridge. "...This is Harvey Markson. From Canada. I know Mr. James is still in Hong Kong and won't be back until next week. If you're talking to him, though, I just wanted him to know I have arrived and am at the Dorchester until the weekend if he wants to get a hold of me. I'm just phoning to confirm our meeting next Tuesday. I'll be back in town after the weekend, but not sure where I'll be staying."

Promptly at ten o'clock, the hotel front desk phoned up to ask permission for a visitor to come up to the room. Harvey spent the next two hours with the man from Zyg's recruitment agency scheduling the next two days' six appointments with the short-listed candidates. No sooner was that task completed than another call came from the doorman to say that the estate agent (his new employers Ponton Greenwell Utterbridge had arranged to have someone show him apartments) had come round for him and was waiting at the front door.

The agent was an affable, heavy woman in her late fifties with a set of misaligned teeth (the English must abhor orthodontists). In her youth, according to her, she had had flaming red hair, but time, in her words, "had put out the fire and left only the ashes." She paid little attention to her appearance and even less to the traffic. Such an attitude doesn't help anybody get used to cars turning off and on streets from the wrong lane.

"I remember from my time living in Brussels. I know how important it is to situate oneself properly in a new city. You'll love the flats I'm showing you. Perhaps not so much the first one, we'll see, but..." She talked on as if silence was a sin. The first day's outing was intended only to orient Harvey to the London housing market. No need to rush into anything. For Harvey, life was on idle that week.

The first five places Harvey saw were out of the question. One had no furniture, three had no charm and the last one made you feel you were camped on the median of a six-lane throughway. All, however, were priced within reason. The sixth place Harvey was taken to, over in Knightsbridge on Ashley Square, just around the corner from where he'd dropped Katherine the day before, was different. The houses formed a square around a small park with its perimeter marked by hedges and a black iron fence about three feet high. In the midst of the park sat a tennis court intended, the estate agent said, for the exclusive use of the Square's inhabitants. If Harvey played tennis, she pointed out, how easy it would be to get know the neighbours. "The American couple who lived in the flat previously blended right into the community. The husband was an extremely busy film producer, but he just loved having a place to play tennis. He got to know the whole square."

Since university, Harvey hadn't been part of a community where people who lived close by knew each other. Inhabitants of big cities all have their own lives to live. Seldom do they have the desire to meet new people from other cities or, worse, from other countries. Without access or connections to the native citizens, you can live in city like London as a complete stranger, and feel, even if you live downtown, on the outskirts of everything.

Furthermore, the agent pointed out, to travel to Ponton Greenwell's offices Harvey would have to make only one *tube* change. For shopping, two steps would take him to Brompton Road and Harrod's. And, further yet, a good address like Ashley Square was "essential and absolutely vital to make one's way in the City." Ennismore Gardens, Hyde Park, the Palace Gardens were all within a convenient walking distance, she told Harvey.

Before it would open, the front door to the flat needed an

extra shove from the agent's broad shoulder. The stairway up was dark, dingy, narrow and extremely steep. During the climb Harvey rejected the place. Once inside the flat, however, it was different. The spaciousness, which meant he could pace up and down just like in his old condo, the high-ceilings and the large, ornate windows gave the feeling of openness and of freedom and comfort. The three fireplaces, all of which worked supposedly, would give Harvey the comfort of knowing that one way or another he need never be cold. The unevenness of the floors added to the sense of history about the place. It had a musty but not unpleasant smell, and none of the stale, leftover cooking odours of the other places he had seen earlier. The beige curtains with tasselled folds framed windows that looked out on to the square and the tennis court. The sofa and chairs looked a little worn, that's true. From the living room you stepped down one step into the raspberry-walled dining room with a long antique oak harvest table. The kitchen, its floor of yellow, shiny Spanish tiles, contained all the appliances including dishwasher and microwave oven, both of which looked brand new. That could not be said of the bathroom's fixtures.

The loo defied time. The pedestal sink and four-footed bathtub displayed aged surfaces mottled with thin black cracks. Three or four of the shower's tiles had split. And in the farthest corner of this reasonably sized room, just below the ceiling, perched a large porcelain tank, a chain hanging from it almost down to the toilet seat. Time had won.

"Charming, don't you think?" asked the agent testing Harvey.

"All the apartments looked the same in the building I lived

in. On the elevator you felt like a bee sent off to your appointed place in the hive."

"You would never get that feeling with this flat. There are no others quite like it," said the estate agent. "You know what's especially nice about it? The minute you walk in, somehow you feel right at home."

At home. Jesus!

Let me just ask you to picture the farmer in ancient Egypt who looks out his front door. Instead of pestilence carpeting his land, he sees yellowy-brown wheat shafts grown from seed he sowed, shimmering under a bright sun and undulating in the early morning breezes. At that moment, wouldn't the farmer feel he was in the right place, wouldn't he feel at home? Today, with all the cacophony and impatience of large cities, how many places could you find where you felt at home? A place, perhaps, with a hearth and a wood fire and the primitive smell of wood smoke, a place that you accepted as yours—and which accepted you in return. Chez toi.

"Flats like this rarely come on the market and never for long," said the estate agent as she drove Harvey back to the Dorchester, trying once again to move him to action. "But my people are anxious to get it rented. They don't like it vacant."

"What did you say the rent was?"

"They'd let it go for twenty-six hundred quid a month. Four thousand U.S."

"That's way, way out of my budget. That's not practical for me."

"It's never gone vacant for more than a week," said the agent.

"Tell your people I'll take it."

Starting anew takes energy. Inertia and the prevailing wind is always a head wind. How Harvey had lasted to this point is not easily explained. So little sleep before he got on the plane, only a restless hour or two of it on the plane. Then there was that Procrustean couch the night before to accommodate Katherine the Ingrate in hopes that she might accommodate him someday.

When the estate agent woke him at nine the next morning to say she was dropping off the lease for his signature, it felt like the middle of the night. But he had to get up anyway to interview Zyg's candidates.

None of the three candidates from that first day impressed Harvey, much like apartment hunting the day before. The first one had worked at a small American firm specializing in bond trading and seemed lazy. Another one had never been involved with sales to large institutional clients like insurance companies or pension funds, which was really the core of Sheardon-Cassidy's clientele. The third, a very presentable man in his early thirties had lots of talent but no management experience.

About three o'clock that afternoon, having had watercress sandwiches and tea in the lobby restaurant of the hotel, Harvey headed out for a better look at his new city of residence. A block down the street at a corner of Hyde Park he got on a red double-decker tour bus.

"Is it better to sit below or up on the deck," he asked as he stepped on.

"Guv'nor, they only pay me to take tickets," came the surly-voiced answer, "I'm not the tour guide."

London is nothing if not a city of sights, a postcard collector's dream. The buildings and monuments over-tax the mind (and likely the inhabitants). All that history crammed into one space—playgrounds for the aristocracy, battlefields for politicians, elevated perches for heroes. The cityscape of central London struck Harvey as an unending memorial to individuals who in one way or another had shaped the country and its history, a sort architectural statement that man can mould his own destiny. By the time the bus drew up on one side of Pall Mall so the tour guide (not the ticket taker) had the time to sketch out a brief history of Buckingham Palace, Harvey was convinced he had come to the perfect place to start a new life.

Rule, Harvey...

After the sightseeing tour, he took a cab along Oxford Street down to the theatre district and picked up a good single ticket for that night's performance of *Shadowlands* at the Shaftesbury Theatre and strolled for a while around Regent Street, Piccadilly and Soho looking at the shop windows and wandering like a tourist without destination. The smell of burnt diesel oil from the buses pumping up and down Regent Street resembled, molecule for molecule, the smell given off by the buses of Toronto plying Bay Street—except the fumes, somehow, if you can imagine it, smelled freer. The honking horns and screeching brakes sounded the same too, perhaps not quite as harsh. Somehow London's cacophony sounded more melodious. Or maybe the sense of freedom had flipped Harvey out. Harvey lost track of time and had to bolt down a Ploughman's sandwich and a pint of bitters at The Rose and Petal to make it in time to his theatre stall.

When he got back to the hotel later in the evening the desk

clerk handed him three small pieces of yellow paper taken from a cubbyhole with Harvey's suite number on it. Norman James's secretary had phoned with a message to confirm their meeting the following Tuesday at 10:15. Zygmunt had called and wanted Harvey to call him. And the third message slip had a full eleven-digit phone number under the words "Please call. Katherine." When he got up to the suite, Harvey threw the messages in the wastebasket by the desk, went into the bathroom, brushed his teeth, got into his pyjamas and slipped into his prized bed. It had been a good day in London.

"Did I wake you?" It was Katherine.

"No."

"You weren't going to call me, were you?" Some static crackled over the phone line. "The phone system in Mallorca is a bit antiquated."

"Maybe not."

"How can I explain? I was scared to death. I didn't know you. I didn't know the city. I never feel that comfortable in a new city anyway. And all I had to my name was fifty pounds."

"You told me that." Harvey kept his distance.

"When I went through the story with my aunt I realized how utterly awful I'd been."

"No need to explain. I'm not sure it was pure altruism on my part."

"My aunt gave me, I don't know, a scolding." Katherine laughed. "She thinks she went to University with your father. Mind you, she thinks she went to school with everybody's parents. Truth is she dropped out in first year university to get married. Anyway she'd love you to come down for the weekend. She wants to show her appreciation to you for having saved her little niece from the perils of London. We have tickets for the *corrida* in Palma on Sunday. You told me at dinner you were determined to see a bullfight again. You'll love it here. Harvey, it's so beautiful. One day—that's all it took me—and you feel like a completely new person. It's so beautiful. Do come down."

"I've made arrangements to go up to Oxford for the weekend and drop in on an old professor of mine. I'm sorry."

"A likely story. Can't you go some other time? Two of the best bullfighters in Spain are here on Sunday. You can go up to Oxford any time."

A long pause. "Thanks, but..."

"I can't persuade you?"

"He's made all kinds of arrangements for me. I can't ask him to change them now."

"Are you sure? Too bad, I thought it might work. But, look, we'll be back in London a week Sunday. The Monday, I have an interview in The City with the president of Commonwealth General. My aunt, in the background, says then you must at least come round for drinks. I fly home the next day. My aunt will be a terrific connection for you in London; she knows everybody. She's under Amelia Russell on Eaton Place. You will call us? It would be really nice to see you."

Do you think a day or two of sun and rest can change a person? Not likely. Once you've sighted the cold, icy side of a woman's nature, not to give her a wide berth would be a mistake of titanic proportions.

"I'm not sure of my schedule. With a new job and a new apartment and all," said Harvey.

"Try."

One phone call cannot alter geography. Between Katherine in the south of Spain and Harvey in London there remained a huge gulf.

A time comes, just before parting from the day, no matter how raucous that day's been, when people like to savour a moment of peace and reflect on the day's events and to contemplate those of the next. Harvey had just gotten off the phone with Katherine, turned out the light, slumped back down between the cool, fresh-smelling sheets and contemplated the inherent wisdom of changing the venue of his life.

"A town full of the most fabulous women in the world and old Harvey Markson's snuggled in by—what time is it there?—eleven?"

"D'you phone four thousand miles to check up on my sex life, Zyg?"

"How's the set-up?"

"Quite acceptable."

"Goddamn right, Harvey. I told my secretary to get you the best suite in the house. How'd the interviews go?"

"Not bad. I met with three guys today. Three more to go," said Harvey.

"Good-good."

"They weren't really the Sheardon-Cassidy type. They don't believe in sloth and greed."

"Not funny, Harvey. I'm counting on you as a good friend to help me turn that goddamn place around before The Pig has me for dinner."

"The first two didn't have much international experience. The third guy had enough talent but I don't think enough management experience. Tomorrow's candidates look much better. Actually one guy, McKendrick, or McKissick, I think his name is, looks really good on paper." Harvey sat up in bed and lit a cigarette.

"Just figure out the three best. And, Harvey, you're right on, the guy doesn't have to be a quantum mechanic. You know, just somebody that understands the investment business. Somebody that can count and that I can count on. And make sure the guy can start in two weeks. Sooner'd be better. I need to turn the goddamn thing around in a hurry."

"We've been over that."

"Okay-okay," said Zygmunt. "What are your plans?"

"I'm off to Oxford on the weekend to visit an old professor of mine who taught in Toronto for a couple of years. I get back Monday and take possession of an apartment I've rented over in Knightsbridge. I signed the lease today. I'm supposed to start down at Ponton Greenwell maybe next week. What's up with you?"

"The goddamn computer company, you know, The Saviour. I've got to raise some more dough. The Pig won't put another cent in. I think he figures if he holds out, the company will go south and he'll get control. You know Sir Oink—why take your fair share when you might get the whole trough. The guy the writes the tech column for *The World of Finance* raved about it. He said that "The Saviour was so good it could organize a religion."

"Look, let me sit this round out until I'm settled in, Zyg. Unless you really need it..."

"Jesus, Harvey, I wouldn't let you come in if I wasn't sure this deal'll make us a fortune. I'm trying to make it a world in which my dear friend Harvey won't have to take crap from jerks like Leon. We'll talk about it next week when I get over there. I've changed my schedule. I'm off to Paris on Monday. I need to see what's going on there. I get to London on Wednesday. I'll meet with the candidates in the afternoon. Let's have dinner that night. We can figure out who to hire. At Annabel's. You make the reservations. See you at eight."

"Okay," said Harvey. "Hey, you ever run into a guy by the name of Tyrone Ridell? A neurosurgeon over at the Toronto General?" asked Harvey.

"Yah, I met him at a couple of parties years ago when I was a broker. Years ago. Why?"

"Umm, on the plane I met someone who knew him."

"He makes Leon look like social worker. Arrogant as hell. We talked about the market all night. I phoned him three times with some red-hot investment ideas. He should've been a lawyer—never returned my calls. Not sure I'd know him if I saw him today. But I'll tell you one thing, Harvey..."

"What?"

"I'd know his wife—anywhere. Can't remember her name. A young Amazer, just like Grace. Not the kind that bowls you over, you know, on first glance. But when you take a second look, everything's perfect—the face, the nose, the eyes, everything—not a hair out of place. Great sexy voice. Fabulous body. She moved her hands and arms like a...like she was performing in Swan Lake or something. And smart too. She worked for some think tank, the Hudson Institute or someplace. The only thing I never could figure out is why the hell she'd want to marry an absolute jerk like Ridell."

"I guess Katherine can't figure that out either."

"How do you know?"

"She was the person on the plane who knew him."

"Harvey, you picking up strangers on a plane now? That's not you."

"I used your old match trick," said Harvey. "Sort of."

"What the hell's gotten into you, Harvey? You know the real reason I'm coming over there? To see what you're up to. I told you, I think you've flipped out. See you. Wednesday at Annabel's. Eight o'clock. And if you can get me a date with Katherine, I'll throw in a couple of thousand Saviour options next time you buy shares."

The magic of compound interest.

Tonight she would sleep on the island of Mallorca and he in the British Isles, thousands of miles apart. Later, maybe something would develop between them. Nothing serious, not at the beginning, not right after a marriage break-up. A Platonic relationship to start with perhaps. If Katherine did come to London live and work, The Holy Sacred Task would be well worth taking up again. Perhaps these two insular existences would come together. Or even sequentially.

Looked at in the clear light of day, life is nothing but a feast or famine of hope. Harvey had his best sleep in months.

As the door opened, after he had put his shoulder to it, he heard a scraping sound. Caught under the door was an envelope from Ponton Greenwell Utterbridge (since 1892), which he shoved in his coat pocket. Then he lifted up again the two large black and brown suitcases (one black, one brown) and began the climb up the long, steep stairway of twenty-two steps. He though it would be appropriate to line the stairway with portraits of Tenzing Norgay and Sir Edmund Hilary.

Of all the tasks that lie before us in life, few surpass in repugnance that of moving in. So Harvey felt relief rather than anxiety when he opened the letter from Norman James's secretary and found out that Norman James's return from Hong Kong would be delayed and that they could not meet until Friday, instead of the next day. Some question remains whether Harvey, even with those extra two days, would have ever gotten properly moved into Ashley Square.

Most of the time on the train ride back from the weekend in Oxford Harvey had spent jotting down items for the ever-present to-do list. In case of sickness or an accident, Rupert had always insisted that all members of the staff keep an up-to-date list of tasks. It is a fact that the day after Rupert's death, Harvey knew exactly where to take up the reins simply by looking over the carefully printed list in Rupert's desk drawer. One reason Harvey had made even a small investment in Zygmunt's Saviour was because he knew only too well the need for a "personal coordinator," especially one that overcame the tendency to get the easy things done immediately and the distasteful ones only out of sheer necessity or to draw a little horizontal arrow adjacent to an item. It stood as a never-ending joke around Winkes' offices that the only thing people did was make up to-do lists. And though it was part of the reason for Winkes' reputation for reliability—you did what you said you'd do—Leon mocked the list-making so much the staff stopped doing it.

For every item deleted from his list two more appeared in its place. Shades of the early days of Project Vamooski. Even with a so-called fully furnished apartment, task upon task presented itself. For one thing the apartment lacked a decent can opener. For another, the left shift-key on the notebook computer still needed repair and so in the list, revised two if not three times daily, some words went uncapitalized:

Can opener
Cleaning lady
Telephone
Spot remover
The World of Finance
Barron's
The Economist
international investor
Financial Times
Wall Street journal
South Asian journal
la Financière
Handkerchiefs (6)
Stationery
Bank account
Newspaper delivery
Shoe polish
Change of address to bank
Robbie Elliot – call

The list for food and staples and pharmaceutical supplies was itself two pages long.

No longer was Harvey ridding himself of things. He had begun to build. Harvey had begun to put down roots, dig a foundation, start a home, return to civilization, find a place in the universe, a home.

On his way out that day, he encountered the couple, tennis racquets in hand, from the flat below. He introduced himself. The couple spoke with accents so heavy Harvey barely understood them. The wife had bad teeth and stood at least two inches taller than her husband. He had worked for National Westminster Bank in Liverpool until two years ago. They played tennis, obviously, but at a private club over in Kensington, never on the Ashley Square court. In fact, that the only person ever to show the slightest interested in playing tennis with Harvey in Ashley Square was Katherine's aunt who had given the game up forty-eight years before.

"I loved the game. I used to play every day. It's a marvellous game. I still go to the All England Club out at Wimbledon whenever I get a chance. Never give it up, Harvey. I made a great mistake," said Katherine's aunt as she offered Harvey more smoked salmon on Melba toast. "But tell us about your flat, Harvey. Do you like it? I mean really? It's such a marvellous location for you. And London, what do you think of our London?"

The paintings that hung on almost every wall of the aunt's townhouse portrayed people, never landscapes or abstract ideas, only ballerinas, clowns, children in a park, strollers along a beach, men and women at different ages and in all economic circumstances.

"I'll to have to lose a little weight before I enter the Grand National this year," she said as she reached the top of the stairs puffing heavily. She led Katherine and Harvey into a small room covered floor to ceiling with either photographs or shelves with photographic albums of voyages to India and Asia, Australia and Hawaii, North and Central and South America. Most of her life must have been spent on a trip or planning the next one. Among the pictures was one of her in conversation with Queen Margaret of Denmark and another in a group with President Mitterrand of France and another at a tea party with the Queen and Prince Philip.

In the next room with a big bay window and shelves as full with books as poor Rupert's old office, the three of them sat down around a French-polished captain's table that held a silver tea service, a plate of jam-covered scones and dishes of macadamia nuts, almonds and candied fruit.

The chatting went on for an hour. Chatting may not be quite the right word. The aunt related stories about the royal family and about business people she had known, like Lord "Somebody-Somebody" whose name she couldn't remember for the moment but who was the head of Rolls Royce before the takeover. There was almost no need for Katherine or Harvey to say a word.

"What's the name of the company you'll be associated with Harvey?"

"Ponton Greenwell."

"Norman James? I've known Norman and his wife for years," said the aunt. "He's an absolutely wonderful man. You'll love working there. They have a very good reputation. Sound as the rock of Gibraltar. And Norman always struck me as one of the most perspicacious men I have ever known. One night we'll all get together. We'll have drinks at your flat to celebrate your arrival here and then I'll take you to a new place I just heard of that has the best Thai food in the world, when Katherine gets back. I'm sure Commonwealth General will want to hire someone as bright as my Katherine. If not, I'll knock their noggins together until they come to their senses."

Katherine had volunteered to walk over to see Harvey's

flat. “I’d like to see it. My aunt doesn’t need a permanent boarder. If I come back I’ll have to rent one.”

As they walked up Eaton Square, the remnants of the late afternoon sun cast long shadows along the sidewalk. Katherine began to chat incessantly like a schoolgirl just let out of school or from under a talkative aunt’s wing.

“If my interview goes well tomorrow and they offer me a job, I don’t know what I’ll do. I’m on automatic pilot these days. My friends think I’m crazy. My poor parents, they don’t know what to think. Their lovely little cum laude daughter had all the trappings of a great and wonderful marriage—house, status, clubs, influence, oodles of disposable income. You have to think twice before you abandon all that and…my son.” She paused as they waited for a traffic light to change. “Why am I saying all this? I’m a very private person.” Her voice dropped. “I guess because at this moment home seems so very far away.”

Two bowler-hatted men ogled Katherine as they walked by in the opposite direction.

“All those trappings just felt like a trap. All Ty seemed to care about was his hospital and his golf game. I think he figured if he got his handicap below ten he could take over the world. Spiritually, I might as well of been living in the Falkland Islands, sort of nowhere. I felt deprived. No, not deprived, confined. Confined. That’s the first time I’ve found a word for it. Confined for life. Have you ever felt like that, Harvey? Have you ever felt constrained just by the air about you?”

Had Harvey ever felt confined? Jesus, is peanut butter made out of peanuts?

Rule, Harvey.

Harvey clasped the underside of her forearm and helped her down the curb.

"How old's your son?

"Seven last month. I miss him. But he's best off with Ty, I guess. For now, anyway. At least he'll have a decent golf handicap when he grows up. He's pretty angry with me just going away for ten days. And his father will fight tooth and nail to get custody. Anyway, I don't have the resources to fight. Or the strength at this moment. But the thought of living without my son is almost unbearable."

"You must have talked to friends."

"I said my prayers for a while. Just like in high school. Didn't make very much difference. I went to see the local minister. He told me to get a hold of myself."

"What do you think you'll do, Katherine?"

"Go home and think about it, I guess. One minute a quiet housewife in Toronto. The next an economist in London. I don't know. You get all excited about these things and then when they happen you have second thoughts. Maybe a quiet housewife in Toronto is where I belong. Why am I going on like this? I'm so inside myself these days," Katherine paused. "You start work in The City tomorrow?"

"Norman James, the man your aunt mentioned, got held up in Hong Kong. So I don't quite know when I start."

"I hope everything goes okay," she said as they started up the face of the steep stairway to Harvey's flat, the only wall decoration a picture of Tenzing Norgay, with snow goggles on the top of his head. "Does your flat need drapes? I love to sew. If I come back I'll make drapes for you, I promise. I owe you."

IOUs, if Dr. Robert John Leon Kelpner, D.D.S., Dip. Perio. had taught Harvey anything, are not something to bank on.

Zygmunt and Harvey had not been seated for two seconds at Annabel's when Zygmunt said, "Let's get the business out of the way first. Then we can talk about important things. But, god, you should have seen the woman Jean-Claude fixed me up with in Paris last night. She's a high-fashion model and I think I'm in love."

"Is that the third or the fourth time since Valentine's day?"

"Next to Paris, this town is dead. Waiter, bring us the '93 Mercurey? Be sure it's not too warm, will you," said Zygmunt as handed the wine list back to the man. "Harvey, don't let me drink too much tonight. I got to be sharp in the morning."

"You always say that."

"I got to fire that jerk that thinks he can run our office here. But I might just hop over to Paris tomorrow night and come back in the morning," said Zygmunt. "Before I forget, The Amazer sends her love. That's what she told me, that and not to forget to tell you that. Sara's in New York studying away. Mrs. Avogadro wants you to stop playing around and come home. I saw Zuzu at a party the other night. She wanted to know when you're coming back. Roi Swasont sent his best regards as did Señor Fkup. That guy drives me nuts. He said he'd give me an order for a ton of The Saviour's shares. Then he changes his mind. Gives me a quarter of what he promised. Typical. Anyway, people miss you. Not me. I'm glad to have you out of my hair."

"What do you tell them?"

"I tell them I didn't know what the hell you were up to, a holiday or some sort of self-imposed exile."

"But you do. You know goddamn well. I'm not coming back. And that's exactly why I left. Everybody there wants to tell you how to live your life. You know what I like best about London? I like it because it's not very friendly. That way you can come and go as you please. You don't have to figure out who'll be offended if you stay home one night."

The waiter held the bottle of wine in front of Zygmunt who put his hand on it. "That's at about room temperature for a sauna. If you could get it down to sixty-five degrees, I'd be extremely grateful." The waiter took the bottle away. "The English like their wine about ten degrees below boiling. I don't know how they can drink the stuff."

"Zyg when you don't like something you always make it sound like the offender broke eight out of the Ten Commandments."

Zygmunt ignored Harvey's comment. "You should be a headhunter. The first two guys weren't bad, but I agree with you, the last guy, McKissick, sounds like my guy. He's got everything going for him and he can start next week. I'd give him the job except for one thing—he liked you. Well, no one's judgment is perfect. I'll give him the job anyway."

"With McKissick here, I can let Jean-Claude go now."

"Jean-Claude?"

"I like Jean-Claude. We've had some really wild times. But I liked him a lot more when he was a big producer. And he's gotten as lazy as the moon. I set that territory up. I know the accounts. But I find out half of them hadn't seen him in months. One account we went to see thought I was Jean-Claude. And Gottfried de Holger—the best goddamn money manager in Europe—doesn't even return Jean-Claude's phone calls. Gott has an IQ of about two thousand. He really liked some of the stuff we did when I was handling the account. I always got special research for him even if I had to buy it from some independent analyst in New York. I did a ton of business with the guy. Jean-Claude can't even get him to return a phone call. No wonder we're in trouble."

The waiter returned with different bottle. Zygmunt put his hand on it. "Better. Much-much better. Better label, too. Same price though, right, waiter?"

"Of course, sir," said the waiter as he opened the bottle and poured a small amount into the glass for Zygmunt.

Zygmunt swirled the glass, then slurped a sip of the contents over his tongue. "Very nice. Very nice. You're a good man." The waiter departed. "What's the apartment like, Harv?"

"Terrific. A lot to do though. Furniture's not bad. I thought as a house present you might send Zuzu over to give me a hand."

"I want to save your dough for the software company. Save Your Time looks fabulous. For a start-up couldn't look better. But with the Asian situation right now nobody wants to invest in anything but Coca Cola. Four different companies are after the U.S. distribution rights for The Saviour. I can get you some warrants to buy the stock at two bucks." Zygmunt's face became taut.

"Do I have a choice, really?"

"Don't do it to please me."

"Okay, I'll take a little more, but it's against my better judgment."

"Done. Thanks, Harv," said Zygmunt. "Enough of that

crap. Now let's get down to business. What's with what's-her-name?"

"Who?"

"Tyrone Ridell's wife?" insisted Zygmunt.

"Oh, you mean, Mrs. Ridell?"

"No, I actually had the Queen Mother in mind."

"Would you like to order now, gentlemen?" the waiter intruded. The waiter took down their orders along with Zygmunt's usual long addendum of instructions on how each item was to be cooked, with the carrots specified as al dente and preferably not touching the julienne potatoes.

"I remember now. Katherine. That's her goddamn name. Katherine Ridell. What are you up to, Harv?"

"As far as I know, nothing. I met her on the plane. Gave her a lift into town. Helped her out of a little jam. She thinks she might come to work in London. She seemed about as interested in male companionship as the summit of Mount Everest."

"Is she going to stay in London?"

"She doesn't know."

"If she comes back to Canada, why don't I give her a call?"

"I thought you were in love with the model in Paris."

"I was kidding. You know what the trouble with me and love is, Harv? Love's a game, right? A game. Well, once I score I can never can get my offensive team back on the field."

As he related it to Harvey, in the summer of 1955, having completed his final examinations to become a Chartered Accountant and won the gold medal, Rupert H. Winkes, intent on life as a banker, like his father before him, sailed on the Empress of Scotland across the ocean to live in England and learn his trade at the Lombard Bank. Seven years later he realized he didn't want to be a banker. Or as Rupert put it, he came to his senses and returned to Toronto to work for an investment counselling firm. Those seven years provided Rupert with many anecdotes; many of the happier ones involved Norman James with whom he worked at Lombard's in those early years, but who then moved on to Ponton Greenwell, eventually becoming the managing director. The two men had always kept up the connection.

However many fortunes the partners of Ponton Greenwell had made for their clients and themselves, it was obvious that only the minutest portion had found its way into the furnishings and decor of the company's offices. In the dowdy, gloomy, time-tired reception area there hung only one picture, a landscape remarkable only for its drabness. On a weary pinewood coffee table scarred with black circles and small, black rectangular blotches lay magazines three months out of date. Suppressing expenses often leads to wealth, we know. But this demonstration of corporate frugality struck Harvey as cold and extreme and he began to have doubts about working there in such a place—totally unnecessary doubts.

A tall, older woman in olive green whose black bangs hung down almost to her eyebrows led Harvey into the boardroom with unusually low ceiling. Harvey sat down in the closest of the dozen brass-studded brown leather chairs that circled the boardroom table. Unlike most of the investment management companies back in the old world, Ponton Greenwell had a history that was displayed in the eleven portraits of former chairmen. The torch had been passed, you could assume, from one to the next through wars and depressions, through good times and bad without a hitch in its hundred-odd year history. And nothing much looked to have changed in those years.

"Sorry to keep you, Harvey. So sorry," said Norman James as he entered and extended his hand, "How good to see you," he said quietly as the two men sat down facing each other at one end of the table. James reached over a picked up a Chinese lacquered box from the middle of the table, opened it and first offered Harvey a cigarette, which was refused, then took one himself and lit it. After blowing out a long stream of smoke, he gave out a deep breath accompanied by a quiet sigh. "I was sure I was done with this filthy habit years ago. It's come back, worse than ever, regretfully." Norman James rubbed the cigarette against the rim of the ashtray trying to scrape off an ash yet to be formed. "Such a bloody shame about Rupert. The earth lost a mountain in him. Except for a professor of mine at Christchurch, I don't think I ever met anyone as intelligent as my friend Rupert. No computer today—I don't care what its processor speed—could ever, ever hope to process information faster than Rupert. No matter how quickly he came to a conclusion it was always laden with common sense. He claimed he made a lot of mistakes. Other than the odd bit of misplaced faith in the management of this corporation or that, the only serious error I ever saw him make was in his choice of female companions. I wouldn't say this if he was alive, of course, but when we were at the bank together he always ran after the sluttiest little tramps and treated each of them as if she was the Virgin Mary. Sex and women seemed areas in which he was, to speak frankly, a consummate imbecile. God has his ways of compensating those of us with limited brains. I shall miss my friend Rupert, miss him awfully." James held his breath for a moment. He looked down towards his vest and tried to brush away some spot. "Whenever I had a tough decision to make I'd ask myself, what would Rupert do? You must feel that but a hundred times more."

"When he died things changed I must admit. And I hadn't realized how much of my thinking was really his."

Norman did not reply immediately. He stared into space as if flipping through his memories like cards of an index file. He rubbed the side of his face as if to help his thinking processes, his lips tightened, his eyes moved up and then to the side, then up and to the side again.

Then, abruptly, he said, "H.R. Winkes & Associates, how is it getting along without the two of you?"

"They've brought in an economist to run the show."

"An economist? Rupert abhorred them so." Norman gave a little laugh and then his tone changed completely. "Harvey, you'll have to excuse my brevity. I have an unexpected meeting about to begin. But I'm afraid I've got some not very good news for you." He took a long inhale on his cigarette. "The delay in Hong Kong was due to the completion of a merger between our company and an Asian investment house. It was an on-again off-again sort of thing for so long I'd given up on it when I talked to you back in February. We had had great difficulty coming to agreement with these people in Hong Kong. All of sudden, with the changes in the market, they had a change of heart and met our conditions. As with any merger, we're going to have to let some people go, some who have been with us a long time. We can't hire anybody new at this point. That wouldn't be right. We'll pay all your expenses..."

What no job? How would he support himself? Leon could stall payout on the Winkes & Associates shares for months, forever. Most of the cash from the condo sale back in Toronto went to the mortgage company. Or into shares of the stupid software company. What a stupid move that was! With a rent of twenty-six hundred pounds a month and everything else costing a fortune in London, Jesus!

Confronted by a steep drop in the price of some stock, say, shares of The Save Your Time Software Inc., which, to demonstrate its faith in the system, The Street calls a "correction," no matter the range of possible outcomes, the mind of the amateur investor sees only one: the company will blow up, get wiped out completely and all will be lost. In the face of this little correction to Harvey's personal cash flow, experienced market professional that he was, Harvey's mind could foresee no more than one outcome: he would have to return from whence he came, return defeated, return to that homeless feeling he was trying to escape from, return like some failed vagabond.

"No, I understand, Mr. James."

"Still Norman to you. Did I bring you all this way—"

"No, I'd made up my mind to leave Toronto, anyway, regardless. I always wanted to work in The City. I guess that came from Rupert."

James handed Harvey two business cards. "Here's my card. The other is that of a fellow I rang up this morning, a very good friend of mine. He thinks he could use someone who knows the North American capital markets. I've made an appointment for you this afternoon at two. He's just on the next street. I don't make a habit of lying, but I did tell my friend you were a good fellow." James smiled. "You will go round and see him this afternoon?"

"That's very kind. Don't worry about me. With the merger you have enough on your hands. Yes, I'll go over this afternoon. Very thoughtful of you."

The two men stood up.

"When things settle down here—I'm sure they will in a fortnight or two—you must come and spend a weekend with us in Surrey. And you must keep in touch at any rate. There could be other opportunities. If you can't get a hold of me, keep my secretary up to date on your whereabouts and send her a list of all your expenses. Paying those is the least we can do."

Harvey walked up one street of The City and down the next. It was just after twelve. He passed a half dozens pubs but didn't feel like lunch. On the way to Ponton Greenwell he had memorized the names of streets he crossed. Now he couldn't be bothered. The scurrying, bowler-hatted people, one of which he might have been him had things worked out with Ponton Greenwell, seemed from some foreign country. It was a bright day. The sun was having a lovely day frolicking in the sky. Didn't matter. "Some not very good news" as Norman James had put it. Yes, some not very good news indeed.

At two o'clock, Harvey took the elevator up to the fourth floor of 8 Basinghall. He stepped into a warmly lit reception area. The red wing chairs looked almost new and they matched the dark red plush carpet, A young girl, Swedish-looking, greeted Harvey with an enthusiasm completely lacking at Norman's office. She offered him tea. The day's *Herald Tribune, Financial Times* and *The Wall Street Journal* lay neatly on the coffee table along with the four most recent copies of *The Economist* layered neatly on top of each other.

Norman's friend, quite short in stature but as amiable as Norman, established a rapport with Harvey almost immediately. And he said how impressed he was that Harvey had worked with a man of Rupert's reputation. Peering over the mountain chain of beige file folders on his desk, reminiscent of Robbie Elliot's cluttered desk (and cluttered agenda), the gentleman agreed he could definitely use someone with Harvey's talents, even if only one of the two major pension accounts they were after came through. One of them looked like it would agree to terms by the end of the next week. But, of course, it could be the week after that. Pension trustees don't make decisions in a hurry. They had already taken four months, it was explained. "Bloody slow, pension trustees."

"Keep in touch," the man said. "I can't commit this bloody moment. But I'm confident I will be able to in the next couple of weeks or so."

"Of course," said Harvey, a sort of reflexive response.

Out on the street, again, he found one of the red, multipaned phone booths you see on every corner in London. He stepped into the booth and, as he did so, took out a plastic card from his wallet.

After a silence broken by a second or two of static he heard a ringing sound. It rang eight times. Harvey was about to hang up. The offices might have been closed for the day for some reason.

"Gladdening Wright. Please hold."

Was it a minute later? A day? A millennium? The voice came back on.

"Gladdening Wright. How may I help you?"

"This is Harvey Markson calling from London, England."

"Please hold."

Pause.

"Good morning. Gladdening Wright. How may I help you?"

"This is Harvey Markson calling—long distance—from England. London, England. May I speak to Mr. Robert Elliott?"

"Certainly. I'll put you straight through immediately, Mr. Clarkson."

"Markson."

Another long pause.

"Hello! This is Robert Elliott. I'm not available to take your phone call at the moment. I'm either on the phone or away from my desk. Please leave a detailed message after the beep and I'll get back to you just as soon as I possibly can."

"Robbie, goddamn it, it's Harvey. First of all, where did you train your telephone receptionist? At the Gestapo School for Bad Manners? Secondly, what the hell's happening with Leon? He's over a month late with the payment. I haven't heard from you in weeks. For Chrissake, will you let me know what's going on? The only thing I ever get from you is invoices. Send me a telegram. Or something. To Second Floor, Seven Ashley Square. London. S. W. One. I don't have a phone yet. Let me repeat that. Second Floor Seven Ashley Square. London. S. W. One. Thanks, Robbie—I think."

Some days nothing connects.

At heart, London's a quick-change artist. One moment a city of heroes, then—in an instant—an arrogant array of old buildings and meaningless monuments, of rude people with no sense of service, waitresses and desk clerks surreptitiously fighting some class war. A city living off past glories, a city of noise, frying meat, spent fuel and over-priced restaurants that purvey overcooked, taste-free food. A city with the evanescent charm of a three-act play with only a good first act, a human settlement, worn out by history, of cab drivers you can never tip heavily enough.

There is a certain momentum to life that carries us from day to day. Face to face with a crisis, that special compound of faith and ignorance which holds our days together, that metaphysical glue, dissolves. Only then do we begin to realize how precarious our little perches on this earth are. Only then do we see that, in truth, existence is nothing more than a bunch of conditions gathered in some irrevocable sequence we call life. What's more, in those despondent moments we see how little control we have over those conditions—our own genetic makeup, the phases of the moon, the fluctuations of the currency exchange markets, unapproachable beauty like that of Katherine. We see that, for the most part, no matter what precautions we take, no matter how nutritiously we eat or how safely we drive, our well-being, our being-at-all, is, in the end, out of our hands, every bit as much as was the life of the deer-slain Rupert Haldane Winkes, dedicated conservationist, health fanatic. In the end his god-like wisdom was as disposable as a gum wrapper or a twist-off beer cap. Goddamn it.

Yet we continue to see ourselves as the sole agents of any change for the better. No financial statement ever attributes an improved financial picture to pure horseshoe luck. Never in an annual report will you read an expression of gratitude to the Chairmen of the Federal Reserve for loosening up the money supply (the way he did in 1999). Nor will you read anything about the fortuitous bankruptcy of a major competitor. Nor a word of thanks to Nature for holding off the bubonic plague during the latest ad campaign. Why? Because in his own vain heart the CEO, not unlike the rest of us, sees his efforts, his thoughts, his judgments as the critical factors that brought about the two-cents-per-share increase in the reported quarterly earnings.

Yet when he wants to identify the cause of an earnings deterioration, the very same CEO hauls out an endless array of causal factors over which he claims to have no control: shortage of raw materials, economic events in far-off Asia or punitive taxes imposed by the silly bastards in Ottawa. In spite of all this evidence to the contrary and all the suffering we see on the nightly news created by hardened voyeurs sticking their cameras into bereaved faces, we do still believe that somehow, somewhere in this universe we can find, if not here and now, somewhere else, sometime further on, a place for ourselves. A home.

More mysterious than all that is, god only knows, why we are not down on our hands and knees eight times a day to curry favour and understanding, to do a little metaphysical wheeling and dealing. Is it because we know—frighteningly enough—that in the grand scheme of things our life has no more importance to some Grand Schemer than does that of some innocent, perky-eared white-tailed deer crossing a slippery concession road?

Yikes.

Harvey had brought back to his apartment a copy of *The Sunday Times* ("16 pages of the best jobs in Britain"), and of the *Financial Times* ("Executive market drops to ten-year low") and, of course, he already had the latest issue of *The Economist*. He scanned all three. The deadline for applications in most cases was a month or two away. So that meant no actual job offer would come forth for three months at the best, maybe six. In all the newspapers and magazines Harvey perused from cover to cover that afternoon, he found only one immediately available job opportunity that came close to matching his experience and qualifications: Associate Professor of Finance at the University of Jakarta. Perfect.

The next morning he went to the phone booth around the corner and called the account manager from the recruiting firm that Zyg had used. Harvey had gotten to know the man fairly well when interviewing the candidates for Sheardon-Cassidy.

"By all means. Put together a CV and come over for a chat. Things are a bit tight in The City at the moment with all the mergers going on. But we'll see what we can do. Look, I'm just going on a business trip to Cape Town and Johannesburg while things are a little slow. Can you call back two or three weeks?"

A quick-and-dirty, back-of-the-napkin strategic analysis of the strengths, weaknesses, opportunities and threats—a so-called SWOT analysis—of the situation looked like this: Harvey was financially illiquid. He was ill-prepared for any of the jobs readily available and Project Vamooski was ill-conceived.

When you manage other people's money, as Harvey had for the last six years, you learn to keep your head when everyone around you seems to have lost his, or hers. Time and time again Rupert had stressed that to Harvey. At the first sign of panic in the rest of the world, like a focused lion salivating in anticipation of a felled wildebeest, a money manager sits and waits for the appropriate moment to pounce. In those moments of panic when the market falls a few hundred points on with an ever-increasing number of shares trading as everybody tries to sell at the same time, as everybody rushes for the door together, Rupert would remain calm, unperturbed, a gleeful little smirk would come on to his face as he put in an order to buy order five hundred thousand shares of Alcan or Inco. "Here's where we earn our keep, Harvey," Rupert would say calmly. "For those with little faith, the fire alarm's gone off. For us, a fire sale has just begun."

That was Harvey's training. But what we had here in London was quite different. More than anything, it resembled one of those inside-out hurricanes from Speaker's Corner with crowds swirling around some turbulent speaker. Everybody around appeared as calm as church ministers on Mondays, while at the eye of the disturbance was a perturbed Harvey, perturbed beyond belief.

To boot, Harvey was sure he was coming down with something and maybe he should find a doctor. He felt weak. He didn't think he'd be able to lift a bag of groceries to take to the apartment. His appetite had disappeared anyway. His neck felt stiff, his throat tight. All he could think of was a futureless future, like Segovia's.

Sounds of a stringless strummer.

XI.

LA RÉPUBLIQUE

Le premier juin, mille neuf cents quatre-vingts-dix-neuf, La Deuxième République d'Harvey Markson a commencé.

Allons enfants de la Har-vay
Le jour de gloire est arrivé.

The day after Harvey emailed Zygmunt that there was no job at Ponton Greenwell, Ian McKissick, the new London manager for Sheardon-Cassidy called and asked to meet with Harvey. They met in a pub down in The City, around the corner from Sheardon-Cassidy's offices. Ian must have shown up on the dot. Harvey had to apologize for being a little late; the phone installer was an hour late coming to his flat that morning. For lunch McKissick ordered a pint of bitters ale and Ploughman's Pie. So did Harvey. The beer was warm and the pie cold.

"Zyg fired Jean-Claude. We weren't getting any business out of the man. To let a key account like that Gottfried de Holger over at the QRS Bank in Frankfurt get away is, can I say, a sin. My theory is Jean-Claude wanted the sack and the severance settlement that would go with it. I'm certain he's got another business in mind."

"What's Zyg think he'll do now?" asked Harvey, more to keep the conversation up.

"Well, he thinks he's going to hire you."

"You're kidding. I told Zyg he was barely tolerable as a friend and absolutely the last person on this earth I would work for. On top of that, can't think of anybody who'd make a worse salesman than me."

"It's uncanny, Harvey. That's exactly what your friend Zygmunt told me you'd say. That's why he asked me to approach you."

"I don't know the first thing about selling stocks."

"Of course not. But it's different over here. The financial institutions are much more sceptical than you people in America. They don't want talk to blokes who can wine and dine them. They want people who can help them do their job."

"So?"

"Who could help them more than some fellow who's done their job, who's worked with one of finest money managers in North America?"

"It's just not me, really. I have really no idea how to close a sale."

"That's the gist of it. Jean-Claude knows how to sell. He

knows how to get into someone's office and ingratiate himself. That's not what the good investment managers want anymore. They want one thing. You and I discussed it at The Dorchester when you were looking me over for Sheardon-Cassidy. People managing money today want more than information about what a company's earnings are or what the revenue numbers are going to look like for the next three quarters or guesses about earnings. Managing investment is much too complicated today." McKissick paused to take a couple of mouthfuls of food and washed them down with a long gulp of beer. Harvey came to lunch unprepared to argue. "They want people who understand the various companies. Who can add judgment and can explain how this or that equity fits into a portfolio. They don't want to be wined. They don't want to be dined. They want value for commissions paid. I mean, old chap, who has the time for chitchat anymore? They want to talk with, and reward, people who can help them do their job..."

"Okay, so I know a little about investing. Let me tell you, managing money is extremely idiosyncratic. Everybody goes about it differently. I haven't any idea how some guy down in Rome or Zurich or Frankfurt does his job. It's bound to be altogether different over here..."

"Zygmunt isn't asking you to sell B shares of some company on the Hang Seng exchange in Hong Kong. He wants you to talk to these chaps about North America, about companies you already know backwards and forward. You know, Alcan, Inco, Bombardier, all those Canadian and any American companies you've studied for years..."

The conversation went on for over an hour. Harvey could

find no way to combat Ian McKissick's quiet persistence. In truth, it was just a softening-up exercise.

After they parted, Harvey spent the rest of the afternoon at the National Museum, grabbed a quick, tasteless dinner at a self-serve off Piccadilly Circus, and walked, instead of taking the subway or a cab, all the way back to his Knightsbridge flat. He had just sat down to read the Employment Wanted pages of *The Economist's* latest issue.

"Do it for a couple of years, Harvey, that's all. The Saviour's going to take a little longer to get on track than I thought. Just go back to being an analyst. That's you're real forte."

"I don't want to be an analyst again."

"What time is it there?" asked Zygmunt.

"Seven-thirty."

"It's one-thirty here. I'll set up a job interview for you in the morning with The Royal Bank. They can't find a decent portfolio manager anywhere. You still have time to catch a late plane home tonight."

"Where's home?"

"Here. Toronto."

"No, it isn't."

"Where is it, then?"

"Jesus Christ, Zygmunt, you jerk, that's what I'm trying to figure out."

"You know how many applicants we had for McKissick's job besides the six you saw? A hundred and seventy-two. Does that tell you something about the job market in London today? All those mergers. McKissick thinks you'd be terrific. He says European institutions are fed up with hot-shot salesmen who know bugger-all about stocks or stock markets. I can open all kinds of doors for you. Old Gottfried de Holger at the QRS Bank'll love you. He loves you intellectual know-it-alls."

"I just wouldn't be any good flogging stocks."

"You know that bald-headed bastard from the squash club who's with the Royal Bank? You know the guy who dances around the court like he's trying out for the National Ballet? I'm going to call him right now. He is desperate for a good money manager. Our limo'll pick you up at the airport here in the morning. I owe the guy big time. He does a lot of business with us. Just email me your flight number. You'll never get a job there. Do you want to try starving to death in London? I know you won't care for it."

"I saw an ad for a teaching job in Jakarta. And there's one in *The Economist* for an immediate opening with the United Nations Relief Fund."

"Look, if you want to help the world, work for us. On Halloween you can give whatever you've saved up to UNICEF. The whole world will be better off—including you."

"Let me think about it, Zyg. I don't mean to play it down. It's kind of you but..."

"This is not charity. I'm trying to save my own neck. You know how much The Pig likes to lose money. He's on my tail day and night about the overseas operations. I figure you and McKissick can put me back in the black over there. I'm guaranteeing you two hundred thousand U.S. plus an expense account. And a fabulous apartment I already have picked out for you in Paris. And you'll get to know all the great cities in Europe. Basel, Frankfurt, Luxembourg, Copenhagen, Rome. Have you ever been to the Vatican?"

"No."

"You've never seen Michelangelo's Pietà? Even pagans like us should go and see the Vatican. It's magnificent. And in France six weeks' holiday is mandatory. We'll take over that stupid apartment you're in now—McKissick thinks he can sub-let in a week. Am I an idiot or does that sound like one helluva deal? I'm not asking you to do it for life. Look at it as a two-year sabbatical from the University of Jakarta with quadruple the pay."

"Maybe. I don't know. I just don't know at this point."

"I'll even throw in Marie-Thérèse, that woman I was in love with in Paris."

"Sex and money. That's what you think makes the world go round."

"Did you take another seminar on negotiating? What more can you ask for?"

"Let me think about it."

"Forget it, then. If you have to think about it, you're not bright enough for the job. I'm not asking you to go up in a space capsule. Hang in for two years. Then come back here. By then the Saviour'll have made you enough dough to set up your own investment counselling shop. And you'll have the seen the world."

"Zyg, you keep thinking I want to come back to Toronto. That's the last thing I want," answered Harvey. "The Saviour's still in business?"

"The stock's down a smidge today. But those guys put together a fabulous marketing agreement. Nothing's firm yet. I'm not supposed to tell you. Looks like we've got the hottest product out there. Start-ups always take longer than you figure and they just burn through dough. But don't worry, in two years you'll be rich. Look, all I'm asking is you think about coming with us in Paris. Paris, for God's sake. Copenhagen. Barcelona. Geneva. Rome. Most people would give an arm and a leg to be able to traipse around Europe all expenses paid. What's the matter with you? Are you sick or something?"

"I told McKissick, you and Eldred wouldn't be my first choice for employers."

"Are you implying, my good friend, Harvey," said Zygmunt, "that The Pig, the esteemed leader of Sheardon-Cassidy, might have a character flaw? Are you implying, for example, that he thinks the only thing that makes the world go round is money, forget about sex?"

One of the many items in Rupert's notebook taken from Santayana: "The human mind is not rich enough to drive many horses abreast and wants one general scheme, under which it strives to bring everything."

No matter how little attention you pay to the religious aspect of your life, an old and very large church plunked down in your front yard is bound to make you question your connection to the Universe. Even though the twentieth century chose in the end to ignore the life of the spirit in any social form other than sports events, and even though it turned the care of the spirit over to a new breed of shamans, called psychiatrists, other people in other times did ask profound questions now and again.

The moment Harvey stepped through the courtyard door of No. 38 and out on to the Quai d'Orléans, the cream-coloured towers and the noduled black-green spire of Notre Dame cathedral threw themselves up, up above the tangle of flying buttresses, up, up into the white-blue sky, proclaiming that, at some period, through the streets of Paris, faith had run rampant.

When he wasn't in a hurry, Harvey would stop and stare at those towers and the buttresses and the interwoven facets of its structure, trying to imagine the minds of the people who, as the French say, caused to build this great church. He might walk to the other side of the street and sit down on the stone wall that runs around the perimeter of Île St. Louis and watch the tourist boats, the Bateaux Mouches, and the long black barges that would slowly chug their way up or down the muddy Seine. And watch the gulls soar above the river.

Time had changed its rhythm. It had begun to lope. The air felt soft and gentle, the river breezes warm. How Paris does it we'll never know, but even to newcomers it exudes a mysterious sense of familiarity. Its outward presentation—the buildings, the streets, the parks, the monuments—by-passes the intellect and speaks to something deep inside, more in words of poetry than the stolid proclamations of mere stone and iron and glass.

Harvey's enlivened senses seemed to overcome all feeling of restraint: the smell of chestnuts warmed in copper stoves by street vendors in blue aprons, the magic aroma of frying garlic and of burning cigarettes, Gauloises or Gitanes, from the restaurants. And, when on his way walking to the office, the earthy smell of fresh vegetables, leeks and cabbages and mounds of flat beans, offered up by the shouting vendors of the street market just across the bridge, who on market days (mercredi et samedi), noisily unfolded their stalls, like Arabs in reverse, and set up their canvas-roofed shops. This was a different world, a new world, a strangely comfortable world that made time slow down and gave life a chance to breath.

Thanks to Zygmunt, Harvey found himself in the perfect apartment. Of all the arguments for and against island living, one reigns supreme: the mind takes great comfort in limits. No matter what you need, short of a soccer stadium, you know it is to be found within the ten or eleven city blocks that compose the Île St. Louis, residing as it does in the middle of the Seine. In a day, two at the most, that little island will reveal itself to a foreigner in a way that no other Parisian quartier or arrondissement would dare think of doing in a decade.

So it was not long before The Île's newest resident, on the rare days when he was in residence, found himself whistling his way to the boulanger to pick up a baguette of bread and to hear as he left the sing-songy, child-like chant of Madame la Boulangère—"Merci, monsieur. Au revoir, monsieur. À la prochaine fois, monsieur." In all his years, though, granted, far fewer than those of the old towers of Notre Dame, no one had ever thanked Harvey for the simple act of buying a loaf of bread. Yet it was not only Madame la Boulangère who thanked Harvey for his patronage. So did the white-smocked Madame la Pharmaciste farther along Rue St. Louis-en-Île whenever Harvey stopped to buy Gravol pills for his plane flights and *préservatifs* for flights of another kind, for his goings, on the one hand and, on the other, his comings. And so did the blue-smocked man in the hardware store on Rue Le Regrattier thank him. And so did, for his soiled shirts, the swarthy Spanish woman with the pointy nose and the twenty kilos of extra weight who ran her blanchisserie with all the haste of a tethered barge. The man at the "Tabac" kindly taught Harvey to begin counting with his thumb not his forefinger when he wanted to ask for two packages of Dunhill cigarettes. Island dwellers are always friendly. Unlike inhabitants of mainlands and peninsulas and isthmuses, they know they can't survive without a sense of community.

At least from an academic point of view, and at least in comparison to the First Republic of H. Markson (often referred to in the literature as The Short-Lived Republic), which tended to be characterized more by earnestness than anything, this upgraded version appeared to lack discipline. The influence of Zygmunt had skewed the design of this new Republic much more towards hedonism and the acceptance of Nature's tendency to distribute bounty unevenly. Even working as hard as he was during the early days to get things going for Sheardon-Cassidy and attending language classes Saturday mornings in the Place des Vosges, Harvey felt like he was, just as Zygmunt had said, on sabbatical. More importantly he felt *maître chez lui.* He felt he could come and go as he wanted—exactly the objective of Project Vamooski begun so many months before.

One day in the middle of June of that year, he'd only been on the job a couple of weeks, Harvey took sick. He woke up on a Saturday with a high temperature. His throat felt like he'd had just consumed a bowl of boiling oil and his head as if stuck in some metal vice slowly being tightened. First thing in the morning he went over and discussed the symptoms with Madame la Pharmaciste, as best he could in French, one hand clinging to his head the other to his throat. Madame showed Harvey several kinds of *ampoules,* elixirs which the French have concocted for every identified disease and condition, including fatigue, depression, nervosité and bad school marks. He went home, took the suggested ampoules, but they failed to help. Nothing happened. And he kept wondering whether he needed a doctor to cure him or a *notaire* to make out his last will. He was desperate. He called Marie-Thérèse with the number Zygmunt had given him. She came right over. And, as it turned out, never went back to her apartment. With doses of some special tea, lots of water and hot rum drinks Marie-Thérèse, as if a saint in training, nursed Harvey back to health in twenty-four hours, never leaving the bedside except to get nourishment for the patient. She could give Mother Teresa a run for her money.

Mère-Thérèse was about to give up her apartment in the 6th arrondissement, not far from the Eiffel Tour. Her roommate was getting married to an Air France pilot. With fewer modeling assignments over the summer, when everybody in the business would be away on holiday, she couldn't afford to keep the apartment on her own. It seemed only reasonable, then, that she move into the spare bedroom at 38, Quai d'Orléans that overlooked the quai, the room with the white and blue toile curtains and a quite small bed. She could save on rent and in return, she herself suggested, she would look after the apartment as a sort of a live-in femme de ménage. It seemed a very reasonable arrangement to newcomer Harvey. But it didn't last. About three o'clock in the morning of Mère-Thérèse's second night in residence, the garbage men, true to habit, began what sounded like soccer practice out on the quai with the residents' *poubelles*. It frightened Mère-Thérèse. Compassion alone forced Harvey to offer the good woman a place in his bed.

Harvey's language classes at the Place des Vosges became almost redundant. Instantly his French began to improve, especially in his use of *tu* and *toi*. Harvey's teacher at the Place des Vosges, a heavy-set man who once in his chair never got up from it, spent most of the time stroking his beard and accusing the students of *bêtises*. He noticed Harvey's fluency improving quite quickly and began holding Harvey up as an example of what any student could achieve through scholastic effort. And on more than one occasion, Harvey worked the subjunctive mood into a short conversation with Madame la Pharmaciste down the street. The bed makes an excellent seat of learning. And compassion, like an over-priced credit card, has its rewards.

Paris is a walking city. Every turn offers something to intrigue: the ludicrous optimism of the fishermen on the Pont Alexander with the lines from their long bamboo poles dropped into the Seine, a river doubtlessly fished out centuries before; the way concierge ladies in worn slippers tend the red and blue flowers of their street-level window boxes; the sad faces of the chestnut vendors; the exuberance of the young boys in short pants, too short, charging at each other as if the Luxembourg Gardens were a pitch for jousters; and, that phenomenon of phenomena, the boule players who cannot throw their silvery iron balls without a cigarette end stuck in one corner of the mouth or the other; the metal plaques on buildings that proclaim that some great thinker or great artist had lived there two or three hundred years before or where some resistance fighter died—died! —on that spot in 1944; the statues of Balzac or Montaigne or Jean Jaurès, the unexpected vistas, the long boulevards lined by plane trees their foliage and branches manicured, their mottled trunks coloured in every tone and shade of green and gray and yellow. Most astounding of all were the green-smocked men with their plastic brooms pushing water and refuge along the street gutters because no automated street cleaning equipment could ever get near the curb, every square centimetre of which was covered by a parked car. In Paris people would park on top of each other if they could.

Every chance he got, Harvey would walk to, or from, the office of Sheardon et Cie., 21 Place Vendôme, just around the corner from the Tuileries Garden and the Louvre, a twenty-minute walk at most from the Île. A rickety elevator, inserted into an ornamented 18th century stairwell, designed without anticipation of twentieth century technology, carried Harvey lurchingly, clangingly up to the third floor. The Sheardon et Cie office was made up of two rooms. The first held a waiting area of a couch and two black leather armchairs, desks for two secretaries, two very large painted armoires which served as cupboards, one for stationery supplies and one for coats. On the far wall beneath the windows, *le fax* and *le photocopieur*. To the left of le fax, through majestic double doors you entered a larger room that served as the office for the *directeur du bureau*, formerly Jean-Claude, now M. Harvey S. Markson, B.Com., M.B.A. A giant Louis Quatorze desk—a reminder of another life and Zuzu Hornfeldt's notion of functionality—sat in the middle of the room, piled as high with papers as any lawyer's desk. The ceiling was painted with cherubs and clouds on a light blue background, confirming Harvey's feeling that this could be as close to heaven as he was ever likely to get.

Jean-Claude had left a list of clients and contacts on Harvey's desk. At various times of day that first week Harvey would call and introduce himself to the Banque Nationale de Paris, Banque Parisbas and even the disgraced Credit

Lyonnais rescued from utter humility some years before by M. Balladur, the Prime Minster of France that year. Harvey spent much of the following weeks traveling his territories. Three days for Amsterdam, Brussels and Luxembourg. A week on the "Swiss swing"—Basel, Zurich and Geneva. Then the "Northern swing" to Frankfurt, Copenhagen and Stockholm. The weekends would cart back a totally exhausted Harvey, ready for peace and rest, back to his well-tidied residence on the Île, back to an ebullient roommate ready to show him the sites of Paris and its environs.

Feature for feature Mère-Thérèse was far from beautiful. Her brown eyes, impish and lively, were far too large for her face. The occlusion of her teeth pushed her lower lip beyond the upper, an arrangement that made it much easier for her to form the mouth configurations necessary to speak French authentically. Her lips were soft, the softest Harvey's had ever felt or tasted. Any studio camera would be charmed—no, fascinated—by a face that looked so different from every angle. Mère-Thérèse was in the habit of dressing as if on assignment, short skirts or well-tailored slacks or plaited culottes. When she was concerned about something or somebody a little worry-triangle would furrow itself into her forehead. When she wore a head band, usually one of brown velvet, it pushed her ears out and made her look life an elf, a loveable elf. Some might say she worked too hard at her appearance and Harvey in an honest moment would have confessed that he preferred the understated attractiveness of a Katherine the Ingrate. Some might say the good mother laughed too readily and too often. But from the standpoint of sheer comfort, Harvey had never met a woman more skilled at smoothing out the ups and downs.

One of the reasons Harvey's French improved so rapidly was that Mère-Thérèse spoke barely a word of English. She seemed content a few handy phrases he taught her such as "nice guy," "hard worker," and "fabulous fornicator."

One Sunday morning as they walked over the small bridge, the Pont St. Louis, to cross over to The Île's sibling island in the middle of the Seine, the Île de la Cité, Harvey found himself a pace or two behind, as he had with Katherine. He was observing the stares directed at Mère-Thérèse not only by the male passers-by but by the women too. Suddenly like a mother disciplining her son, she turned around and chastised him. "La vie n'attend jamais les lents. Dépêche-toi, chou-chou. 'Urry up, chou-chou."

They laughed, they hugged and kissed right in front of the young boys doing loops and turns with their skateboards. In Paris people kiss on bridges all the time.

Cliché or not, Harvey could have died and gone to heaven and not known the difference that moment. The only thing to be heard above the blub-sounds of the skateboards crashing down on the pavement of the little Pont St. Louis was the screeching of the seagulls skimming by overhead in search of a free lunch like a flock of cackling stock brokers. It was the two-week anniversary of their relationship. If the poets told the truth, it would not have been out of place for the bells of Notre Dame to peal out in joy. It was a Sunday morning but nobody knew a miracle had occurred.

Mère-Thérèse did not mind in the least the responsibilities of maintaining the presidential residence of the Deuxième République. She kept the apartment immaculate. And almost every day that Harvey was not on the road, she would do the shopping so that there would be fresh baguettes and fresh ingredients—beans, zucchini, cauliflower, lettuce—for the dinners she made. Absolutely no pre-prepared foods full of chemicals. If she had a headache, she'd take some herbal remedy, never an aspirin, never any kind of pharmaceutical. And perhaps from her upbringing in the Perigord, she served *foie gras* a little more often than healthy. And she always set the forks on the table upside down like the French do. And occasionally from the kitchen the odd "zut" or "merde" could be heard from the Good Mother when a soufflé refused to rise or an oyster slipped from her spoon. She thought, too, Harvey had better things to do with his money then spend it in restaurants. Besides, she insisted on earning her keep as the femme de ménage and chef de la cuisine. When Harvey brought her flowers from a street vendor or a scarf on his return from one of his trips, she shrieked with a little child's joy.

No question, life for Chou-chou Markson had slowed up, slowed up beautifully. Every once in a while he would stand on the sidewalk outside his apartment and look up at the looming towers of Notre Dame and take a moment to try and savour his insular life on the Île, try to taste it as it rolled by. The rhythm was just right. Time loped.

Sheardon-Cassidy - July 8 1999 - Toronto, Canada - Fax: 416- 601-3375

CONFIDENTIAL PRIVATE CONFIDENTIAL

To: H. Markson
Fax: 33 (01) 43 16 34 62
From: Z. Adams,
At: Sheardon-Cassidy International Capital Markets Inc. Toronto, Canada.
Our Fax: 1 (1) 416-933-3375
No. of Pages including this cover page: 5

Should you have any difficulty with transmission please contact our office in Toronto, Canada: (416) 601-2100. The Information contained herein is confidential. Kindly destroy this document if received in error and notify sender at fax number (416) - 933-3375

Page 1 of 5

Sheardon-Cassidy -July 8 1999 -Toronto, Canada - Fax: 416- 601-3375

Harv: Nice order from UBS. Love to see those orders coming in. Great start. Yes! But our beloved Chairman is wagging his curly tail again. He wants to double the business from Europe. Gottfried de Holger at the QRS Bank can make that happen—overnight. My cousin in Frankfurt will set up a meeting for you as soon as you can be there. Call Gustav

Meyer at (49) (69) 797041. It's all arranged. With your smarts and all that bloody knowledge you've stuffed in your stupid head, Gott will be on the phone to you twice a day. Once the other money managers find out Gott deals with you (make sure they do) the orders will pour in.

One tip: Gott is the most organized man you'll ever meet. He won't be a second late and everything will be prepared. He loves order. Not a hair on his head will be out of place.

Keep me posted.

Z.

P.S. Social notes: Saw Roi and Ferdy Swasont at the track on the weekend. They send their best regards (I'd bet on that. You know I like long shots). Roi was particularly interested to hear you're with Sheardon-Cassidy now. Met your new friend Katherine at a dinner party last week. Small world, isn't it? She said you had been extremely kind to her in England. I told her it was out of character. Commonwealth General Insurance offered her a job over there. She didn't sound interested. Too bad. With Mother Teresa in Paris and Katherine in London you could re-write *The "Tail" of Two Cities.*

A couple of pieces of news attached.

Page 2 of 5

Sheardon-Cassidy, - July 8 1999 -Toronto, Canada - Fax: 416- 601-3375

Your Financial World June 28, 1999 Page B2

SAVE-YOUR-TIME (Vancouver) $3.25, up 25 cents
The Save Your Time Software Corp. signed a definitive agreement yesterday to distribute its breakthrough time management program through Software Miracles of Owings Mills, Maryland. Creswell Duncan, president of Save Your Time, expects to meet the sales target for 1999 of 200,000 copies of their latest version (1.51). He expects the company to begin to show positive cash flow by their December 31st year-end.

[The "200,000" was underlined by pen and a note added in handwriting "The president's name is Duncan Creswell, not Creswell Duncan."]

Sheardon-Cassidy - July 8 1999 - Toronto, Canada - Fax: 416- 601-3375

The World of Finance - June 30, 1999 - F9
"Goings On" by Halvart Tulvin

Univest Lands Two Biggies

Associated Freight Forwarders awarded their 3000-man pension account to Univest Investment Management yesterday. The day before, Univest agreed to manage Everybody's Favourite Grocer Employee Pension Fund. Both accounts were formerly managed by R. H. Winkes & Associates. This brings Univest's assets under management to $4.5 billion.

"It's only natural when you have a change of management style, in our case to a more aggressive one, you'll lose some assets to other managers," according to Dr. Leon Kelpner, D.D.S. Dip. Perio., Winkes' new CEO. "But we think the new economy is here to stay. The Internet companies will produce the best returns for our clients over the next decade."

The troubled R.H. Winkes has lost several clients since the death a year ago of its founder, Rupert H. Winkes, and the subsequent departure of other senior management. Executive Vice President, Harvey Markson who resigned last winter when overlooked for the presidency which went to an outsider, noted and respected economist and journalist, Lawrence Lipakowski.

["Respected" was underlined by pen.]

page 4 of 5

Sheardon-Cassidy - July 8 1999 - Toronto, Canada - Fax: 416- 601-3375

end.

Should you have any difficulty with transmission please contact our office in Toronto, Canada: (416) 601-2100. The Information contained herein is confidential. Kindly destroy this document if received in error and notify sender at fax number (416) - 933-3375.

page 5 of 5

That Katherine would not return did not come as a surprise. Nothing would have likely come of it anyway. What chance did a relationship have that, even at forty thousand feet about sea level, couldn't get off the ground?

Harvey put the name Gott on his to-do list.

Out of nowhere, into the tranquil island existence of the Deuxième République, came some of the same old pressure from the pre-Republic days. The serpent had slipped back into paradise. And an old familiar urban rhythm intruded itself—busy-ness. Haste was back big time.

In European financial circles the pronouncements of Dr. Gottfried de Holger, Harvey found out subsequently, carried with them all the authority of somebody writing Scripture. Almost every week that year some publication—*Financial Times, Der Spiegel, Le Figaro*—headlined some comment or other of de Holger's (in 20-point type or larger): "EURO TO FALL"; "U.S. MARKETS TO TUMBLE"; "GOLD TO WEAKEN IN 2000."

Formerly a law professor at the University of Heidelberg, Dr. Gottfried de Holger was the Director of Investments for the QRS Bank in Frankfurt. That meant he was responsible for the prosperity of assets that translated into roughly €153 billion (prior to adopting the Euro that would have equalled about 300 billion Deutsche Marks). Over the years, he had amassed, it was said, a fortune of his own. His pronouncements evoked a certain reverence, either from the fact that he controlled €153 billion or from his reputation as an advisor to Helmut Kohl and many top officials at the German Bundesbank, or from the fact that he had been on a first name basis with the likes of Brandt, Schmidt, Delors, Chirac, Heath and Thatcher, Major and Blair. And, though certainly not on a first name basis with the late Deng Xiaoping, it was known that Dr. de Holger had had an exceptionally long audience with the chairman in Beijing the winter of 1991. Though not everybody agreed with his ideas and, often enough, his forecasts required revision, no one could deny that Dr. de Holger had the ear of anybody who was (or had been) anybody in Europe, that subtle kind of power and influence that outlasts any politician's, true power.

It was a Friday in late July when Harvey finally got to meet with Dr. Holger. Even with the strings Zygmunt had pulled, a meeting originally scheduled the week before had to be postponed to accommodate some big mucky-muck (might have been Chancellor Schroeder). Harvey got the phone call less than a half hour before Harvey was to leave from his Place Vendôme office and catch the plane at Charles de Gaulle for Frankfurt.

Dr. de Holger's office enclosed roughly the same amount of space as the Saint Chapelle in the Palais de Justice across the street from Notre Dame. It was huge. The elaborate ceiling, which displayed what looked like family crests of the nobility with eagles and eagle claws, a repeated theme on a celestial light blue background, was held up by walls of books in greater number but in the same proportion as Rupert's office. Some of them seemed familiar, such as the works of Heidegger and Hegel, and there were even copies of Peter Drucker in English and in the German translation.

The office/chamber held several different seating arrangements: one with a large rectangular mahogany table surrounded by twelve chairs, another area over by the huge walk-in fireplace made up of four high-backed armchairs around a low circular antique table with several inch-thick reports stacked neatly at each place in preparation for another meeting. At the far end sat a huge desk ornamented with inlaid wood and gold; in front of the desk sat two comfortable looking armchairs, behind, a high-backed chair and a huge mural of a ship on a white-capped sea.

The male secretary had ushered Harvey in exactly at the

appointed hour. Immediately, as if in the presence of one of his first-name dignitaries, Helmut or Otto, Wily or Margaret, Dr. de Holger ended his phone conversation, slid out of his chair and approached Harvey almost at a jog his hand held out, a friendly grin on his face. His shoes shone like an army sergeant's. His tailored, double-breasted, dark blue suit showed not a crease, its exact shade of blue picked up again in the paisley tie. His eyebrows and eyelashes were so blonde they disappeared against the background of his yellowish complexion. After a firm handshake and a nod of his head in the direction of the armchairs, they sat down. As Zygmunt in his all-knowing way had predicted, not one hair on Dr. Holger's head stood out of place for not a single one resided on his Holger's shaved scalp and most likely had not for many, many years.

The phone rang.

"Yes. Nein. Yes. Nein. Tomorrow *morgen. Dankeschön.* No more calls," said Gott and placed the phone back in its cradle. "I'm so sorry about cancelling our last meeting. I hope you understand. All these people like to consult me for some reason. I don't know why the think my guesses are better than theirs. So I go along with them. Do you speak German?"

"I took it at University, but I haven't spoken it in some time," said Harvey, omitting mention of how he had deployed the language one night on the plane when he tried to pick up Katherine the Ingrate. "Which would be more comfortable for you, Mr. Markson, my broken English or your unpractised German?"

"Your English certainly doesn't need any practice."

"Tell me how my good friend Zyg-moont is," said Gott.

"He sends his best. He's hoping to get over and see you."

"Such a rogue. He'll never come to see me unless he's given

up women. I would say to him: Zygmunt you are a rogue, a genuine one hundred per cent rogue. And Zygmunt would smile at me and answer 'Of course.' And then he would laugh. And I would laugh. In zis business, you meet rogues every day. But in all my years, bless him, Zygmunt was the only man I ever met that would admit he was one."

It took no more than five minutes of conversation for Harvey to realize that, like Rupert, Dr. de Holger had read all books that covered the walls of his office. They weren't there for decoration anymore than the inhabitants of the walls of Rupert's old office. When the conversation came back to investing de Holger said, "Frankly, Mr. Markson, I'd lost quite a bit faith in your company. Your predecessor—allow me to speak frankly—seemed so...so unreliable. He would promise me reports. Then never send them. So I took special trouble to verify your reputation and that of your late colleague, Herr Winkes. What a tragedy a man of that quality had to leave us so early. You don't mind my little investigation, I hope. In my position one has to be careful, very, very careful. Some people say that's the only reason I'm in this position. May I offer you some tea?"

"Thank you, no. You have quite a remarkable reputation yourself."

De Holger just smiled. "To the point. *Retournons aux nos moutons*, as the French say. I don't like the market. I can't find anything to buy. Too much optimism around. Unless the capital markets have changed drastically—and maybe they have, I don't know—we are in for some very, very rough weather ahead. I rarely try to predict that sort of thing," said de Holger. "What do you think, Mr. Markson?"

"Things seem a little out of hand. But the market is the

market. Most, if not all, of the time it seems completely unpredictable. If for no other reasons than there's too many factors at play and it's too difficult to tell how and when they will collide."

"True, but you can hardly read a financial statement of an American company where something doesn't look like bad fish. I have no faith in the market. None. Most of my portfolios hold a great deal in short-term bonds. And I don't know that governments or their agencies these days are—how can say?—capable of doing what they need to do. Not many people agree with me. It's a little lonely. That may be a good sign though."

"Rupert never tried to predict the market. We just searched for companies with a good future and waited until we could buy the stock at a good price. We particularly liked companies that had intellectual capital that didn't show up in the stock price."

"Our people are not equipped to handle that kind of analysis. And all I get is stories from brokers saying: buy, buy, buy. Never sell, sell, sell. I don't want to buy stocks anymore. I want to buy the companies themselves and then take them private for a few years. Companies we can help grow with our financing and contacts and management expertise. But we don't want to run them. Some companies are much better off out of the stupid race to show better earnings every quarter, don't you think, Mr. Markson?"

"A company like Lehigh Robotics is doing highly innovative things with computers but gets lumped in together with established ones like IBM or Compaq."

"I like technology. As long as nobody else likes it. The more complicated the technology the better. Anybody can understand a hamburger. What is it that Lehigh—have I the name correctly? —does?"

"They design robots for automotive assembly lines. Their robots are also intricate communications tools. Nobody can touch their design skills. They keep coming up with great ideas. And they know how to implement those ideas. Almost no staff turnover. One woman's husband was transferred to the west coast and it almost broke up the marriage; she didn't want to leave the company. Twelve per cent of their revenue goes into research."

"What's it capitalized at?"

"3.4 billion U.S."

"What do the earnings look like?"

"They should quadruple in the next five years."

"Have you any material on it."

"I'll put something together."

"I'm going on holiday for August. Scandinavia. Can you have something for me when I get back? And don't show it to my hungry competitors in Switzerland until I've had some time to study it. Maybe you and I can do some business. Agreed?"

"D'accord," Harvey blurted, then corrected with, "Gut."

When Harvey arrived back at his office in Paris the next day, he called McKissick. "...Ian, I haven't done a report in the kind of detail de Holger wants for ten years. It's a ton of work. If it's slipshod, we'll lose him forever. And I can't neglect the other clients or they'll think I'm another Jean-Claude."

"It'll be a lovely bonanza for you, Harvey. At my former job I worked with a bloke, not very likeable mind you, but a very good salesman. He claimed he made a ruddy fortune out of the QRS Bank. How long before we got some word back from de Holger, Harvey?"

"Five, six weeks if we're lucky."

"Six weeks?

"He's on holiday in Sweden for August. My report won't be the most pressing matter on his desk. All the big politicians call him all day long to hold their hand."

"You mean I'm going to have Zygmunt on my back the rest of the summer?"

"I need all the time anyway. Getting the company and industry data doesn't take long. Getting the info on the competitors, some of them are private companies, can take forever. One thing: I promised de Holger it would be on his desk by the end of August. It will be."

"Zygmunt keeps asking if we've had any orders from Gott. He doesn't want to call you and put the pressure on."

"Next time he asks, tell him if Sheardon-Cassidy had decent research, we wouldn't have to go through all this."

"Why does he keep saying he needs better numbers for the barnyard? The barnyard?"

"That's just Zygmunt. That's his name for the directors' meetings run by the chairman with a nickname of Piggy. The chairman has a magnificent home in the country that Zyg likes to call The Sty."

"That chap holds absolutely nothing in reverence," said McKissick. "I told him whatever you do will take a few weeks."

"What'd he say?"

"I don't know. We got disconnected or he hung up."

Harvey began working the long hours. Trips to Zurich and Brussels, Amsterdam, Milan, Copenhagen meant getting up for the early flights, then meetings all day and working on the report for Gott at night. And there was all the reading to keep up with: *Financial Times, The Wall Street Journal, The World of Finance,* on a daily basis; and on a weekly, two private news services, *"The Triple I"* (*The International Investor's Intelligence Report* from Manchester, England) and *Jellcott's World Politics and Economic Events* out of Palm Beach, Florida, eight pages of which were faxed every Friday. Then there were at least a half dozen magazines like *The Economist* and *Forbes, Technology Today* and, once in a while, the *Financial Analysts' Journal.* And, of course, there were mounds of reports from the Research & Economics Department of Sheardon-Cassidy, but they required no more than a quick glance.

Thank God for August. Everybody in Europe goes on holiday in August. So Harvey could spend less time on the road, less time with clients and more time on the Lehigh Robotics report. There were phone calls to make to all parts of the world, letters to write, faxes and emails to send and acknowledge in order to gather the economic, industry and corporate information necessary. It was a rare night that the taxi dropped him back at the Île before nine that August.

Even with that workload, or maybe because of it, since an unchallenged mind attracts doubt and anxiety, those days in the summer of 1999 were among the Deuxième République's best.

How much Paris, which is usually the first to take credit, had to do with this contentment would not be easy to say. If the anchor and steadying point for contentment is feeling you're in the right place, then Paris was the prime cause. From the moment he set foot on The Île, the quiet longing to be somewhere else vanished. Why would he want to be anywhere else? The Île, he was convinced, was the centre of the world.

That summer the only time Mère-Thérèse and he got to spend together was at late dinners. Or on Sunday. Twice Harvey ended up flying home Friday just in time to have dinner only to fall asleep almost immediately after. They had talked about getting away again for a weekend, to London or Rome or even just down to the Loire country to see the chateaux. In August Harvey had to spend even Sundays in the office working on the Lehigh Robotics report. The Good Mother took it all in stride.

"Il faut faire, chou-chou, ce qu'on doit faire," she commented with her usual acceptance of the strange way in which the world imposes obligations upon us.

The next day a message from McKissick said that a Ms. Katherine Ridell, who had recently joined Commonwealth General Insurance, had called his office.

"It's good to hear from you. When I met your friend in Toronto he gave me his card and he told me you now worked for the same company but in Paris."

"He told me you weren't serious about the job in London. Where are you staying?"

"With my aunt, for now. We're off to Deauville this weekend. Would you like come up and join us?"

"Things are a little involved over here at the moment."

"Harvey-Harvey! I turn my back for a few weeks and first thing you know there's another woman in your life."

The Swiss money managers were first to recognize that Harvey was no run-of-the-mill salesman. As time went along, Harvey found the phone calls he made to his accounts returned in a quicker and quicker fashion. Orders to purchase stocks began to trickle in. Most of them were for shares of major Canadian mining or oil companies that Harvey had followed for years and knew inside out. A request for information on five New York stocks came in from a small private bank in Switzerland. They had a long relationship with Sheardon-Cassidy that went back, supposedly, to the times when Colonel Cassidy used to stop off briefly on his way to the Villa d'Este on Lake Como. So he could write his vacation off as a company expense.

Some small orders came in from the Belgians and then one from the ABN Amro Bank in The Hague. One large order came in for fifty thousand shares of Alcan to be purchased over the next month (at limit of $49 CDN) from the Banca Commerciale Italiana. That gave Harvey a reason to arrange a business trip to Rome for a long weekend with Mère-Thérèse.

"Cripes, Harvey," said McKissick on the phone. "Congratulations. What a lovely order that one from the *bonka commerchelee*. Zygmunt will love it. You must being doing something right. Those updated figures you wanted for them on Canadian National Railway I just received by the way. We're expecting third quarter earnings of about one dollar five. I'll fax the whole story on to the *bonka* in Rome today and copy you."

"I've never even met the guy that placed the order. Just talked to him over the phone a couple of times. He went to college in the States. I told him I'd get down to Rome. I think we could do a lot of business with him. He seemed very receptive."

"I'll have a small toast to you tonight."

A week later they had a similar conversation. More orders

had come in, still not large, but they were what McKissick called "sprouts of hope."

"Every time I speak to Zygmunt he still asks me about Gott de Holger."

"Goddamn it, tell him I'm a money manager, not Joan of Arc. I don't do miracles. Is he at his office now? I'll call him."

"No, he's on a cross-country trip visiting all the Sheardon-Cassidy Canadian offices. Then he's off to Lima to get participation for us in a bond issue the Peruvians are coming out with. I think he's going to be awfully difficult to catch up with for the next while or so. He said he had some thought of going on a car rally down to Tierra del Fuego. Is that possible? Did I get that straight?"

"I need to talk to him anyway. I've got way too much tied up in some stock he talked me into. He faxes me all these clippings. I'd like to sell some of my position. It's not really my kind of stock, anyway. If you're talking to him ask him to call me, will you? I can never get him. He's always in meetings or on the phone. Or I am, when he calls back. And, Ian, tell him, too, nobody's going to get to Gottfried de Holger overnight, for chrissake. Good research takes time. If you want some examples of bad research read any of their reports Sheardon-Cassidy sends over."

"Is there any way I can help you?"

"It's taking forever. Either I can't find the information I need or I can't find the time. I got a lot information on Mitsubishi and Matsushita, Lehigh's two biggest competitors. But there are also two small competitors, one in California and one here in France, and it's practically impossible to make contact with anybody there. I didn't realize the world comes to a stop over here in August. The only other person here in my office is the junior secretary, and she doesn't have time to do anything for me with the phone and all the normal office work. I've had to input a lot of the stuff myself. It should be ready by the end of the week. It'll be on time for Gott for sure, don't worry. It's almost finished. Another day or two. The report looks pretty good. Everything over here's looking pretty good."

In the stock market, in a court of law, on a squash court, on a lush green fairway—anywhere—is there a more dangerous thought than to think you've got it made? In a world as competitive as ours, more points, many more, are lost by thinking they are about to be won than because of an opponent's cleverness or skill. One example comes to mind immediately. No sooner had Harvey hung up from this long conversation with McKissick, then the junior secretary knocked on the door and told Harvey the Mère-Thérèse had called. She had important news and wanted him to call her as soon as possible.

"Arvey, je viens de trouvé un boulot absolument incroyable," she shouted over the phone. "A job, chou-chou."

Mancur Sebastiano, Paris's hot couturier of the moment, had hired her and three other models to introduce his new fashion line across North America. She would be gone for a month. "Plus longue, peut-être," to quote the good woman herself.

They would celebrate in Rome on the weekend, Harvey suggested.

"Dommage, chou-chou," she said, "I quit Paris tomorrow. I'm vachement sorry. If faut faire..."

That night Mère-Thérèse and Harvey celebrated her good luck of at a small outside restaurant over on Boulevard Raspail instead of at the three-star restaurant he had planned in Rome. And it was not until the following night when Harvey went to brush his teeth and noticed that the white ceramic holder, screwed rather carelessly to bathroom wall above the sink, held only one toothbrush that the significance of her departure struck him. Taking his shirts in his string filet to Madame at the *blanchisserie* the day Mère-Thérèse left turned from a quaint activity to a chore. The suddenness of this sea change shook the Île. With the departure of Mère-Thérèse, much of its charm drifted away as if just so much flotsam and jetsam.

Nature's specialty is turmoil. One minute the world seems stable as the North Star. The next it's a meteor flaming across the sky out of control. What was supposed to happen was that on the Saturday the "Good Mother" would fly down to Rome with Harvey for the weekend. All the arrangements had been made: airport limos, hotel suite, dinner reservations at La Terrazza dell'Eden, and a guided tour of the city. Everything was set. Except Mère-Thérèse.

You have to do what you have to do.

"...Harvey, I'd love to. I've always had such a good time staying with you in some elegant suite like we did at the Dorchester," Katherine teased.

"Wonderful."

"But, Saturday, my aunt's having a dinner party for me. She's fixed me up with the son of a friend of hers. Lord Somebody-Somebody. I'm so (at least she did not use *vachement*) sorry. What a shame. We never seem to get our timing quite right, do we?"

On the Friday, the 27th of August, the junior secretary, a woman who spoke French with such a heavy Italian accent Harvey understood barely a word, brought him a neatly wrapped package from the printers. Inside the brown wrapper rested four copies of Harvey's report: a cover page, a concise one-page summary, and eighty-two pages that dealt with Lehigh Robotics Inc. of Allentown, Pennsylvania in every aspect. Every aspect. Not just the financial numbers and the EBITDA projections that any accountant could put together. But such items as: general strategy; human resource practices; competitive advantages; size of existing and potential markets; its mission statement; organizational structure; management philosophy; suggestions how the next growth phase could be financed and how much capital it would take; clients' opinions of the company and its products; competitors' opinions of the company; a thorough write-up of the strengths and weaknesses of the major competitors; innovation practices; employee turnover statistics; employees' opinions of the company; copies of the last three months of the internal newsletter called *The Lehigh Listener*; detailed biographies of all key personnel; an industry analysis of economic factors at play; the trading patterns of its stock; as well as an original attempt to describe intellectual property of the company and even attribute a value to it.

Enough information, in other words, to make a takeover bid for the company. A corporate chef d'oeuvre. One copy was couriered to de Holger in Frankfurt, another to McKissick in London and one was sent by air mail to Zygmunt.

He probably never got to read it.

XII.

A ROMAN BATH

By the time Alitalia Flight 9161 had climbed to its cruising altitude of 9,500 metres in the Saturday sky, Harvey, flying solo, having read just the first two pages of *Jellcott's Investors Intelligence International,* the printed word had lost its meaning and he fell to sleep. And for all he knew the flight between Charles de Gaulle's airport and Leonardo da Vinci's encountered no turbulence. And since he also slept on the ride into Rome from airport, he might just as well have entered the city via the catacombs. Not until the porter at the Excelsior Hotel threw open the curtains of Suite 1802 did Harvey get his first real glimpse of that magnificent old city, that age-old shrine to faith.

"Ee-na-joy," said the porter as he lifted Harvey's suitcase on to the wooden luggage rack.

"Grazie," Harvey replied and handed the man a five-euro bill.

"Buon giorno." The porter drew himself to attention with a soft click of his heels and bow of his head, backed out of the suite.

Harvey walked over to the window and stared down at the tile-roofed grandeur of the city, steeples poking out here and there. Except in age, the view reminded him of the one from his old condo apartment back in Toronto overlooking the little church that Donnis tried to relocate. In Rome, the same result. The churches never move.

On his way in, Harvey had the concierge cancel the dinner reservations at La Terrazza dell'Eden. ("The favourite haunt of Italian politicians and other power brokers" according to Fodor's.) Harvey's had scaled down his evening plans to a bath, an early dinner, and an early to bed. No power brokering.

While he was unpacking an envelope was slipped under the door. No surprise, McKissick had promised to fax over some new fact sheets on Alcan Aluminum, Canadian Natural Resources and Encana Oil and Gas for the Monday meeting with the Banca Commerciale. Harvey picked up and opened the envelope and sat down on the bed to check through the contents and make sure everything needed was there.

TO:
MR HARVEY MARKSON
EXCELSIOR HOTEL, VIA VITTORIO VENTO, ROME

DATE: SATURDAY AUGUST 30, 1999

YOUR FAX: (39) (06) 4836205

FROM:

MR. IAN MCKISSICK
OLD MARTIN'S BARN, WALMSLEY STREET
TUNBRIDGE WELLS, KENT
ENGLAND SC2V 5DB

OUR FAX: 00 44 1892 4435028

PAGE: 1 OF 3 INCLUDING THIS COVER SHEET

THIS COMMUNICATION IS CONFIDENTIAL AND INTENDED SOLELY FOR THE ADDRESSEE. PLEASE NOTIFY US AT OUR COST AT THE ABOVE FAX NUMBER SHOULD YOU RECEIVE THIS DOCUMENT IN ERROR. WE APPRECIATE YOUR COOPERATION.

I. M. MCKISSICK
TEL: 00 44 1892 443599
FAX: 00 44 1892 4435028

Harvey, call me when you've had a chance to read this over. I wanted to give you some time to think it through. Things are in a bit of a mess. I hope you're sitting down. A man by the name of Ferdinand Swasont called me this afternoon here at my home in Kent to say that yesterday Zygmunt resigned from Sheardon-Cassidy.

He told me the parting was amicable and that Zygmunt had simply felt it was time to go on to other things. That sounds quite odd since evidently Zygmunt had phoned in his resignation from Lima. He was down there trying to get a piece of a bond underwriting the Peruvian government was doing with a couple of the big U.S. shops. I think I told you that part. After the business meetings he was supposed to go on some car rally in Argentina.

According to Swasont, Zygmunt had wanted to resign for sometime. He finally admitted there had been a bit of row with Mr. Donnis and Zygmunt over an investment in some software company that had gone sour. So there must be more to the story. At any rate, where does that leave you and me?

Unfortunately my news does not get any better. The Sheardon-Cassidy Board held an emergency meeting late last night. Ferdinand's brother, I believe his name is Roy, whom evidently you know, is the new president. Here comes the difficult part. Ferdinand was appointed the executive vice-president in charge of international operations. They decided to close down the Paris office immediately. I am to go to Paris next week and with your help let everybody go.

You'll be paid until mid-October (How very generous!), but there will be no office, territory or job for you in Europe according to Ferdinand.

He wants me to get rid of my staff here in London. They say they'll send people over from head office on occasion to do the rounds. I am to remain on as sort of the curator of a smaller London office to keep a European presence and do some sales on my own. I suppose I will, least while I look around.

PAGE 2 OF 3

I. M. MCKISSICK
TEL: 00 44 1892 443599
FAX: 00 44 1892 4435028

I've a great many connections in the City and know how exceptional your work is. Will that stupid lot at head office ever know how good the Lehigh Robotics report is? Swasont didn't seem the least bit interested when I tried to explain. Perhaps I have some ideas on where you might relocate should you want to come to London.

No doubt this is most unsettling for you. When you have had a chance to reflect on these events, call me at home in Kent. I'll be here the rest of the weekend.

Sorry it has all worked out this way. Maybe it's for the best, we never know.

Ian M.

PAGE 3 OF 3

"Gawwwwdamn it," shouted Harvey. He actually shouted. He got up from the bed, crumpled Ian's fax and threw it full force at the large window that looked out upon the serene city. With a quiet thud the paper ball bounced off the glass, fell down onto the gray-green carpet and lay there motionless, lifeless.

Roi and Ferdy? Those two fornicating fornicators.

Aux armes, citoyens!

Formez vos bataillons!

Marchons...

Harvey went over to his attaché case, took out his Palm Pilot and then sat back down heavily on the bed. He grabbed the phone and began to punch the keys. Click. Click. Click. Click. Pause. Ring. Ring. Ring.

"Roi and Edith are not available right now. Leave a message after the tone and we'll get back to you as soon as it's convenient for us," said a voice difficult to tell whether it was Edith's or Roi's.

Smash. Click. Click. Click. Click. Pause. Ring. Ring.

"Ferdinand Swasont." Words pronounced like a salesman at his desk hoping for an order and the pronouncement of the name normally followed by, "How can I help you?"

"Ferdy, where the hell is Zygmunt?"

"Who's this?"

"Harvey."

"We don't know. Somewhere in the Andes, we think. Went down to Lima for us on business. Then he was to go on some car rally down to Terra del ...Terra del somewhere."

"How do I get a hold of him?"

"Nobody knows."

"What the hell's going on?"

There was a little pause, that special little pause that Ferdy always needed in order to shuffle the truth. "Zygmunt and Eldred had a disagreement about raising some capital for that stupid software company. I advised Eldred to wait and see if they really did have a marketing deal. Then for some reason Zygmunt when he got down to Lima, out of the blue phoned Eldred and quit. Just quit. Eldred brought us in—Roi and I [*sic*]—to get things back in some order."

"In order? You and Roi couldn't get a nun into some order."

"All I know is we're gearing down European operations. Roi and I spent last night going over the numbers. Roi thinks there's not a hope of Sheardon-Cassidy ever making a red cent over there."

"How would you and Roi know, Ferdy? You're thousands of miles away. If you guys had managed anything other than that lemonade stand you called an investment bank, you'd know enough to talk to McKissick and me first." Harvey brought a match to the cigarette he had just put in his mouth. "What's happened to Save Your Time?"

"It went south. The software catalogue house that was going to buy a couple of hundred thousand copies of the program backed out at the last minute. Everybody else is making a killing in this market these days and I'm out a packet thanks to your friend Zygmunt."

"Ask Roi to call me, will you? Write this down. My room number is eighteen zero two, that's at the Excelsior in Rome. The international code for Italy is thirty-nine. The area code in Italy is zero six. And the number here at the hotel is four seven zero eight one. My suite number is eighteen zero two. Tell Roy to call me. Doesn't matter what time. You got that?"

"Yes. But, Harvey, there's no need to get upset. We have some ideas for—"

The phone receiver made a blub-sound like a skateboard landing on pavement as Harvey slammed it back into its cradle. He took another number from his Palm Pilot and began dialling. Click. Click. Click. Click. Click. Pause. Pause.

"Allo, allo," a voice said almost instantly.

"Mrs. Avogadro? You're home. It's Harvey. I'm calling from Europe. Europe. How is everything?"

"Not nice, Mister Harvey."

"Do you know where Zygmunt is?"

"Sout America."

"When's he coming back?"

"No soon," she said in a hushed voice. She explained that Mr. Adams had called and asked her to check his new house regularly until he got back to Toronto. "Mister Harvey? You come back. Dunna-be a deep-steek."

Just after nine o'clock the next morning, Sunday, the phone rang four times before Harvey picked it up. It wasn't Roi. Of course not, it would be the middle of the night for him. It was the concierge from downstairs. The car and driver that Marie-Thérèse had set up from Paris awaited Mr. Markson and his party for their tour of the city.

Harvey didn't know what to say. For one thing he was hardly awake, though he couldn't remember anything other than tumbling around the bed the whole night and a long bath just before dawn. And in his new state of unemployment, it seemed extravagant to be chauffeured around Rome. It's one thing when you're Director of the Paris office of an international brokerage house. Then, of course, pomp and pretense are to be expected. Quite another, however, when you're jobless and a big chunk of your assets just disappeared, thanks to a high-flying start-up software company crashing to earth. The prudent thing to do was to cancel the tour.

Within ten minutes, an unshaven Harvey, party of one, enthroned in the rear seat of a very large black Mercedes, his green Michelin guidebook at hand, was driven away from the Excelsior and off to see the great sites of Rome and The Vatican, as if he were some grand potentate from some far-off country. He felt a little guilty, but perhaps he was not the first person with those destinations in mind to feel that way.

The driver, a stocky, bald-headed man who had some difficulty wedging his barrel chest between the front seat and the steering wheel, over which he could barely see anyway, spoke next to no English. As it turned out, it was better that way. Harvey was not in the mood for conversation.

The sunless sky had switched the city's brownness to an unbecoming gray. The limousine drove onto the Via Veneto and immersed itself in the usual iron chaos of the modern city. It stopped a few minutes later at the first of five churches, San Carlo alle Quatro Fontane. Harvey went in and came back out shortly and got back in the car. The Michelin guide said that the architect of the church, the great Francesco Borromini, never gained the fame of his rival Gian Lorenzo Bernini, that he had lived a life of incessant anxiety and in a fit of anger and anguish ended up one night committing suicide.

The city of Rome paraded its churches and monuments: Victor Emmanuelle Monument, The Forum, Castel Sant'Angelo, The Coliseum, The Spanish Steps. None of these great treasures for all their magnificence could alter Harvey's focus. The city seemed like scenes from an oversized coffee table book. It had that same sense of unreality he'd felt that day he decided to leave Toronto. Everything looked like a stage set.

So magnificent Rome, that day, was not a city but a mood. Its history seemed more preoccupied with death than life. The powerful spent most of their time in schemes to kill one another off. The saints got to have a tibia or fibula encased in glass and placed in the middle of some church. For many others, either a mausoleum awaited them or dust and oblivion. Death seemed just part of a marketing scheme to attract adherents.

As the Mercedes drove up to St. Peter's Square the driver said "Magnifico," supplying a little colour commentary as he parked the car. Harvey got out and trudged past the stately columns and up to the front of the domed Basilica. He walked up the steps and through the Holy Door and then over to the glass-protected *Pietà* sculpture. He stood in front of it just staring, unmoved by the sculptural genius of as great a communicator as this world has ever known; but at least he'd be able to tell Zyg he'd seen it.

As matter of fact, the only thing that impressed Harvey as he left the Basilica was how nicely dressed the Swiss Guards were, in their silver helmets and lavish blue and yellow and red uniforms. The guards looked like very peaceful and decent people, not like the usual kind of guard—gap-toothed, fat-fingered and Kalashnikov-toting.

As Harvey walked back to the car on the other side of St. Peter's Square, a crowd had gathered in front of the palace next to the Basilica. A cheer began. "Il Papa. Il Papa." From a balcony, four or five storeys up, with a purple cloth hanging from it, a small hunched-over man dressed in white waved to the crowd. No, not so much waved as moved his forearms up and down, then from side to side, slowly, gently, in arcs. The cheers from the crowd in the Square grew louder and louder. Harvey just kept on walking and didn't even look around.

When the limousine got back to the Via Veneto, the street was hopelessly clogged with traffic. A block from the hotel Harvey lost all patience, paid the driver and walked the rest of the way through the acrid fumes, past the stationary, iron-bound, angry, honking citizens of Rome. The Polizia were escorting away a gypsy beggar in ragged clothes and torn shoes, just the way they would have hauled away Segovia when drunk. How cold the world looked. Harvey hurried back to the hotel and into warmth of a bath.

The only two possible agents of instant succour—Marie-Thérèse and Katherine the Ingrate—had chosen to minister to others. And as Zygmunt had foretold, H.R Winkes & Associates looked well along on the road to self-destruction. One significant drop in the stock market and Leon would be back scraping plaque-packed teeth full time and Lipakowski would be back to producing his mendacity for print. And the software program, the supposed Saviour, looked to have been sacrificed on the altar of mismanagement. To boot, Zygmunt had jumped ship somewhere in the Peruvian Andes and taken off on a car rally— without a word. The Pig had chosen to crown Roi Swasont as the head of Sheardon-Cassidy and Roi in turn immediately beheaded the head of the Paris office.

In short, Harvey's female relationships, his job, H.R. Winkes & Associates, Save Your Time Software Inc., and Zygmunt Adams on his way to the end of the earth, all looked, to use The Street expression once again, headed south, very south.

Only a highly skilled theologian would be in a position to argue for a connection between the accidental blessing Harvey had received in St. Peter's Square not an hour before the divine intervention that followed.

"It's Grace, Harvey."

"What time is it there?"

"It must be six, the sun's just coming up."

"I just got back from a sightseeing tour."

"How are you?" said Grace. Her voice with its quiet assuredness could, in a second, quiet the world. She spoke with a slight lisp. "How are you really?"

"Okay. It's been a busy couple of months. I meant to call when I got settled in Paris. Except I never really got settled in. At the moment I'm a little...it's good to hear your voice. How are you? How's...Sara?" It was difficult to remember her niece's name. The good times at Bon Chance seemed from a different era.

"Sara's taken a job at the MOMA museum. She always asks about you, but she's enchanted with New York."

"She always wanted to live there."

"But, look, I called to talk about you. Roi wants you to come back and take over Sheardon-Cassidy's research department."

"Grace, you ever stop trying to patch up the world?"

"I can't blame you for being a little cynical at this point. Look, Eldred's not going to be around that much, his doctors want him to take it easier. His blood pressure is dangerously high. The new arrangement is that Roi runs the show. He has tremendous admiration for your abilities. Sure you get Ferdy in the bargain, but he's harmless, really. You'd be a full partner. They really need you. Evidently, I'm told, after your recent experience with European institutions you know they have a serious problem with research."

"Right now, at this moment, I don't know what I know."

"Think it over, Harvey. You don't have to rush. Europe's lovely. I adore Europe, you know that. But you're always such an outsider there. Zuzu told me you could probably get back into your old building next to the Church of the Redeemer."

"Grace, at this point, to tell the truth, I really think I'm beyond redemption."

"Look, Harvey, I'm not calling because Roi asked me to, which he did, by the way, obviously. I'm calling because I care what happens to you, Harvey, the way you cared about me when I was having all those problems with Eldred and Roi's wife. I'm your friend, Harvey. I care. This is a terrific opportunity for your career. In Europe you can never really feel at home. You'll always feel like a tourist wandering around with your hand glued to a Michelin guide."

"Grace, I don't know what to say. Or think. I didn't come over here to be a tourist the rest of my life. That's the last thing I want to be. I need a time-out. At the moment nothing makes a hell of a lot of sense..."

When the spirit protests, why is it that the only way it knows how to speak is through anger and anguish like some frenzied mute? To give voice to its discontent, why does it have to paralyze your arms, lash at your shoulders, burn your insides and hollow them out? Why must it make you feel so frail, so weak you can barely lift your hand up to wipe the sweat from your forehead? Why can't the spirit come right out in the plain, ordinary, everyday English that language philosophers laud so much and say, "Me no like, shit-for-brains"?

A simple email to Roi—that's all it would take—and everything could be rolled back as if you clicked your laptop's "undo" icon. Easy as that. No need to go through the agony to put down roots in the inhospitable terrain of this new world. No need to be an outsider. A visitor, a tourist, a tourist in perpetuity.

"Jesus. I don't know. I don't know," said Harvey out loud—directed at what we'll never know—as he lay in his hotel bathtub filled almost to the brim, a holding tank in the midst of a city the celebrates miraculous releases from the woes of the flesh.

Look, not only have the great poets misled us, so have the great painters, like David and Delacroix, whose works Harvey would ponder on his visits to the Louvre with Mère-Thérèse. The decisive moments in history don't really need a backdrop of crowded ramparts or snarling armies or swirling seas. We know now that most of the fiercest battles in history were fought not at the foot of majestic mountains nor in front of grandstands full of fanatics or in small ships hovered over by giant waves. Most often, nothing whatsoever festoons those little momentous moments upon which our lives of seeming inconsequence turn. The setting is, sadly enough, completely incidental. Anywhere will do.

All the same, water often somehow comes into the picture. Would Moses have made it to the Scriptures without the Red Sea? Could Thales have built his reputation as the first great pre-Socratic philosopher without his notions of water and energy? Would Nelson have made it to his perch in Trafalgar Square without a victory at sea? What would a waterless Venice look like? Could the Île St. Louis be an Île without the Seine? Or here, Rome, could it be Rome without the winding Tiber?

Lolling in a couple of cubic meters of water—his fourth bath since his arrival the day before—facing two gold leaping fish that served as faucets, ornate enough to have been designed by Bernini himself, lay our Icarus, his flight to a new world grounded, wondering where in God's name things had gone so wrong.

Where in God's name was his mind, he wondered, when he decided to go ahead with Project Vamooski and give up everything in Toronto? Why had he not stayed there with all the comforts and security and found a job on The Street instead of tossing himself out half-crazed on the world's boulevards? Why in heaven's name had he made himself into an international vagrant? How unbelievably naive of him to snap up that disappearing act in London referred to as a "job waiting for you when you get here." Easy come, easy go, everybody knows that. And how unbelievably stupid to have let Zygmunt—Zygmunt of all people—persuade him to take the Shearson's job in Paris? How stupid! How goddamn stupid! Stupid. Stupid. Stupid.

The sounds of a stringless strummer.

As he had done so often for a company in whose stock he wanted to analyze, Harvey performed a quick, down-and-dirty net-worth calculation (a sort of back-of-the-soap-dish analysis). Things did not look good. A couple of small locked-in deposits at his old bank branch at King and Bay (the one in front of which Segovia used to bring his guitar and camp stool); an oversupply of shares of Save Your Time Software Inc. [SAV -$0.38 – 26%] on its way down in a free-fall from $12.80; a bundle of about-to-be-worthless shares of R.H. Winkes & Associates, his old firm; and, with all his furniture sold when he moved out of his Tuscan Plaza apartment, virtually no fixed assets. Mind you, no debts at this point. But cash flow was about to dry up like the Gobi Desert in summer. The fact was that the only liquid thing that Harvey could get his hands on at that moment was the tepid water in which he lay immersed.

As if it might salve the burning within, with his right foot Harvey pushed the handle of one of the gold faucets. A quick burst of hot water plunged into the bath slowly rippling the glassy surface. Then everything went silent.

From within the watery realm, a washcloth floating above his loins, Harvey spread his right arm over the side of the marble bathtub. Without any forethought—none whatsoever—the middle finger of that outstretched hand rose to the vertical, the other fingers and the thumb folded themselves together tightly against his palm. Then his forearm began to move upwards in slow, determined, repeated vertical flicks.

"No, goddamn it. No," he said in a muted shout. "No Roi! No goddamn Roi!"

With that cry, "No Roi," La Deuxième République d'Harvey Markson, there and then, in that very instant, in that Roman bath, miraculously, died. That second little attempt at a metaphysical uprising—intended to alter his relationship with Whatever-Is—evaporated into the (moist) thin air of the marbled bathroom. The burning within subsided, as if the struggle had ended (ha!). A peacefulness overtook Harvey, much more profound than even the tranquility he'd come to know on the Île St. Louis. It was as if he had stepped out of the momentum of his life much as you would a bath.

It was a Sunday, a Sunday in a city brimful of churches. Not one bell pealed out to mourn the death of The Second Republic. True, one of the gold faucets gurgled, but with a definite air of indifference.

XIII.

LA RETRAITE

The two possible places of refuge on the Île St. Louis—the Hotel Deux Îles and the Hotel Lutèce—were both fully booked when Harvey went to move out ten days later from his apartment, Sheardon-Cassidy no longer willing to pay the rent. So he took the advice of his closest acquaintance on the Île, Madame La Pharmaciste, and retreated to the Hôtel des Écoles, next door to the Sorbonne, into a reasonably priced room but one with the bathroom down the hall.

Ex-îled.

The two secretaries in the office on Place Vendôme who had seen business pick up so briskly since Jean-Claude left were astonished (*étonnées* was the word they used) when Ian, who had flown over from London for the day, and Harvey told them of the Board of Directors' decision to close down the office. And, for their part, Ian and Harvey were equally *étonnés* by the number of details and amount of bureaucratic *chinoiserie* they had to deal with, from putting the phone on call forwarding to the London office, to paying the entire rent up front for the office lease that still had thirteen months to run, and guaranteeing salary payments to the secretaries for the next two years in case they could not find other employment in that period. France does not make it easy to unemploy. An exception, of course, was Harvey himself who joined the 8.9% of the country's *chômeurs*, completely without grounds to claim compensation from any state, institution or corporation.

Undeployed.

Ian offered to put Harvey in touch with a couple of brokerage firms and an investment manager in The City. But in England financial groups were all consolidating and re-organizing themselves right, left and centre. If you did get a job, how could you be sure it wouldn't disappear the next week when the company merged with another or absorbed some recent acquisition or got absorbed itself? Harvey had been burnt on his first go-round in London with Ponton Greenwell Utterbridge. Once was enough, more than enough. And the miracle, or whatever it was, in the Roman bath had made Harvey's mind up. He would fax Roi his regrets, perhaps in the same way you might send on RSVP for some party you couldn't attend. It was just a matter of the right wording. On the next to last day, before Harvey got the words right, Roi called the Place Vendôme office.

"Grace asked me to phone you, Harvey. The Amazer agrees, it would be best for everybody if you'd come back and run our research department. She told me I had to make a deal with you whatever it took."

"Is there anybody in this world kinder than her? But thanks, Roi, nice of you to call. I won't be coming back."

"Just tell me what it is you want, Harvey. Anything."

"In Rome I thought it over very carefully after Grace called. I came to the conclusion that nothing in the whole world could get me to come back. Absolutely nothing!" There was a silence. "But thanks for calling, Roi. That was kind of you, too. Thanks. Thanks anyway."

Thanks? Jesus Christ, Harvey! Was there no learning process going on here? Was Roi some sadistic airport security guard who kindly frisked you five times, twice carelessly in the crotch? Thanks for what? For the vote of non-confidence? For the consultative style Sheardon-Cassidy deployed in their decision-making? For his outstanding demonstration of a lack of faith? It's always the same with those Street People. Everybody's supposed to put their faith in them, but they don't have to trust another living soul. Surely someone in the last couple of millennia has pointed out that faith is a two-way street.

And if there was a neuron of doubt rattling around in Harvey's brain from his refusal to return to Toronto, it disappeared when *The World of Finance's* latest edition arrived at his Place Vendôme office his last day with this little item in tow:

> "Goings On" by Halvert Tulvin
>
> *If At First:* In the recent Sheardon Cassidy re-shuffle of its overseas offices, Director of European operations went to Ion [*sic*] McCassock [*sic*]. Harvey

> Markson, former second-in-command at ailing H.R. Winkes & Associates, was again overlooked. He left Winkes when wunderkind Lawrence Lipakowski was brought in as president and chief investment officer. Could it be that the highly experienced Markson finds himself once again out on the road looking yet again?

Sick. Sick. Sick. Out on the road? Can't that fat-necked dipstick get anything straight? Crissake, out on the street was more like it!

Almost two weeks had passed since Zygmunt had resigned from Shearson-Cassidy. Harvey hadn't had even a two-word email from him. Of all the things that had happened since leaving Toronto nothing distressed Harvey more than Zyg's silence. He had to be healthy or he wouldn't be going on a car rally through the Andes, for God's sake. Of course, Harvey had recognized Zyg's recklessness long before, in the way Zyg treated women, in the contempt with which he treated competitors, on or off the squash court, in the high-risk chances he took in business. All the same, and regardless of how unalike they were, Zygmunt and he had built that special rapport which flourishes between two men who enjoy each other's company. They can come to believe that—no matter what—the one would never willingly let the other down. But one had. One had abandoned the other. It was like a death, a disappearance from being.

Even the short email that arrived a day later from Buenos Aires, felt like too little too late. All it said was: "Sorry, Harvey. The Zyg had to zag."

Outside of death and sickness few things disturb the mind

as much as misplaced trust. Profound misjudgments about trust cause injury to the spirit. The mind loses faith, not in the world, but in itself, in its own judgment. If it could be deceived in that particular case, then why not in others? Each instance of unwarranted trust eats away at our links to the world. A link here, a link there and next thing you know you're ready for the nut house. If you can't believe in your own consciousness—what you see and hear and think—what the hell can you believe in?

On reflection the only truly profound comment—lots of good observations and wise cracks—Zygmunt made in all the years was at dinner one night at Thrace's. He was talking about how the market had gone against him badly that month: "You know, when you're a devout atheist like me and things go against you, there's no goddamn place to go. No church to run to. No mosque to visit. No chants to chant. No special breathing exercises. Not a goddamn thing to do but flail about and wait for things to right themselves."

Flail and wait.

Such were the thoughts on Harvey's mind as he took the jerky trip down in the outdated elevator for the last time from Sheardon et Cie. He walked out on to Place Vendôme. Then he just kept walking, walking without any particular destination in mind. He crossed Place de la Concorde, with its buzzing merry-go-round of cars and trucks and motor bikes—safely. He walked across Pont de la Concorde, but without his usual pause to look over the side to catch a glimpse of the Bateaux Mouches and the barges and the garbage boats as they slid up and down the Seine. He continued up the Boulevard St. Michel and up to the Jardin du Luxembourg. He wandered through the Jardin, along its earth pathways, just looking at life: the children sailing their boats across the muddy, octangular pond in front of the old palace, the tennis players who shouted "zut" when they overhit the ball, the half-finished cigarettes hanging from the mouths of the boule players, two students on a bench embracing each other with shy passion. Two men in blue smocks argued as they passed by him, leaving a cloud of Gauloise smoke with its biting scent, a smell that, before, created excitement. Not now. The excitement of the city had vanished like the sun on an overcast day. Without even the minutest tectonic shift, the great capital of the Fifth Republic of France no longer occupied the centre of this earth. For everybody else in the park that day, life seemed simple, straightforward, uncomplicated. They had nothing to worry about but their tennis swings, their boule games, and their small boats. And they would all surely know, when it came time to leave, when the sun started its descent into evening, how to find their way home.

Now and again, the scene seemed blurry and unfocused. Harvey bought some hot chestnuts from a vendor over by the children's swings. Like all the chestnut vendors of Paris, the hunched man carefully placed an extra chestnut in the little brown bag he gave Harvey. That used to bring on a good feeling, a feeling of being an insider, of sharing a secret ritual. That afternoon, the gesture had no significance. In truth, that day Harvey was out to teach even Nature Herself a trick or two about indifference.

Harvey sat down on an unoccupied bench. He ate one chestnut and then a second. They were tasteless. The rest he threw in a wire basket full of discarded newspapers. He took a heavy breath and then walked out of the Jardin, winding his way aimlessly from street to street, one looking not unlike the other, stacked with gray six-storey buildings. He ended up, much by chance, way over at Les Invalides at the Église du Dôme, staring at the red sarcophagus that was the tomb of Napoleon: the confrontation of two ex-îles—one very much dead, the other not that much alive.

Certain events trick the mind into quick judgments about the future. A sudden twenty-five per cent drop in stock prices, a goal that puts your team two down with only a few minutes to go or, say, the sight of a woman, with whom you are enchanted, on the arm of another man, like Lord Somebody-Somebody, slipping up to a hotel room. Events like that convince us overwhelmingly that the outcome so desperately desired is the least likely. In the mind's strange logic, the worst of all possible outcomes is inevitable. We lose hope. To steal from Pascal (who had lived not far from the Jardin), neither the boule players in the Jardin with their wily strategies, nor George Boole with his Boolean symbols, nor the great Aristotle with his syllogisms could ever capture the logic of the heart, of the spirit.

Harvey, once an inhabitant of the Île, an inhabitant of the city of Paris, a Parisian, had returned to mere tourist, taking cues from the green Michelin Tourist Guide of Paris like some newly-arrived. A visit to the La Défense on the other bank beyond the Arc de Triomphe rated two stars in the Michelin and so the next day he walked all the way over there, had a *croque madame* for lunch, and walked all the way back. The day after that (or was it the day before?) he walked out to the Père Lachaise cemetery where, according to the Michelin, in May of 1871, one hundred and forty-seven insurgents were lined up against a wall in the southeast corner and shot. "Don't wait dinner for me, ma chère, I've been invited to a little get-together over at the cemetery this aft."

Like some *clochard* who sleeps on the subway vents of the sidewalks, no doubt like our Segovia when he wasn't in concert back in Toronto, Harvey wandered the streets of Paris, without purpose, without destination, without the slightest sense of urgency. Now and again he would stop to read a plaque on a fence or on the wall of some buildings or on some black iron fence that commemorated a citizen who had lived or died at that very location. Or every once in a while, he would stand motionless to stare at a statue of some great French *citoyen* like Michel de Montaigne or Jean Jaurès or Balzac, in an attempt to discern in their physical features the essential quality of those that triumphed over the day-to-day.

It was late afternoon before he got back to his hotel from Père Lachaise. The woman on the front desk smiled and said "Bonjour, Monsieur" in the usual sing-songy way. She took out from one of the pigeon holes in the wall behind her a key, fastened to a heavy bronze medallion along with a note with the word *Urgent* scrawled across the top.

"Good thing you left me your number," McKissick said on the phone. "Gott called. Gott de Holger. He wanted you. I got on the blower and told him what had happened. And you know what the bloke said?"

"No idea."

"He said 'Gut. That means I should not have to steal him away from you chaps.' Got said—and I'm not exaggerating, Harvey—your Lehigh report was the finest analysis on a company he'd ever read. I think what really got him was that valuation work you did on Lehigh's intellectual property. He said he'd never seen anything on the subject as astute. He said it was a work of art, he just loved it."

"He said he loved it?"

"I swear he told me exactly that. He bloody well loved it, my friend," McKissick said almost in a shout.

"Well, it's nice somebody likes my ideas."

"Not somebody. The best investment manager in all of Europe, Harvey. And he wants you do to fly up to Frankfurt and meet with him."

"What's the point now?"

"They're re-organizing the entire QRS Bank investment operations from stem to gudgeon, he told me. That's why he's been so tardy in getting back to you. He wants you to go and work for him as his special assistant."

"To do what?"

"I don't know exactly. I'm not sure I did a good job for you, Harvey. Here I am on the phone with the great Gott de Holger. It's like speaking to God himself. I was pretty excited, I don't mind telling you. He talked of buying out companies all over the world. You'd report directly to de Holger himself but comb the world for acquisitions like Lehigh. He said it wouldn't matter where you lived as long as it wasn't too far from an airport. You'd just travel the world from one end to the other. He said to have you call his secretary. She'll make all the arrangements for you. Call her first thing tomorrow. Gott wants to see you soon as possible."

XIV.

THE PROMISED GEOGRAPHY

There was something unidentifiably familiar in the air the next night when the stewardess who had greeted Harvey with her hazel-eyed Nordic smile aboard the Lufthansa's Airbus bound for Frankfurt placed on the pull-out table before our Harvey a glass of Riesling. On the flight-path monitor in front of him Harvey followed the take-off from De Gaulle airport, a particularly smooth, gentle drift into the lower heavens as the plane pointed itself towards Frankfurt.

Harvey was reading a brochure on Bermuda that he'd

taken off the Net back at the hotel. He had decided that's where he wanted to live. He'd buy a house. It would mean a mortgage, but so what? In time he'd join a tennis club and, maybe, the yacht club and a resident's association. Start a garden. Put down roots. Get himself out of the tourist category once and for all. Bermuda would be perfect. Warmer weather. Halfway between the old world and the new—a little farther away, the brochure pointed out, from London than he had thought, but only two hours from New York. He could go and visit Sara if she was still at the MOMA. Maybe she'd come over help him to get settled in house. Life would be much like it was on the Île except for garbage-can soccer in the middle of the night. And in Bermuda, you could probably even find parking spots.

At that point, those miscreants from The Street might as well have dwelt in another universe, the memories of Leon and Larry and Ferdy Fkup and Roi and all their corporate thuggery dimmed with every kilometre the plane traversed. Though it might mean running into The Pig from time to time, Harvey intended to keep in touch with Grace, of course. It might even be easier to do that now that she'd be living in Nassau, an hour or two's flight from Bermuda. Marie Thérèse, whenever, and if ever, she returned to Paris, now that her cash flow had picked up, would probably get an apartment again back in the 6th arrondissement.

His one regret was Katherine the Ingrate. She sounded pretty serious about that Lord Somebody-Somebody. He wouldn't be able to resist someone with forearms as magnificent as hers. Maybe she'd end up marrying the guy. Maybe she and Harvey were not meant to get together in the first place. How else can you explain the shoddy synchronization of needs? Nature at work.

What Lufthansa was carrying that night, though, was a somewhat different Harvey—seated in the first row of the business section—a Harvey about to be empowered to wander the world. An elegant canon of Pachelbel's that played on his earphones sounded perhaps like an introduction to an entirely new arrangement between Harvey and the world, one completely free of political boundaries. This new arrangement would allow Harvey—in an *un-stated* way—to wander almost everywhere, his comings and goings unbidden, unfettered, and unhampered. No matter where he was he could feel at home—*chez lui*. A new, modern—postmodern even—kind of republic unhindered by geography...

Markson. Markson. Uber alles...

Hold on. Hold on. This sounds too familiar. Haven't we been here before?

Looks like we've run into a small problem. The stated objective of this little metaphysical romp was to discover in which, or in what, prison Harvey had landed himself. Remember all that talk way back at the beginning about the generous array of prisons Nature has laid out for mankind? About gap-toothed, fat-fingered, Kalashnikov-toting guards? Have we tramped our way through thousands of words, all that wearisome chatter, only to discover no progress whatsoever has been made?

Well, perhaps our notion of progress is quite mistaken. If you end up where you started, does that mean no progress has been made? Can't you be wiser for the journey, if wiser only in the knowledge that you would never, never take that trip again, not in hundred years?

Or, from another point of view, when you come right down to it, a fair number of people feel completely at home in prison. Some people say they're happier on the inside: no parking problems, no fenders to repair. Maybe life itself is a kind of prison. Some poets have said that.

Out the plane window, the moon, steady in the centre of the sky, shone so brightly you'd think the sun was doing night shift. And we know there are no churches forty thousand feet above sea level. And this may sound contrived but a bell rang out, a bell. It certainly sounded like a bell—a jubilant bell tolling out celebration and glory. Could it have been that sweet-sweet, joyful sound that rings out when defiance—No Roi! No Roi!—finally gets the recognition it deserves?

Nope. It was the fasten-your-seat-belt sign being turned on. The plane had begun its descent. The plane's captain announced they would be landing soon and thanked the passengers once again for flying Lufthansa.

The world would change in Frankfurt. Harvey wasn't going off to join some pipsqueak firm like Sheardon-Cassidy International that couldn't even sustain a crummy little office in Paris. He'd be allied with one of the world's largest financial groups—€800 billion in assets, more than 2300 facilities in seventy countries. Seventy countries! God knows in how many cities! €800 billion in assets! In this venture with Gott and an €800-billion bank, how could Project Vamooski go awry? Not even Ferdy Fkup could fumble away an arrangement like that. To boot, McKissick, a man you could trust without question, had sworn that Gott loved—those were McKissick's exact words—Harvey's report on Lehigh Robotics. With Gott's love in tow and with a €800-billion bank as a fallback, where could Harvey possibly go wrong?

The clanking sound of the plane's wheels being lowered made Harvey glance at the flight-path monitor in front of him. The plane was approaching the airport in a southerly direction.

But maybe the Gott thing would not turn out. There were still dozens of details to work out—responsibilities, salary, benefits, titles, reporting requirements, cultural fit. These deals are seldom simple. What if this didn't work out, then what? Then what?

Sounds of a stringless strummer.

Maybe this was just another pipe dream, like London and Paris turned out to be. Maybe Harvey's dreams, like the plane, were headed once again in a southerly direction.

Very southerly.

Several years later, shortly after Gottfried de Holger's elaborate retirement party in Frankfurt, the banking world once again blew itself up. This time it was not sovereign debt problems, as it was in the eighties. Nor was it the premature anticipation of the Internet's power, as at the turn of the century. No, just as in the early nineties, the real estate markets headed south. To help shore up its weakened balance sheet, The QRS Bank sold the "private equity" arm that de Holger had established with the friendly takeover of Lehigh Robotics and nineteen subsequent major acquisitions.

Later that same year, in Hamilton, Bermuda, a resident of some time incorporated a company under the ampersand-free name of H. Markson and Associates, International Investment Counselors. In need of a research analyst, the new company ran an ad in the *Financial Times* of London.

One of the forty-six replies demonstrated exactly the type of experience and qualifications the company was looking for. The applicant was a Canadian, originally from Toronto, who had worked for the last several years as an investment analyst in London, a woman twice-divorced. The sole blemish on her record was that of having once practiced as an economist. The covering letter attached to her resume stated that, no longer enjoying life in large cities, she would love to come and live and work in Bermuda. (All three? Yippeee!)

As the sun performed its customary afternoon dance upon the blue and turquoise water, white-mantled waves, not fifty feet away, lapped upon the beach and undulated in and out, in and out. The resident turned from the window of his home office, tugged up his knee-length socks and leaned back in his desk chair. Then he cupped his hands behind his head and began to think about various kinds of alliances that might be formed with the applicant and even the possibility of a union of some sort.

Hold on. Hold on.

An alliance? Maybe even a union of some sort? What kind of a union? But-but, Harv, a union would put the kibosh on our independence forever. Harv—Jesus—you out of your fornicating mind, I protested at the top of my lungs.

In return, there was only a lingering silence...

FURTHER TESTAMENT

When Leon took over Rupert's office he sent most of the books on to the Campbellville Library, as Rupert would have wished. With the consent of his sister, he gave Rupert's notebooks to Harvey. Harvey read them cover to cover in that period awaiting settlement with Leon. In earlier days, before the lawyers got involved, Leon saw no need for Rupert's lifetime subscriptions to *Harper's* and *Atlantic Monthly* around the office either, so they were put in Harvey's name.

Here are just a few of the many hundreds of ideas Rupert had collected in his notebooks over the years, and a couple Harvey added later.

From the Notebooks of Rupert Winkes:

"If economists could manage to get themselves thought of as humble, competent people on a level with dentists, that would be splendid."

John Maynard Keynes, *Essays in Persuasion*

"Over himself, over his own body and mind, the individual is sovereign."
J. S. Mill, *On Liberty*

"On the journey though life, why, in God's name, do most of our dreams end up in the lost and found?"
R. H. Winkes, 1995

"The great events of the world are, at bottom, profoundly unimportant. In the last analysis, the essential thing is the life of the individual, here alone do the great transformations take place, and the whole future, the whole history of the world, ultimately springs as a gigantic summation from these hidden resources in individuals."
Carl Jung, *Modern Man in Search of a Soul*

"Faith is the substance of things hoped for, the evidence of things not seen."
Hebrews 11.1

Added later to the Notebooks by Harvey:

"A true friend is the most precious of all possessions and one we take the least thought in acquiring."
La Rochefoucauld

"Is a dream a lie if it don't come true, or is it something worse?"
Bruce Springsteen

"La chair est triste, hélas! et j'ai lu tous les livres.
Fuir! là bas fuir!"
Stéphane Mallarmé, *Brise Marine*

"In fact, we all live with our thoughts always in the forest of the future; we are filled with vague cravings, and are finally impelled to wander amid the trees to find our destiny there."
David Brooks, *Atlantic Monthly*, December, 2002

"Freedom, after all, is not merely emancipation, meaning the relaxation of rules imposed on people by society, church, or state, by the tyranny of a ruler, by a minority, or by a majority. Freedom means the capacity to know something about oneself, and the desire to live according to the limits imposed on oneself rather than by external powers."
John Lukacs, *Democracy and Populism* excerpted in Harper's, April 2005

About the Author

John received a B.A. from the University of Toronto, a Diplôme d'Étude from the Sorbonne and an M.A. in Philosophy from the University of Waterloo. After that, for the error of his ways, he spent more than thirty years in the financial services business, mostly on the fringe.

He likes to think about things.

Acknowledgement

Without the professionalism of my editor, the manuscript for this book would have remained no more than that. To Victoria White, many and much thanks.